Praise for

The Amazing Absorbing Boy

NATIONAL BESTSELLER
WINNER OF THE TRILLIUM BOOK AWARD
FINALIST FOR THE CITY OF TORONTO BOOK AWARD

"Genuinely detailed and lyrically apt. . . . Sharply satirical."
National Post

"There is an engaging, surreal quality to the story . . . [which is] a hallmark of all of Maharaj's books. . . . Samuel's story is the story of Canada." *Ottawa Citizen*

"Think you know Toronto? Then it's getting another perspective. You won't find a fresher one than in *The Amazing Absorbing Boy*." *NOW* (Toronto)

"To those long-established metaphors of immigrant identity, the patchwork quilt and the melting pot, we have now to add the comic book. . . . Sharply observed and entertaining. . . . [A] rich exploration of the immigrant psychodrama of attraction and repulsion, welcome and paranoia, perception and misunderstanding." *Toronto Star*

"*The Amazing Absorbing Boy* walks our streets with fresh eyes, taking us to places we've been many times and showing us what we've missed. This is a book Canadians have been waiting a long time to read." Steven Galloway

"An exhilarating interpretation of immigrant experience. . . . Maharaj superbly articulates the longing for home, on the one hand, and the dream of success in Canada on the other." *The Globe and Mail*

"Toronto provides an ideal if unsurprising setting for an assimilation story, and Maharaj expertly captures the varied carols of its urban multiculture." *The Walrus*

"Maharaj is a sensitive observer who renders the familiar new and strange in this bittersweet tale of an everyday hero navigating a new land." Camilla Gibb, author of *The Beauty of Humanity Movement*

"To read Maharaj's novel is to laugh at ourselves, to wonder at ourselves, and most importantly, to understand ourselves. If you haven't yet discovered Rabindranath Maharaj, discover him with this novel." Gail Anderson-Dargatz, author of *Turtle Valley*

"Charming. . . . In telling Sam's story, Maharaj also allows the reader to see Canadian society through a pair of fresh, unprejudiced eyes. . . . A touching tale of discovery." *Winnipeg Free Press*

"*The Amazing Absorbing Boy* has its amazing moments: Maharaj is an often funny, sharply observant stylist." *Calgary Herald*

The Amazing Absorbing Boy

RABINDRANATH MAHARAJ

Vintage Canada

VINTAGE CANADA EDITION, 2011

Published in Canada by Vintage Canada, a division of
Random House of Canada Limited, Toronto, in 2011. Originally
published in hardcover in Canada by Alfred A. Knopf Canada, a division
of Random House of Canada Limited, in 2010. Distributed by
Random House of Canada Limited.

Vintage Canada with colophon is a registered trademark.

www.randomhouse.ca

A glossary of Trinidadian vocabulary can be found on page 329.

Library and Archives Canada Cataloguing in Publication

Maharaj, Rabindranath
The amazing absorbing boy / Rabindranath Maharaj.

ISBN 978-0-307-39728-7

I. Title.

PS8576.A42A73 2011   C813'.54   C2010-903831-2

Book design by Jennifer Lum

Printed and bound in the United States of America

4 6 8 9 7 5

For Darin, who shared my love for comics.

Gulp!
It's too late. He's beginning to change.

A comic book, somewhere

Chapter One

THE NOWHEREIAN

When my mother died four months after my sixteenth birthday, I felt I had already received glimpses of all that would follow. Like if I was once again sitting on a dusty, silvery asteroid and could see through lanes of swirling space dust and dark, puffed-up clouds, right through the samaan tree in our front yard where the shadows of our Mayaro neighbours cast a crooked picket fence on the coffin. I could even make out Uncle Boysie still looking funny in his black suit, staring again at the road as if in this replay my father would suddenly appear in a big puff of sulphurous smoke. But my father was not Nightcrawler the teleporter, and I was not Doctor Manhattan who could see into the future.

Yet, until that morning in June when her life passed away and Uncle Boysie held my hand and pulled me out of the house—as if it was suddenly a dangerous place—I always expected my mother to recover. I say this even though she had been sick for the last four months with all her wavy hair falling out so that instead of looking prettier than all the Mayaro women, she began to resemble the caged monkey inside Lighthouse rumshop. I held on to this faith even when she returned from the clinic in Rio Claro walking so tiredly that I had to support her into the house; when a few of the neighbours began whispering nonsense about *obeah* and *maljeaux;* when we both moved in with Uncle Boysie and he began to treat me more kindly than any time before.

I think my mother was responsible for these thoughts because three weeks before she died, we returned to our house on Church Street, just a quarter mile from the beach. I was relieved and felt that everything would soon get back to normal. She would stop vomiting and become stronger and the kitchen would once more smell of *shadow-beni*, ripe plantain and cassava *pone*. And the dripping sink would sound like faraway cymbals for the high-pitched Bollywood songs she was always humming.

I was convinced of her recovery when, during those three weeks, she began dressing up in fancy clothes I had never seen before. Each afternoon when I returned from the Mayaro Composite School, I saw her in a new and unfamiliar dress. They looked expensive, with sashes, embroidered collars, and frilly hems. She appeared paler too, though whether this was from the powder on her face or from her sickness, I could not say.

Some evenings Moolai, the village midwife who doubled as a nurse, would be there forcing my mother to drink some nasty-smelling potion. Whenever Moolai saw me, her small eyes would get lost in the loose skin, making her look like a spiteful river turtle, a moroccoy. Uncle Boysie came each evening and stayed with my mother for an hour or two. Except for the day Auntie Umbrella, my father's sister, turned up. That evening he took one look at my aunt and left in a hurry. She had come armed with her prayer book and her old umbrella strengthened with bicycle spokes. From my bedroom, I heard her preaching about salvation and rapture and Abraham's bosom.

The following day my mother was in bad shape and when I saw her vomiting into an enamel bowl held by Moolai I really did not want to go to school. All day I thought of her but in the afternoon she was dressed up even more than the last few days. She was wearing rouge that made her cheeks look bonier—like a wrinkly lady taking a deep drag from a cigarette—and instead of the veil tied tightly around her bald head, she had on a wig with the hair plaited just like in the picture of her that used to be above the front door. She had recently replaced this picture together with all the other happy ones removed over the years.

She was sitting by the window as usual and as Moolai was not there, I pulled up a chair from the kitchen. She put her hand on mine and I looked out of the window, trying to match her view. I saw the breadfruit tree with leaves like huge moth wings, and scattered all around, sword-shaped balisier with sickly yellow flowers. In the field of balisier, there was a path that led to the main road and I wondered whether my mother was watching and waiting for someone to turn up. With her fancy dress and powdered face and new shoes and plaited-hair wig. I got distracted by the cornbird nest swinging from the breadfruit tree. About two years earlier, when I was fourteen, my mother had spotted me with a slingshot and asked from the window if the birds had ever done anything to me.

On my way from school the next day, I wondered whether it was the same family that had been living in the nest for all these years or whether the baby birds had grown up and had their own children. Uncle Boysie's station wagon was parked in the yard and when I opened the door, I saw him and Moolai supporting my mother. "Where all you going?" I asked them. My mother was wearing a completely white dress with bows by the collar and she smelled of some strong perfume.

"Help, boy." Moolai sounded grumpier than usual. I held my mother's arm and supported her to the steps and into the station wagon. Just before they pulled off, Uncle Boysie, as if the question had now registered, said, "To Liberty cinema. Sylvie, your mother, want to look at a show."

"I could come?"

My mother closed her eyes and leaned her head against the seat. Uncle Boysie told me, "Better you stay home, boy. See the house."

"I could come the next time?"

My mother's eyes opened weakly and she seemed to smile a little.

Three days later she died, and I moved back to Uncle Boysie's place, alone this time.

The day after the funeral, Uncle Boysie asked me how I was holding up. He must have seen me staring at the boys around my age in his Anything and Everything shop gathering fishhooks and corks from the lower shelves and women stretching to reach some kitchen gadget strung on nails on the wall. I told him I was okay because I didn't know what else to say, and his eyes got watery and he started to cough to hide whatever was going through his mind.

He began to quarrel even more, though never to me, and whenever I heard him I wondered if he felt that Cockort, the short, spongy postman whose oversized shoes were always flapping as he walked, or Latchmin, the "sign-lady" who claimed she could predict all the deaths and births in the village, were responsible for my mother's death. "Damn pussyahs," he would say, managing to make this rude word sound like a pet. But as one week passed, then two, I realized that in my uncle's eyes this position was reserved for my father. He never said anything point-blank and at first, I wasn't even sure who he was talking about. One night as he was closing up, dragging the heavy bolt against the door, he said, "You would expect that he would at least show up for the funeral. You would expect *this.*" A couple days later, while he was searching for some plumbing part in one of the cardboard boxes stacked with unions and valves, I heard him saying, "Useless! Completely kissmeass useless *nowhereian.*" That was the word he used most often to describe my father—*nowhereian*.

The box crashed to the floor and when I went to help him he said, "Keep a eye on the door before any of them blasted *locho* walk out with a whole box of fish hook." As his temper got shorter, I began to wonder at this arrangement with Uncle Boysie.

It was strange not having my mother around. A few boys from my fourth form had one parent missing, but none as far as I knew were complete orphans. That was the word my English teacher, Miss Charles, used and her texts made it seem as if I had a horrible life waiting for me, eating gruel and treacle and just waiting for someone named Sid or Mano to introduce me to a life of pickpocketing. I think Uncle Boysie was afraid of this too as he soon began to shoot off little proverbs like, "Birds of a feather frock together" and "Rolling stones gather in the mosque," and I never bothered to correct him because most evenings he seemed quite tipsy, drinking from the bottle of Johnnie Walker on the shelf behind the counter. Like all the adults in Mayaro, he normally drank on weekends at one of the bars close to the beach but this every-day drinking was new and a couple times, I saw him gazing right in front of him as if he was in a big empty space.

When I began coming to his shop later than usual he seemed not to notice and so I didn't have to explain that I now took a roundabout route from school that bypassed our house. It meant walking along the beach and cutting into the track next to Plaisance where the dead mangrove crabs looked like birds that had lost their feathers and pitched to earth. The evening high tides usually washed ashore dozens of silvery fishes but their eyes shone so brightly it seemed as if they didn't want to die. Sometimes there were families from the town gathered around their cars with the women hiding behind towels and the men drinking beer from their coolers. They glanced at me with my bookbag and school uniform and always asked the same questions: "Which school you from, sonnyboy?" and "How come you walking all by youself?"

Because I am a *nowhereian*, I thought once, and immediately the word seemed flavoured with recklessness. Like an adventurer moving from place to place with no friends or family to hook on to him. Like the Silver Surfer but with no Galactus to command him. Uncle Boysie would have been shocked.

I believe it was three weeks after the funeral that I first went into our old house. As was the custom following a death, the curtains had been removed and there were drapes and doilies over all the pictures. On the first evening, I sat on the chair facing the window and looked out at the road. I must have fallen half-asleep there and when I heard a sound from the kitchen, I bolted up and ran straight down the road, not stopping until I reached Uncle Boysie's shop. The next day at school, I had to share Pantamoolie's textbooks, and I believe it was only because I had left my bookbag in the house that I decided to return. I pressed my ear against the door before I nudged it open. I saw my bookbag on the floor and took a few steps forward, keeping my eyes on the kitchen door. I heard the sound again, a gentle tapping, different from the breadfruit leaves scraping the galvanized roof or the wind blowing through the jalousie.

I must have stood there in the middle of the living room for about three minutes, convincing myself that no one would dare come into the house to steal because they knew Uncle Boysie had contacts with all the drunkard policemen from the station on the junction. I didn't think it was my mother's ghost or anything, and even if it was, she would not harm me. Soon after the illness had weakened her I overheard her telling my uncle that although I was getting a bit *ownway* I helped her in plenty ways. I think she meant I had stopped *liming* around after school with my friends and now came home early to assist around the house and run to the grocery for little kitchen items. Some of my friends called me a "housey-bird" because of this.

In a way, I would have been happy to see her floating above the stove but when I went to the kitchen, I heard the tap dripping into the kitchen sink. I turned it off and walked around the house. Everything looked exactly the same apart from the missing curtains and the drapes on the pictures.

I removed these and gazed at the photographs, one by one. I believe my mother was proud of the big one that hung over the bureau in the living room as I had often seen her watching it while Moolai was massaging her. Her wavy hair was around her shoulders and the way she was looking up at the photographer made her eyes look big and mischievous. It was hard to connect her with that picture. She was more normal in the old black-and-white picture with a wooden frame that stood above the doorway to the kitchen. There, she was standing next to Uncle Boysie and they seemed to be going to a function or something because her hair was plaited and Uncle Boysie was wearing a tie and a jacket that surprisingly did not push against his belly. When I went into her bedroom, the first thing that struck me was the smell of camphor and Limacol and I wondered whether this was the odour of death some of my school novels mentioned. On her dresser was the tree-shaped picture holder. It was not covered, maybe because there were missing pictures from some of the branches. The tree looked as if it was dying. I was in two of the branches though, one as a baby with my mother holding me up and the other for my fifth birthday.

Over the years, most of the pictures had been removed from the walls and whenever I asked my mother about it, she would say it was to repair the frames. In one, my mother and father were sitting together and the only thing I could remember was that his shirt was unbuttoned and she was staring sleepily at his smoke rings. I believed she removed it after Matapal, the old half-crazy fisherman who delivered moonshine, bonito, and *carite* every other Friday, made some joke about it.

I don't think my mother ever liked Matapal, because he smelled of rum and dropped a trail of fish scales from the front door to the kitchen. She always left the kitchen while he was scaling the fishes and during that time, he would tell me nonsense about how he had discovered gold chains and necklaces inside some of the fishes. Once he said there was a picture on every scale and he held up one against the window and said he could see a scene of my mother there. "Funny little scene, boy.

Never imagine you mother like this." When he was describing these pictures, he would stretch his arms like a big seabird and his beard would seem to get longer and his face blacker. One night during a storm, he went to untangle a boat's anchor and no one ever saw him again. I have to say that I missed his stories but more than that I missed the newspapers in which he rolled up his fish, for it was there that I first saw the comics of the Phantom passing on his secret to his only son and Mandrake discovering a whole race of people who lived behind mirrors and the miserable little girl who was always pulling away the ball from Charlie Brown.

After Matapal drowned, it was my job to buy fish from the Mayaro market. I enjoyed going to the market because it was always packed with *caimite* and *sapodilla* and *soursop*, and vendors who sold *doubles* and *pone* and pickled *pommecythere*. Some of the vendors still referred to me as "Danny's boy," which was strange, as I had not seen my father since I was six and even then he was always leaving home to go on his trips. Once, Pantamoolie's father, who sold *dasheen* and cassava, called me "the *nowhereian* son," which was the first time I had heard the word.

Uncle Boysie always used the word in an insulting way so I was surprised when a month or so after the funeral he too said, "It look like you will come a *nowhereian* soon, boy." We were about to close up the shop and I felt then he had found out about my evening trips along Plaisance but a couple days later he asked me, "So what you think about Canada?" Like everybody else in Mayaro, he pronounced it as *Cyanada*.

"I think it have bears and thing." I couldn't tell him about Captain Canuck and Wolverine because I was sure he didn't know about superheroes.

He looked at me suspiciously before he said, "Oho. You mean the hairy kind." After a while he added, "You know it have a lotta people who does go up there. Picking apple and grapes."

The next day at school, I asked Pantamoolie, "So what you think about Canada?"

"These Cyanadian people have a special gland below they armpit which does keep away the cold." I was about to laugh when he added, "Shave ice does fall from the sky. In all different flavour and colour. Lime and orange and chocolate."

"Who tell you that?"

"*Reader's Digest,* man. You don't read or what?"

I should have known better than to ask Pantamoolie, as he was a big liar. For years, he tried to get us to call him Panther but nearly everybody chose Panties instead and he soon grew resigned to it. He claimed that his father who sold in the market was really an undercover agent, and that he had once seen Mr. Chotolal fingering Miss Charles in the staffroom. In form three, he tried to convince the class that Hanuman, the monkey god, was the world's first superhero as he had super strength, could fly, had a mace as his weapon, and his name ended in "man." But Pantamoolie's picture of shaved ice stuck in my head and during the lunch break, I went into the school library and pulled out a really old book with pictures of Eskimos spearing seals and dogs pulling people in sleds. Some of the names of places like Ottawa and Toronto reminded me of our local Carib ones like Arima and Mayaro.

I think it was maybe four or five days after Uncle Boysie asked the question that he told me he had written my father.

"About Mummy?"

His face hardened a bit and I thought he was going to say something about how my father was a useless nowhereian but instead he said, "About you."

"Me?"

"Is time he take on some responsibility."

I wondered if my father was coming from Canada to live in our house. I pictured him wearing one of these white gowns like a crazy scientist as he tried experiments from *The Wonder Book of Wonders* that was packed with directions for making magnets and flashlights and water clocks, and crystals from ordinary cupboard items. Soon after he had left for good, I discovered the book in the closet in my mother's room. It was hidden beneath neatly folded jeans and overalls, and the minute I opened the book I knew it had been my father's.

But why would he come now? When I was in primary school, my mother used to make up stories of him soon sending for us, but as the years passed and he did not show up, she began repeating some of Uncle Boysie's criticisms. He was "a dreamer" and "was always running away from his responsibilities" and he "made promises he could never keep." I stopped asking her about him as it was sure to put her in a bad mood, so I never mentioned *The Wonder Book of*

Wonders or his drawings of strange, triangular fishing boats, and seines with bulbs instead of corks, and lawnmowers with wings, or even the fancy Timex watch he had sent for me on my tenth birthday.

One day after our term exam in July, I told Pantamoolie my father would soon be coming to live with me. Immediately he asked, "He will bring down any of these Cyanadian gadgets?"

"Yeah, man. Some that he invent himself."

"You think he might bring a motorbike?"

"I don't think that will fit in a suitcase."

"He could fold it up. A German Lugie then?"

"Luger?"

"Same thing. Or a Gatling gun like the one Django the movie *badjohn* had."

"I really don't know. Might be illegal."

"What about one of these gadget that could see where it have fish below the water? Tell you exactly where to fishen."

"Yeah. Yeah, I believe he might."

During the following weeks while I was packing away small tools in Uncle Boysie's shop I sometimes imagined my father and myself together on a boat, riding the breakers until we were past the Bocas and could see Venezuela. Sometimes in these scenes we actually landed on Venezuela and chatted with the Warahoon Indians who were so impressed with all my father's gadgets that they loaded us up with *tattou* and 'gouti and rainbow-coloured macaws and playful baby monkeys. Each day I waited patiently for Uncle Boysie to tell me, "Well, boy, he coming tomorrow." But as the months passed,

I began to feel that my uncle's promise was no different from my mother's, when I was much younger. Just ole talk.

I soon began to see myself living my entire life right in Mayaro. Maybe I would inherit Uncle Boysie's shop, as he wasn't married and had no children of his own. I would also get a big belly and sit behind the counter quarrelling with the children for interfering with the stocks and appliances. I might even go to Lighthouse rumshop by the beach every weekend for a nip of Puncheon rum. One Friday after school I did exactly that but for two beers instead and when I arrived at the shop trying to fight my drowsiness, my uncle glanced at me, pushed his hand beneath his shirt and began scratching his belly. He usually did that when he was thinking of something. In the following weeks, I saw him scratching, too, whenever I took down one of the comics fastened with clothes clips to a line of polyester twine across the haberdashery section, and when he saw my shoes muddy from searching for Loykie, my sick friend who lived in the mangrove with his mother. To tell the truth, I soon forgot Uncle Boysie had ever mentioned my father but exactly nine months after my mother's funeral, he told me, "He sending for you."

"For me? Who?"

"You father, boy."

"You mean to go up to Canada?"

"Righto pappyo. Cyanada."

This was too much to digest. I had imagined my father would be joining me in Mayaro so Canada was the furthest thing from my mind. "What I will do there?"

Uncle Boysie reeled off a list of jobs he had most likely picked up from his rumshop friends. He made the place seem only slightly different from Pantamoolie's crazy land. And he kept this up during the four weeks before I left, joking about "white chicks" and some Canadian wrestler before getting serious with warnings about *ownwayness*. On the night before my departure, he gave me a long speech that sounded as if he had crammed it from a book, because it didn't resemble any of his previous advice. But I was really not paying him too much attention as my mind was already far, far away. I was on a plane zooming through fluffy patches of clouds to a land where flavoured shaved ice fell from the sky. A *nowhereian*, at last!

Chapter Two

THE WONDER BOOK OF WONDERS

In the months before she died, my mother stopped talking of my father. Uncle Boysie took over and sometimes from my mother's quietness, I felt she didn't agree with my uncle's criticisms even though she once used to say some of the same things, except in a more resigned way. Her silence took me back to the time after his last disappearance from our house. I remember how she fussed about fixing this or that around the house to surprise him when he returned. She tried to convince me he was on a ship travelling from port to magical port and he would one day return with gifts spilling from his pockets and stuffed inside soft velvety boxes. She kept that up for months, even when that final disappearance lasted longer than the others.

Once I heard a neighbour telling her, "Is the good-looking one and them who does cause the heartache, Sylvie. Real charmers but *skeffy* like hell." From my mother's little smile I felt they were talking of my father. He appeared that way in the pictures, too, with his unbuttoned shirt and long hair and stubble on his face and his bored look. But then most of the pictures were removed (one by one, the happier ones first) and my own memories of his time with us—broken up by his trips away—faded and I began to see him from Uncle Boysie's descriptions: a lazy, good-for-nothing scamp.

So I didn't know what to expect when I landed in the Toronto airport and glanced around. There were a few men with beards and turbans but they all seemed to be working in the building. I walked to a bench and when a middle-aged man with a moustache sat next to me I wondered if he was my father and Canada could make people shorter and fatter but the man hailed out a woman in an accent like rolling marbles.

After ten minutes or so, I went outside but the place was too cold so I returned to the bench. Could my father have forgotten the date of my arrival? Did Uncle Boysie's letter somehow get lost? This was worse than getting stranded in Port of Spain or San Fernando with no money for passage. Then I remembered the five hundred dollars Uncle Boysie had given to me and I cheered up a bit. In any case, I had a visa for six months. By then most of the people from the flight had disappeared with their families so I dragged my suitcase once more outside.

"Your name is Sam?"

It was a man leaning against the wall and smoking. He looked a little like Lee Van Cleef from the Westerns, sort of grim and calculating but then I saw the person from the pictures in our living room. I told him yes and followed him to a bus a little distance away. I hauled my suitcase up the steps and we sat on opposite seats. While we were waiting for the driver I expected that he would ask about the trip or about Mayaro but he just gazed outside. Maybe was feeling shy just like me, rehearsing what to say because we had not seen each other since I was six, which was eleven years ago. Then the driver who was well dressed for a bus man came in and we took off.

I remember how the driver on the Mayaro to Rio Claro route always stopped midway for a drink of Puncheon rum, not caring about the passengers cursing and bawling at him through the windows: "Bring you ass here, nah man. Is government property, not you *mooma* bus you driving." But this driver announced our stops on a mike like if he was a pilot. Dundas. Harbour Castle. Royal York. Everywhere looked neat and organized with lanes and parks bordered by wavy concrete banks. The trees, which didn't have any leaves, were planted in a straight line. People with coats were walking briskly, not chatting in groups like in Trinidad. They all looked faded, like dematerializing comic book ghosts. This was so exciting: I could almost believe Pantamoolie's talk of flavoured ice falling from the sky. I wished my school friends could be with me now to see all the tall buildings and highways with so many lanes.

I glanced at my father. In the evening light he looked pale and sad, like someone sitting in a dark, damp place like the Batcave, and knowing his schemes were slipping away, one by one. When the bus dropped us off at Union, we took a tramcar, which was like a train running on the streets. It was colder than the bus and my father must have seen me shivering because he asked me, "You know what season this is?"

"March," I told him.

"I see. March is a season now. Nice. Very nice." It sounded like a Mayaro joke but he didn't laugh.

It was dark when we got to a place with big, boxy buildings. There were many lanes and a sign before one said Regent Park. While I was dragging my suitcase up the steps in front of a red building, I almost told him that I had discovered the book he had left behind—*The Wonder Book of Wonders*—but I thought maybe he would be vexed at me for leaving it behind.

We walked down a long corridor and he opened a door near the end. "Only a damn fool will come to this place wearing just a raincoat and khaki pants," he told me. He went into a room and returned with two sweaters and a coat. The sweaters were a muddy brown colour with loose threads like a sucked-out mango seed and the extra large coat couldn't zip all the way up. He also gave me something he called mittens, which sounded like little, round animals hiding beneath stoves and fridges.

That first night I sat at the kitchen table expecting him to start a conversation and maybe explain why, after so many years of silence, he had asked me to join him in Canada. I felt it might be rude to ask especially since I knew nothing firsthand about him. When he came into the kitchen, I prepared myself but he just went to the fridge, poured out some reddish juice into a mug with Niagara written beneath its rim, and walked over to the couch. He placed his bare feet on the small laminated table and I saw his toes twitching like river shrimps.

I felt he was preparing some explanation and when he got up, I straightened again and glanced at the chair opposite, but he returned to the kitchen and opened the top cupboards, shifting their contents about. The lower shelf was lined with old newspapers. He got out a package of some sort, sniffed it, and threw its contents into a bucket between the stove and the fridge. There were bread scraps on the tiled floor and a crumpled box of fruit juice that he kicked towards the bucket as he returned to the living room. When he walked past me I looked down at the holes in the plastic tablecloth that made it resemble a Chinese checkers board. Apart from the skinny couch, the laminated centre table, and the box on which the television rested, there was no other furniture in the living room. Two large bricks stood against the far wall and I tried to imagine their purpose. Maybe he placed a trestle there when he was working on his inventions.

He went out to the balcony and asked, "So where you going to sleep?"

The question confused me. I didn't know if it was a challenge or a reproach. I saw his cigarette glinting as he hunched over the railing. When he returned I said, "Anywhere that convenient."

"What you said?"

"I will sleep anywhere."

"You sure about that?" The way he looked at me made me feel like this was some trap he was setting but again he didn't wait for a reply as he disappeared into the bedroom. I wondered if this was a Canadian manner of conversation but I felt uncomfortable talking to an empty, grey wall. He came out with a rolled-up tube of foam and tossed it where a dining room table might have stood. "The blankets in that top cupboard." He motioned with his chin to a built-in cupboard in the hall. It seemed there were so many storing places in this small apartment. I tried to make it more interesting by pretending he had hidden some of his inventions in secret cupboards somewhere. Maybe machines to transform mittens into sweaters and thin socks into warm fluffy boots.

That night I lay on the foam, stared at the ceiling fan and tried to imagine my new life in Canada. The fan was creaking in a regular pattern like an old man coughing some distance away. My mind stalled again and again; I didn't know anything about this place and I could picture nothing of tomorrow or the day after. I thought instead of my Uncle Boysie taking me to the Piarco airport in his pickup van and saying that my mother would have been pleased by this "Cyanadian affair." He had chatted as if I might return in a few hours but that was Uncle Boysie. When, during the trip to the airport, he talked about my mother's funeral, it sounded as if she had died a few hours ago instead of nine months earlier. My father's betrayal—*neemakararam* was the word he used—could have happened yesterday. The way he squeezed all these events into little tubes had lessened some of my worry about this unexpected move to a country thousands of miles away.

I don't know when I finally fell asleep but I had a dream of my high school near to the Mayaro cemetery. My English teacher, Miss Charles, was describing a place called Corfu from some boring novel while Pantamoolie was gossiping about Rita, the pretty girl who sat one row before us. At the back of the class, sitting alone, was Loykie. It was strange to see him without the old sugar bag he always wore when he came out of the swamp. In the dream, Loykie's skin became a milk-white colour from rubbing a stick of chalk and then brown from grazing his finger on the mahogany desk cover and even darker still as he touched a spilled drop of ink. He *really* was the Amazing Absorbing Boy.

The dream of Mayaro, the seaside village, with all its rumshop and churches and wooden houses peeping from behind breadfruit and coconut trees made me a little worried about this strange new place. That I should then miss Uncle Boysie, and Auntie Umbrella who was forever running from the sun, and Matapal the fisherman and Sporty who was always with his Kid Colt comics was easy to understand. This new place seemed too organized and judging by my father, the people too quiet. I didn't know if I could fit into this big mall of a country where everything was so new and so properly arranged.

I got up from the foam, put on an extra sweater, and opened the balcony door. We were on the fourth floor of a six-storey building and even at this late hour, many buildings had their lights on. I couldn't make out the houses and trees properly though, because of the thick fog all around. I had never seen anything like this: it seemed as if we were on an ocean floating to some unknown place. The tips of the trees looked like peeping-out masts. I felt giddy and stepped away from the railing. From the apartment above I heard the sound of a woman's reckless laugh and a man's low voice. I tried to imagine what they could be doing outside on their balcony at this late hour. A police siren seemed to get closer and farther at the same time before it disappeared.

Everything sounded different from Mayaro, where every night I would hear the wind lambasting the branches. There, every bit of noise was familiar: the dog howl from the neighbours' yard, the conversation in the night from drunkards returning from the bars, the misfiring engine from the coconut husking factory close to a mile away. But here it seemed as if these sounds, coming from afar, were squashed and packaged so I could not get their range or their distance. The fog and the washed-out lights from the building opposite made all of this seem very mysterious.

On the way to the Piarco airport, Uncle Boysie had talked about bears and penguins and dog carriages and Eskimos dressed up in animal clothes, which had made me smile because I knew he had picked up this nonsense from the rumshop. Yet when I looked at the covering of fog outside, it was not too difficult to imagine all of Uncle Boysie's creatures walking about cool-cool under the cover of the fog. Some of my worries melted away. This was Canada, where people came for a while and never returned. They sent home money and boasted in their letters about the apples and snow and crazy ice-skating games that ended with serious fights. Some of Uncle Boysie's regular customers like Cockort and Latchmin couldn't believe I was actually moving here. They thought the trip would take a month, like if I was flying to the moon or something. I closed my eyes and tried to separate all the fresh smells brushing up from the fog. I must have remained there for an hour or more.

"Hello." It was my father in a thick, wavy sweater. "People here don't leave the door open like if they still in some *mash-up* Trinidad village, you know." He pointed to a long vent near the floor and I noticed a big tear in the arm of his sweater. "That heating unit there is not just for decoration."

In the morning he added other rules: turn off the lights in the night, don't bathe for too long, wear a sweater in the evenings, never answer the telephone when he not around, don't wait for him to make meals, and check all the appliances whenever the smoke alarm goes off. He told me that children here never depended on anyone but learned to take care of themselves the minute they crossed ten, and by the time they were seventeen they moved away. I wondered whether he knew I had turned seventeen less than a month earlier.

"Where do they go?"

I was just making conversation but the question put him in a bad mood. "Where the hell you expect them to go? Following the Pied Piper to a river? To a chocolate factory singing oompa loompa? Eh?" I decided to ask no further questions but a few minutes later he said, "Nobody does starve in this place. It have shelters and food banks."

I felt this was the speech he had intended for my first night but I soon learned its real purpose the following afternoon. He was poking around in the lower cupboard and grumbling about tins of this or that he was sure he had stored away. I walked over to help him but I saw only the paper packages, their ends tied with rubber bands. The cupboard smelled old and cockroachy instead of ripening plantain and breadfruit. "What you looking for?" I asked him. Maybe I was still thinking as if I was in Trinidad because I expected the cupboards to be stuffed with tins of Ovaltine and jars of guava jam and all kinds of fruits.

He got up without answering and a few minutes later he came out from his room with a green blowup coat that made him look a little like a long turtle. "I going to the supermarket to get some stuff."

I kept on the light late that night even though he had warned against it. While I waited, I made up my mind to finally ask why he had sent for me to Canada. I also intended to ask if I had gone against some Canadian habit for him to be so annoyed with me. He had not even noticed the Timex watch I was wearing.

I got the watch for my tenth birthday, and when my mother said it had been sent by my father I gazed for hours on end at the rotating outer frame and the compass close to the bottom and all the fine writing on the brass back. I fiddled with it so often that it broke after a few months but I continued wearing it for more than a year. Finally I put it on top of *The Wonder Book of Wonders*. I really hoped he would notice and be surprised that I was still wearing the watch and maybe pull out a tiny toolkit and have it up and running in less than five minutes.

Early the next morning I knocked on his bedroom door but there was no answer. I opened the door a bit and peeped inside. I saw his mattress on the floor and a blanket sprawled around a pillow. There were two pairs of pants at the foot of the bed and a couple more hooked over nails in the wall. A small table was pushed against the window and there were a few *Popular Mechanics* magazines on the chair. Beneath the table were cardboard boxes lumped against each other. I closed the door carefully, remembering all the halfway gadgets he had left behind in Mayaro, pushed beneath her bed by my mother. By midday new questions were forming: when was he going to return, and what should I do in the meantime? This wasn't the way I had pictured our first days. I imagined he would tell me about his years in Canada and maybe bundle all his adventures for telling like Uncle Boysie did. I felt he would be nervous and sad at first while he asked about Mayaro School and my mother, but then as he got accustomed to me he would apologize and give some sensible and unexpected reason for leaving. Finally, I would tell him I used to read his *Wonder Book of Wonders,* with all its crazy experiments, and he would say seriously, "They not really crazy if you understand their purpose. For instance . . ." In the weeks before I left, I had practised secretly in Uncle Boysie's little backroom some Canadian words I had picked up from my comic books. Oh gosh. That's swell. Thanks, buddy. How awful. You gotta be kidding. Great Scott.

I really wanted to impress him. They may have been American words but in the comics everyone looked and talked the same. Now it seemed as if all my TV knowledge, too, about hockey and Celine Dion and William Shatner might be wasted. By midday I had a bigger concern: what if he did not return? I reached for one of the boxes of corn flakes on top of the fridge. It was nearly empty, just like the other two, and I finished all three by the next morning. I am not ashamed to say I panicked that day. I was in a strange place. I knew no one except for my father. I had no idea about any of the rules or laws. The apartment looked smaller each hour and I began to feel like these movie actors trapped inside closing-in walls. I rushed to the balcony and watched people walking about on sidewalks and pavements. The soft cushiony fog was gone. I noticed the garbage poking out from a big iron container by the parking lot, and at the side of the container, two overturned carts. Even in this cold weather two boys were riding their bikes. One of them slammed against the container like if it was a stunt and he tumbled on the curb. The other boy stopped and seemed to be laughing. A police car swung out from behind another building that was boxy and stumpy and had only three floors. The car was driving real slow like one of the sharks from *Jaws*. The two boys rode away in a hurry. I dashed back inside.

I opened the bedroom door once more as if my father might be hiding inside the big cupboard. This time I did not shut the door; instead I walked from the kitchen to the bedroom like a madman, over and over again. I must have travelled close to two miles if I counted all my footsteps, and on this little journey I noticed a baby cockroach scrambling up the cupboard, two hand-sized holes in the kitchen wall, a puddle coming from somewhere under the fridge, a watermark that looked like a plucked chicken on the ceiling, and a cord trailing from somewhere behind the couch. The cord was attached to a phone on top of an empty overturned aquarium. I wondered why my father had hidden the phone there and the purpose of the numbers written on the back of a handbill advertising swimming pool cleaning. My father, if he had written the note, had taken his time because FOOD BANK was spelt in neat block letters just like all the numbers on the right side of the sheet. It took a while before I actually made the call and even when I heard the man on the other side, I had no idea what I could say to him. Finally I gathered up the courage to ask if he had food there.

"Yes, sir."

My heart sank fast. Why did he call me "sir"? This was a trap for sure. But it was too late to back out. "What kind?"

"Are you asking about the types of food we have here?"

"Yes. Dried goods or ground provisions?" This was going badly. I tried to recall what the television Canadians ate and rattled out the list that came into my head.

"Yes sir, we do have bacon and tins of sardine but you will have to get your whisky elsewhere."

"And all of this free?'

"Hold on." I heard him talking to a woman about a pickup. He seemed harassed and I pictured a thin beaky man with a few grains of trembling hair on top his head. I put down the phone. My suitcase was resting against the living room wall and I was tempted to take out some money but I didn't know if I should leave the apartment in my father's absence, and in any case, I had no idea if there were groceries or parlours like Miss Bango's nearby. In Mayaro there was always food in the cupboards and fruits in the backyard but this place was bare. I felt like calling Uncle Boysie on the phone and explaining this Canadian affair was a big mistake. Tell him that I was returning to pile pliers and can openers and fish-hooks in his shop. Then I remembered he had packed away currant rolls and cassava *pone* and plastic packets of pickled mangoes in the suitcase's outer pocket. They were squashed and stale but had never tasted better. The next morning it took about two or three minutes before I digested where I was. But I decided that I would not remain all day hideaway or chook up in the apartment. I put on two sweaters and followed some dark Chinese-looking people to the elevator in the outside hall. The elevator bounced a bit at each floor and by the time it reached the ground level, it was full-up with a good crop of plump children. Three of them were so alike I felt they could have been made from a fat little mould. As I walked about, I discovered a small park and webs of little roads all over the place. But the interesting thing was that on some of these roads I saw old Indians in turbans and on others, some black men in big puffed-out coats, and a little distance away these real Canadian people with their fat apple cheeks. Each group stuck to their own paths and as I pushed through a small gate leading to another set of red buildings, I wondered what would happen if the road-builder had made a mistake and all these people found themselves on the wrong path.

Maybe I was rude to smile at this thought because I landed in exactly that situation and by the time I circled back to my father's building, I realized that a lot of parks and buildings looked alike. The apartments were all red and boxy. I felt these were the sort of bullet-box buildings with their many closed windows where a crazy man might be chatting with his cat and aiming his telescope or his rifle outside. On my way back, I imagined Green Lantern from the DC comics surrounding all the buildings with a soft emerald fog that made the place look bushy like Mayaro. When I got to the apartment, my father was on the couch twitching his toes. "You had a nice walk?"

"I went around the block." I wanted to ask where *he* had been.

"Around the block, eh? Nice. Very nice. You met any of Boysie's drunkard friends? Any of your mother's other family? Huh?" I wondered why he was talking in this Canadian accent all of a sudden. "That is why you left the door unlocked? So they could drop in and have a nice little party? A Mayaro *fête* with plenty rum and *bacchanal*?"

"I had no keys." I wanted to add that he had disappeared without a single word and that the cupboards were empty but felt that would further provoke him.

I went to put the bread I had bought into the fridge when something clattered beneath the kitchen table. It was a single key. I felt angry all of a sudden. Did he expect me to pick up the key like a little dog? I went to the table and pulled a chair. I had half a mind to repeat some of my mother's accusations, like how he was a no-good daydreamer who could never hold down a regular job or how he believed he was smarter than everybody else but had nothing to prove it. Uncle Boysie was even more badmouthing. I remember him telling me that every family had one completely useless person who couldn't get along with anybody else and that my father was this person. Once he had told me, "You know what is the problem with you father? A dreamer with no dreams is just a madman."

I saw the key just beneath the table's leg and when I looked to the balcony, I noticed my father's toes curling and uncurling. His hand was beneath his sweater scratching at something and I heard some low mumbling but I didn't want to look directly at him. He got up still grumbling and walked past me with dragging feet. I heard his bedroom door slam shut.

This Canadian affair was getting worse by the hour.

During the remainder of my first week in Canada, I tried my best to keep out of my father's way. This was not too difficult because he, too, seemed to be avoiding me. He left just before midday and when he returned in the night he spent an hour or so smoking on the balcony. I walked around a lot those few days especially on the cold mornings. I tried to put aside my worries about the money I was wasting on doughnuts and muffins, and the busy people who never returned my smile but hurried away, and my unfriendly father in the apartment, and most of all, how I was going to fit into a place where every nut had a proper bolt. I know it might seem strange to say this, but the only comforting thing was that every single day I spotted something else about this complicated housing place that made it seem not like the mall I had imagined on my way from the airport but more and more like Port of Spain. I noticed all the different breed of children running around and the drying clothes on the balcony and the torn and spilling garbage bags and the fancy drawings on the walls. Even the dog smell that hit me the minute I stepped in the building. The only difference was the coldness and sometimes I watched old Chinese couples walking with tiny, pattering steps on the sidewalk, looking like little dragons with their frosty breath.

Whenever my father returned from his job or wherever he had been, he would sit before the television and suck his teeth as three young men, who called themselves mythbusters, cooked up all kinds of contraptions to challenge why this or that couldn't ever happen. I believe *Mythbusters* was his favourite television programme, even though he sometimes switched to *MacGyver*. One night while he was watching *Mythbusters,* he asked me, "So what you intend to do?"

It was the first time he had spoken directly to me in days. "About what?"

"About what." He imitated my accent and it felt like he was mocking me. "That is the way you Trinidadians does operate? Answering one question with another."

As he grumbled, I remembered Uncle Boysie telling me that Canada was designed for young, hard-working boys like me. He had rattled off a list of jobs he had heard about in the rumshops: delivering pizza, watchmanning, mowing lawns, picking apples, pumping gas, packing goods, cleaning rubbish, waitering. He made it seem as if these jobs were just lying on the sides of the road waiting for me. "I don't know anybody here."

"Then why exactly you here?"

"You invited me to come." How could he forget this?

"You think I had any choice in the matter?" He did not explain and because of his nasty mood, I kept quiet. "But the point is you here now and I can't do anything about that."

He went to the balcony for one of his smokes and when he returned, I told him, "Maybe I could get a work with you."

"I see. You mean in one of my big factories that I making millions from? Maybe I could hire you as an overseer to manage one of them. Oompa loompa. You will like that?" This way he was talking got me real angry and I had to remind myself once more that I knew nobody else in this place. "You have any money?"

"Uncle Boysie gave me five hundred."

"And I sure he sell the property in Mayaro for a hundred times that amount. The damn chiseller. Who living there now?"

I guessed he was talking about my mother's board house that she always kept nice and neat with curtains and flowers like zinnias and daisies and ginger lilies. Before she got sick, she was always watering the flowers. "Nobody, as far as I know."

I saw him digging his teeth with his little finger. "He send anything for me? Your Uncle Boysie?" I remembered Uncle Boysie's threatening message but I shook my head. "The damn scamp and chiseller." He got up and put on his green coat. At the door he hesitated and told me, "You better give me forty from that five hundred. To buy some foodstuff."

I got out the money from my suitcase and handed it to him. He returned late in the night and from the foam I saw him placing two loaves of bread in the fridge and a little while later, sitting before the kitchen table, trying to make out the numbers from what looked like a lottery ticket. Every now and again he would glance in my direction and even though in the dark he could not see me awake, I still shut my eyes tightly. About two hours later, I fell asleep and finally had that conversation with my father where he chatted about *The Wonder Book of Wonders* and said he was pleased that my mother had not thrown it away. And then he apologized for not sending any money to us after his first year in Canada.

In the morning, with the dream still fresh in my mind, I remembered how I used to sit on the balcony railing in Mayaro and listen to my mother telling some of the other village women that my father always posted letters with Canadian money; and the women, as if they knew that my mother was lying, just rubbing their hands and saying, "So it is, Sylvie. So it is." After these conversations I would catch her gazing at the framed photograph on top of the old safe that was set close to the window, alongside the sewing machine. The picture was of a couple. The man had longish hair and a scrawny patch of beard on his chin that made him look like a Mayaro pimp. The woman didn't look special in any way except her eyes were shining as if she was excited about going to a party later on. Whenever I asked my mother about this couple, she always said it was of two people who had disappeared. That made the picture interesting and mysterious and I sometimes made up little stories to explain their disappearance. The most interesting was they had moved to one of the misty hills in the forest, past the radar station, where they looked down on a river flowing into the beach and the manatees playing among the water reeds. Even though I knew the couple was my parents.

The next day, with this picture in my mind, I felt a tiny bit of happiness and decided I would try to understand my father's coldness. But I never got the opportunity because he disappeared, just like that, for a full five days. There was no warning except for a note stuck on the fridge. Written in bold letters was: Don't open the door or answer calls from strangers. And scribbled underneath: This is not Trinidad. So you better learn the rules real fast.

Chapter Three

MOTHSKI THE MOLEMAN

When you are cornered inside one place, with just one view, nothing seems interesting after a while. By the second day of my father's disappearance, I had memorized what I could see of our slice of the neighbourhood. I could make out the tops of rows of tall buildings that looked like an unfinished dominoes game. I knew where the school must be because I could see children with bookbags come running home across a big street nearby. The smaller children, bandaged up in coats and fluffy hats, and gloves that looked like paws, would be met by women in veils while the bigger ones loitered around their buildings a bit and shoved each other as if they were about to fight. They never did. I could anticipate when the sidewalks would get crowded, though couldn't say why. I knew when the men with turbans and the little stooped ladies would walk slowly to one of the buildings. Once I saw an old man sitting on a bench feeding pigeons. He had a bag at his side and as the birds got closer,

I felt he would snatch a couple and push them inside but he just continued feeding them. Later, a fat lady came and sat next to him but they didn't seem to know each other.

In the beginning this was interesting because it was all new and I compared the view with that from our house in Mayaro, where each day I would see the spindly coconut trees and the narrow asphalt road and the low concrete houses across the road and the bushy backyards livened with hibiscus and crocus and fruit trees with swinging cornbird nests. After four days, this comparing business became boring and to shut out the dullness, I tried to imagine Spider-Man and Batman swinging from the crane that stood on top of a several-storey building a little distance away. I pictured the Joker or maybe some half-mad Canadian murderer talking to his orange cat inside one of the red boxy buildings and laughing at nothing in particular.

I wanted to get out and roam the city but I remembered all my father's warning so each day I stared at the young boys playing basketball nearby, and fat women holding their grocery bags in one hand and their cigarettes in the other, and every now and then, an old-timer riding one of these scooter-machines. When I got tired of the view from the balcony, I turned on the television. One of the channels talked about the weather, which was far more interesting than the Trinidad weatherman, who said the same thing day after day: sunshine with a possibility of rain.

Then one night the phone rang. I ignored it but it rang again and again. Finally, I picked it up but before I could get a chance to say that my father was not at home, the voice on the other end said, "I will pull out your tongue." I almost dropped the phone but I was too shocked. "I will kill you over and over. Then I will kill you again."

I managed to say, "The owner of the place is not at home."

"Who is this then?" I heard some heavy breathing as if this murderer was puffing a cigarette.

"I am staying here for a while."

"Then you give him this message. Tell him that I will kill him every single day of the week until I get back my teeth."

"Teeth?"

"Exactly." He made a gnashing sound.

That was the end of my boredom. And of following my father's rules about keeping inside. If the murderer knew the phone number then he might also know our address. The apartment was no longer safe.

As I walked through all the lanes and the paths between the houses and the curbs, where there were bicycles hooked onto metal ramps, and posters stuck on lamp poles advertising community meetings, and huge metal boxes overflowing with garbage, I tried to push away this new worry by watching the heap of children all over Regent Park. They seemed to be from every country on the earth and they sometimes shouted in their strange languages as they ran about. This was comforting in a way, because it reminded me of all the different types of people squashed together in the bus from Mayaro to Rio Claro. I always stopped at the edge of Regent Park though, opposite Shuter Street, where the buildings reminded me of the cramped office blocks in San Fernando. Apart from this teeth-murderer, Canada didn't seem to be all that different from Trinidad.

Every time I returned to our building, I would peep from the elevator at the door to our apartment before I headed for it. I pictured the murderer as a big fat man with a thick neck and curling whiskers. His head was shaved and there were rolls of muscles at the back of his neck. He might have a bag with knives and tongs and ice picks. Thankfully, I never spotted him at the door but two days after his threats, he called again. I don't have any Spider sense or anything but when the phone rang, I instantly knew it was him. I was scared but curious.

I picked up the phone. He said, "I am coming over."

I bolted out of the apartment and that morning for the first time, I went outside Regent Park.

I expected the people would stare and know that I was new to this country but no one even glanced at me. I never suspected there were so many black people in Canada, some Mayaro-black but others light brown like my father and wearing long robes. They sometimes stood in little groups and spoke to each other in loud hacking accents. Each day I went a little further, to Sackville Street (which seemed such a sad name) eventually to Parliament Street where I took a bus that went to a place called Castle Frank. There I followed a group of boys down some steps. The boys, who were about my age, went through some shiny arms between two metal boxes but when I tried to follow, the arms wouldn't let me through.

A man inside some sort of glass cage tapped a sign just above a square mug filled with coins. The sign said two-fifty. I pushed three one-dollar coins into the box and waited for my change. The man looked at me above his glasses and then at two spongy women at my back. All three seemed vexed. I hurried away towards another row of steps.

When I was a little boy I had seen this television show where a girl was sent into a room with magic doors, leading to her dead mother in a smoky garden, to her future husband with long wavy hair, and other people she would meet. The minute I walked down those steps I felt like I had entered a place with a different breed of people. A sort of Bizarro world with all the rules reversed. I always imagined these train places as filled with curly-hair women in old-fashioned clothes clutching at a *grop* of children and staring anxiously at the approaching smoke, but here nearly everybody standing before the track looked lost and lonely and worried. I wondered if they, too, were puzzled about why they were here in Canada. The first train pulled off too fast for me to jump aboard but I glimpsed a row of eyes that were either too tired to look away or didn't care what they bounced up. About five minutes later, I rushed inside another train before the conductor could close the door and I almost sat on a woman who looked up at me like a big, lazy fish. She didn't blink her eyes, as far as I could see, for the entire trip. Sitting next to her was another woman whose entire face was covered in a veil. Her hands were white, though, and for some reason she reminded me of these old television science fiction movies like *Dune*.

I rode on the train for close to an hour, surprised there were no conductors asking to see my tickets. I was wondering how far the train would go when we arrived back at Castle Frank.

This Canada was turning out to be an interesting place. Dangerous, yes, but filled with little surprises. When I got back I wished that my father would be home even though I knew he would quarrel about my trip. But neither he nor the murderer was around. Late that night I believed someone was knocking on the door but it may have been a dream. The next morning I headed for the subway train place, and the minute I landed there I was able to put aside all my worries. I felt this was the place to which trapped people came to spend their time. I boarded the train and sat next to a small man with a big funnel nose and two button eyes and hardly any chin. When he gave a little start and looked at me angrily, I realized I had mumbled aloud what was running through my mind. Mole people! I had come across them before in comic books and old movies, plotting and building bombs in underground places, but it was exciting to meet them face to face here.

Don't ask why I began to wonder where these mole people were going because this is the only answer I can come up with: it was another game to get my mind away from the murderer and the situation in my father's apartment. Anyways, for a few evenings I followed them to long, flat buildings with signs advertising manufacturing and packaging goods. Just like the real mole people slaving away below the ground, making ray guns and laser beams for their masters! It was easy to spot them too: they were all dressed in oversized coats, had dirty knapsacks, usually seemed tired and sleepy and kept to themselves, and always headed for what I guessed were factories. I was sure they only came out at nights, too. I think it was a little under a month in Canada that a crazy thought hit me, just like that, without any warning: Was it possible that my father was a mole man too? I remembered his stupid "oompa loompa factory" talk and pictured the train suddenly stopping before a factory and all the molemen filing out in neat lines and singing as they made their way to a big underground factory.

I began to go out earlier, in the mornings during rush time, where, in places like Broadview and Chester and Pape I made another interesting discovery: the mole people were just one of many different breeds. There were also pretty high-boot women who walked straight and stiff like men, and scarf and turtleneck young men who walked in the opposite manner, and Chinese boys who were always glancing through their modern glasses at their reflections in glass windows, and old spotted men who looked so angrily at everyone else I expected a snort to fling out from their fat, red noses at any minute. A couple times I pictured my mother sitting next to me and watching everyone and saying, "You see, Sam. I told you . . ." as if she knew our lives would turn in this direction.

During my walks back to the apartment, I wondered what my friends in Mayaro might think of this place, which—in spite of my first impressions—was so different from what we had seen on television; and how I might describe it if I decided

I had enough and took the next flight back to Trinidad. I felt they would not be surprised that I had tried to soften my problems with these stupid games because we regularly did the same thing at Mayaro School. Thinking of my old friends consoled me a bit but it also reminded me that I was trapped in a place with a father who barely spoke to me and a murderer who might pop up at any minute. One night I wrote a letter to Uncle Boysie. I thanked him for the money and said that it was very handy. I told him the Canadian business was not working out and I believed it was time to return. I lied and mentioned that I missed working in his old store stuffed with mechanical and gardening and plumbing tools.

The next day, with the letter in my pocket, I was in an especially worried mood. I knew what Uncle Boysie would say. That I should stick with the plan and not allow these difficulties to *downcourage* me. He might make some reference to my father's slackness. And he would also say that my mother, if she was alive, would have been so happy that I was in a place with plenty opportunities. I think it was this worry that caused me to get off at Coxwell station where I followed one of these molemen who was pushing out his lip as if he was stretching it to touch the tip of his hat. Tracking a single moleman in the broad daylight made me realize that the movies had given me a wrong idea of trailing for it was far more difficult than I expected. First of all, I had to keep a good distance between us because I didn't want him to swing back and catch me. He also stopped a few times to light his cigarettes and to just stare quietly at the clothes set up inside shop windows so I had to stop too. I followed him to a coffee place, and from a little convenience store across the road, I saw him taking a paper cup to a small table near the wall. I don't know how long he remained there reading his newspaper but eventually the store lady asked me impatiently if I was going to buy anything. Just then the moleman left and I stuck with him as he made his way to a church.

He went inside and after a moment, I did too. It was packed with mole people and they were selecting cans of beans and soup and fruit juice from long tables. Nobody seemed to be paying and I joined a line and grabbed a bag of doughnuts. I felt a little ashamed when I noticed that I was younger than everyone there so I left with nothing else. It was only when I was on the subway that I realized this might be the food bank I had called and asked about provisions and dry goods and whisky. I tried to hide the doughnuts inside my coat, next to the letter to Uncle Boysie, and when I reached our apartment complex, I hurried up the stairs instead of taking the elevator. As I reached to our floor, my doughnuts almost dropped out from my coat because I came face to face with a big shaved-head monster that looked exactly like Bane from the *Batman* comics. I walked straight past our apartment and only when I reached the end of the hallway, I turned around. The Bane man had taken the elevator.

Inside, I double bolted the door and peeped over the balcony rail, but I could not see him. Was it possible that he was living in this apartment complex? I checked the front door again and went into the kitchen. There was a plate on the cupboard and next to it, a crumpled lottery ticket. After ten minutes or so I knocked on my father's bedroom door but there was no reply. Maybe he had spotted Bane and had blazed away. I wondered if this hoodlum was carrying around a bag of sharpened teeth jangling like river conches.

The next morning I was especially cautious as I made my way from Regent Park to the subway. I got off again at Coxwell and scanned around for groups of molemen before I went to the food bank. I felt I needed something solid to pelt at Bane in case he showed up so I took two cans of chickpeas. While I was walking home I remembered Uncle Boysie telling me, "The fella above does always balance out everything but is we who have to tip the scales." I had felt it was his usual rumshop nonsense but here I was, with a murderer on my back at the same time I had more or less solved my food problem. I got home just before midday and immediately the phone rang. I figured that he knew I was here and would come over if I ignored his call so I picked up the phone. It was my father. "Anybody called?" he asked.

"Somebody wanted back his teeth."

"I thought I told you not to pick up the blasted phone." He hung up.

Five minutes later the phone rang again and I rushed to it. "I have urgent need for my teeth."

"My father is not at home," I blurted out.

"You is son?"

He had trapped me. "Yes, but we don't talk to each other much."

"*Now* you talk. To give message. I am in a mood for many killings. You understand?"

I tried to reason with him. "What is the point in killing him more than once?"

"Because I am grandson of Cossacks. It is my hobby."

"I don't know when he will return."

"Then it fall on you. You must come with brand new set of teeth."

"Where I will get teeth from?"

"It is for you to decide. Teeth or money. You make choice."

"How much?"

"I will calculate." There was a screeching sound as if he was adding with his nail on a wall. "It is forty dollars. You bring it to me."

I thought it would be much more than forty dollars. "Where you want me to drop it off?"

"Not drop off. Bring, bring. You understand? To same coffee shop where I give you."

"You didn't give me anything."

"Father, son. Same thing. It is your duty." He seemed angry so I did not interrupt him while he gave me the directions to his coffee shop in Parliament Street.

I was to meet him at noon so I went early to the food bank and got the biggest tins I could find. It took a while to locate the coffee shop even though it was within walking distance from Regent Park and before I entered I scanned the customers. There were just a couple old-timers seated around a table, and sitting by himself, another old man with a Wilson hat and a greyish coat. I walked in, hoping that Bane had changed his mind. The group of old men glanced at me and returned to their staring at each other. I chose a table with my back safely against the wall. The man with the hat came across and pulled a chair next to me. He placed a tightly wound package on the table. I was about to tell him that I was waiting on someone when he asked if I had the money.

I was astonished. I was expecting a murderer, a Cossack, Bane, but this slight old man seated next to me resembled a dry, dusty moth. He was wearing glasses big enough to be goggles and behind it his eyes seemed real squinty. His voice seemed different too—although this could be just because of how safe he looked. He told me his name, which was very long but ended in "-ski." I wondered if I should hand over the money to this harmless Mothski man. He noticed me staring at his package and said, "Teeth. I make for woman from Sri Lanka. Big, long teeth." He measured the size with his thumb and forefinger. "Some prefer big teeth. Sri Lanka, Somali people. Some prefer small. It is their choice. Big one, small one, same price."

"You are a dentist?"

"What else you expect me to be? Zookeeper?

I thought about mentioning a Cossack but instead I asked him, "You made some teeth for my father then?"

"Not some. One. Some cost plenty money. One cost forty. You have?"

When I gave him the money he took off his hat and pushed the bills into one of its inner folds. He replaced the hat on his head. "Now I buy you coffee." He shouted to a pretty orangeish girl clearing a table. The girl came over, frowning, maybe at his rude voice. "Two coffee. One for me and one for my friend here." She looked at me and I noticed how big and nice her eyes were. When she went to get the coffee he told me, "Very pretty. You like?"

"Yes, she is pretty."

"She remind?" I didn't know what he was saying until he repeated the sentence.

I almost mentioned Rita from Mayaro Composite but didn't want to get too friendly with this Mothski so I shook my head. He laughed, making a greasy, whirring sound, and revealed that when he was younger he had many girlfriends. He made teeth for their mothers and fathers back in Bulgaria. "I go to their house," he told me. "And only when parents are dizzy on chair I make my move." The girl brought across the coffee. He drank slowly with a slurping sound I always hated. "You make move on turkey girl?"

She didn't look like a turkey one bit. Just the opposite. Maybe a peacock girl. I remained quiet.

"I tell you something." He dragged his chair closer to me. "If you don't try then you never know. Free advice."

I tried to change the subject. "So you make false teeth?"

He looked at me sternly and I felt he was going to slip into his Cossack voice. "Open your mouth. Let me see." I pulled away because he was clutching at my face with his nasty fingers but it was too late.

I managed to force out, "Don't do that." His grasp was strong and I felt his thumb digging into my cheek. The old people from the other table were staring at us, but blankly, like cows.

He twisted my mouth open. "Nothing spoil as yet." He bent a bit to get a better view and I slapped away his hand. I could still feel the imprint of his thumb. I noticed the orangeish girl staring with her wide eyes and I felt ashamed for having submitted to this slight Mothski man. Maybe I should stand up and pelt some good curses on him. Insult him upside down. "Many people report me," he said sadly. "They say I practise without licence. Not a real teeth-doctor." He said something that sounded like "zebo-lekar." "But it is . . . how do you say it . . . is service for poor people. People from different place who come here. I feel so happy when I see somebody from far away. Rotten teeth. Bleeding gum. Loose molars. Bad filling. Stinky breath. Like if bomb explode inside mouth. I want to fix everything and make new. Like artist. My wife was artist too. I proposed with her father strapped tight on my chair." He took his package from the table and got up. "But that is past tense now. Now I live byself." I saw him blinking behind his goggles as if he wanted me to feel sorry for him but I felt he deserved all his bad luck. "My sons, they all disappear."

"Maybe you treated them badly." Don't ask why this slipped out but Mothski glanced at me for a good minute or so. Finally he got up.

"I go now. But one more free pound of advice. You must make move on girl soon. You are good boy but if you not change in hurry then gifts just pass by, whoosh-whoosh." As I watched him shuffling out from the coffee shop in his goggles and hat, his body bent, I realized he was a moleman. Mothski the moleman. I remained in the coffee shop for another half an hour, trying to digest how this situation had turned out and what it could teach me about my new country, Canada. Every now and again the group in the nearby table would glance in their unfocused old people manner to my direction but I felt that they were looking past me, maybe at the dirty wallpaper.

My father showed up at the end of the week. That same night while he was watching *MacGyver,* I told him, "I paid the dentist for the teeth."

He remained silent but I saw his toes twitching, a sign he was thinking. MacGyver was building a beeping aerial so that he and a woman could escape from a booby-trapped field and when my father said, "Is this sort of assness that does cause problems in this place," I wasn't sure if he talking to them or to me.

Chapter Four

THE GOOD OLD DAYS

Although I continued going to the Coffee Time at Parliament Street I never saw Mothski again. Most likely, he was busy frightening some poor victim with his Cossack talk. I liked the coffee shop though, because it was usually empty except for the old-timers who mostly stared at each other and coughed and read the *Toronto Sun*. Every now and again they gazed sleepily at the tight-jeans girls who carried their purchases outside to chat and smoke in little groups. Once the orangeish girl caught me staring at a group and she looked a little angry, which gave me the idea that maybe she was jealous. Even though I never talked with her, just the idea that there was a pretty girl close-by, who was my age, gave me a nice feeling. Off and on, I would imagine that I was sitting on one of the wooden stools in Mrs. Bango's parlour or the dry goods store that was hooked up to a rumshop, and that the old-timers were fishermen who had just returned with their catch of moonshine and kingfish and bonito, and instead of drinking coffee and staring at the *Sun,* they were sipping Puncheon rum and quarrelling about some alderman who never returned after the elections in spite of all the bribes they sent his way. Talking and listening and never removing the cigarette from their mouths.

Here, most of the old people ate rice puddings and drank soup with trembling spoons and nearly dead lips. There was a telephone nearby and mostly black men would come in to make calls, waving their arms and sometimes glancing at me surrounded by old-timers. Maybe they were wondering what I was doing there with all these people with brown spots on their pink faces. I pretended I was staring at the faded wall pictures of men with hockey costumes and sticks and masks posing like comic book warriors, or at the old clock that was stuck at three o'clock. Every evening a moleman came in and he too would gaze at the clock as he sipped his coffee. This moleman was neither white, black nor brown and I put him down as a *coco-panyol,* a mixture of everything. A few times I thought I should go over and talk with him but he was always concentrating so hard on the clock that I felt he might be mad. Sometimes when I glanced at the orangeish girl with her nice jewellery I would wonder how she might decorate the place if she was allowed to. It might be yellow and pink and orange instead of plain cream colour. She might have a picture of her father and mother smiling with each other just above the counter.

Twice a week, I would head for the food bank. My father, when he was around, never asked where the food had come from and I never bothered explaining. Maybe he felt I had bought it with Uncle Boysie's money but one night he asked me, "You working as yet?" and when I said I wasn't he added, "I see," in his mocking voice. A couple days later he asked where I disappeared to every evening and I remained quiet because the coffee shop was my own little secret.

Although the old-timers never talked with me, just being around the same familiar faces every day removed some of my loneliness. But one day, one of the group, a man of about sixty with a big head, which looked like that of Christopher Plummer from *The Sound of Music,* said something to me in a strange language. He had never spoken with me before and I felt it was to show off to the pretty oldish lady at his side. I had never seen her there before and now the Christopher Plummer man was in a happy mood, laughing and waving around his hands as he spoke.

From then on, she was with him every evening. He began to seem slightly out of place in the gloomy group, but he would wave to me and he would say, "Yaksha mash," or "Ko-me-chi-wa." Though I didn't understand what he was saying to me, his friendliness told me these were greetings of some sort, and I returned them in the Trinidadian fashion by nodding my head quickly, once. And the small pretty lady would pull at his sleeve and tell him that some day he would get into trouble for striking up conversations with perfect strangers. But she always said this loudly and with a mischievous smile, as if she was enjoying my confusion.

Soon, the Christopher Plummer man began dressing like a *saga boy*, with burgundy and navy blue coats and brown leather jackets and medallions around his neck, maybe to match the lady who favoured these light green and yellowish pants. They seemed so different from all the old people I had ever known, not only because of their stylish clothing but also in the way they held hands and seemed not to have a single worry in the world. Sometimes I would play my old game and place them in a Trinidadian setting and I would imagine everyone staring and *mauvais-languing* this grandparent couple for carrying on like carefree teenagers. Me, I was just happy to bounce up a happy face every now and again, especially after the sourness in my father's apartment.

"So where are you from?" he asked about a week after the nice-looking lady showed up. I think this was the first English statement he made to me but before I could answer, he looked at the lady and added, "Wait a minute, let me guess." She glanced from him to me, smiling. "India?"

"No."

"Iran?"

I shook my head and felt some of my shyness stripping off with this game of his. I was surprised that the other old-timers just continued staring at the Sunshine Girls in the newspapers. In Trinidad, they would have joined in the game even if they didn't understand what was going on.

"Are you sure? I had a friend from Iran who looked exactly like you. Could it be Pakistan or Afghanistan?"

"Trinidad," I told him.

"I was wrong by just a few thousand miles, dear," he told the lady. "And I think I know why. He's never spoken to us.

Why don't you say something for us in Trinidadianese." The lady whispered into his ear and he asked me, "Is bashfulness a Trinidadian trait?" I didn't tell him that over there, bashfulness was viewed as a kind of sly weakness. A cover up for some shameful secret. Or worse, a sign of pride that was an even worse vice. *Now,* the old-timers seemed interested and they stared at me as if I had crawled out from a nearby hole. One of them, a short man with a red cap and a nose that resembled a big spreading yam, snorted directly at me. "Just the opposite," I told them. "Everybody like *bacchanal* there." The Plummer man leaned towards the lady and they both stared at me for a good minute or two.

While I was walking back to Regent Park on that cool day in April, I wondered for the first time how all these people on the street and in the subway I was always watching, saw *me.* A couple with a pram gave me the usual one-second glance. Same with a woman who peeked up from her book, and I wondered if she had made an assessment in just one second. But how could this be? How could all of them notice my clothes and shoes and expression so quickly? Unless these things were not important. In Trinidad the glances were long and questioning; they were like the silent beginning of a conversation.

As I crossed Shuter Street I thought once more of the coffee-shop lady question about bashfulness. Once Auntie Umbrella had called me "an only child" like if it was a sickness, but our old wooden house with its concrete posts, just a half mile from the sea, was sometimes crowded with neighbours, usually women who brought along their children.

We would play marbles and top and *zwill* with flattened bottle caps, and *scooch* like the game in the movie *Dodgeball,* and hide and seek between the crotons and ginger lilies in the yard. I grew up with these friends, Guevara and Pantamoolie, and the whole batch of Lopi grandchildren. As we got older, we took these games to the Mayaro High School, and to the beach, where we added *windball cricket* and football and *kite-cutting.* At the beach too, we helped the fishermen pull in their seine nets and were rewarded with shining bonito and moonshine with their scales looking like small silvery shillings, and if the day's catch was good, a nice thick kingfish. We cut classes from school, *lackarbeech* we called it, to hang out with the old coppery fishermen, not only for the little gifts but because of all the stories they told us about getting lost at sea and bouncing up Venezuelan coastguards and spending time in prison there. They told us, between their sips of Puncheon rum straight out of the bottle, about the sharks and barracudas they had caught, and tapirs that had swum out straight from the Amazon River and manatees that looked like pregnant mermaids. The most interesting stories, though, were about the smugglers who chose the nights and the rough coves to drop off their drugs and guns and tons of money.

When my mother heard from my fourth-form history teacher, Mr. Chotolal, that I was skipping school to hang out with the fishermen, she got in a real bad mood and said I was following my father's wayward path, good and proper. Before he disappeared completely, my father had been briefly a fisherman who spent many nights and weekends at sea. And when I mentioned the fishermen's stories to *mamaguy* her, she said that I was becoming an "ole-talker" just like my father.

But after a while, she had stopped complaining, even the few times I came home later than usual after a crab-catching trip in the mangrove. Maybe she was just busy with her sewing and watching her Bollywood movies from the video player Uncle Boysie had given her.

Just thinking of my Mayaro friends and the fishermen and the drunkards who would wake up the whole village with their loud greetings when they came home late in the nights from the rumshops made me sad. I wondered what Uncle Boysie was doing the same instant I was entering the housing complex, and all of a sudden, I recalled my mother's funeral service at the Mayaro Presbyterian church and the crowd of villagers who surprised me by showing up at the cemetery half a mile from the church. These thoughts, especially of my mother sitting by the front window and sewing her clothes in the old Singer with the mournful Hindi song broken up by the machine's clapping pedals, caused a little shock to crawl down my back; and all of a sudden, the place seemed colder and the air heavier and the traffic slower than usual. On my way to our apartment I wondered why my steps seemed so heavy and the distance so long. This mood lasted the next day and thankfully the old couple was not there in the coffee shop because I was in no mood for their scattered happiness.

They showed up the following day, though, and I think the lady must have noticed the new strain on my face because for the first time she lost her smile as her companion was joking around in one of his strange languages.

"Do you have a minute, friend?" The Christopher Plummer man gestured to an empty chair. When I sat, he let loose some foreign words in a fast shouting accent like these Japanese from *Bridge over the River Kwai*. The red cap man sitting with them was wearing a green blazer that made him look like an ugly macaw. He looked at me crankily before he got up with his Zane Grey western and walked shakily to the door. "Don't mind Roy," Christopher Plummer said. "He hates all young people. So?"

"So what?"

"You accepted my invitation. I suppose I should say, *"Mum-moon.* That's 'thank you' in Persian."

"How do you know all these words?" I asked the question that had been on my mind since I first heard him speak.

From his reaction, I think that was a smart question. He pulled his chair an inch or so closer to mine. "I listen to people all the time. And when I begin a conversation in their own language, they open up just like this." He snapped his fingers. *"Ja-tory!"* he shouted to the orange-coloured girl who was wiping a nearby table, and when she waved to him, he told me, "See. It's a special talent."

"So they are all different languages?"

"You must try it sometimes."

"First, I have to learn English properly." I didn't tell them how much I hated Spanish and French classes at school or of a conversation with Pantamoolie. I had told him there was nothing better than comic-book English with the gulp-ing and sighing and constant threatening. Still, I wished I knew some of these languages now so I could impress the girl but the Plummer man didn't give me much time to reflect on this. First he told me his name was Norbert and then he began his story about how he lived in a place called Cabbagetown. From there he had moved all over the place working as a salesman until he ended up somewhere called Brantford. He and the pretty lady were going to start some sort of Internet business to export Canadian medicine to the States. The lady didn't say anything much, just smiling and playing with her necklace as Norbert talked a mile a minute and I wondered if she, too, was imagining this strangely named town as a place where cabbages rolled on all the streets like tumbleweed from old Westerns. And children playing cricket with the small ones and football with the bigger ones.

Norbert called out to me every evening and I soon joined the group of old-timers. From a distance they had always appeared like cows grazing and chewing their cud but I soon discovered that they had many adventures in their younger days, and had worked for a while on trains travelling through Canada. They had lived in England and other places in Europe before they landed here. I learned many other surprising facts. I discovered there were places in Canada where mostly Germans or Portuguese or Italian or Chinese lived. "This is what I like about Toronto," Norbert told me. "Just cross the street and you are in a completely different country. Everybody's here."

The way he said this I imagined that all these people had come as visitors and liked the place so much they decided to stay. I pictured them leaving the ships and rushing straight for Cabbagetown, collecting a few of the vegetables on their way. I hoped Norbert would describe this strange town but Roy glanced up from his *Toronto Sun* to talk about a little girl who was killed while she was waiting for her friends at some nearby street. After this, everybody got quiet and Roy returned to his newspaper.

The next day I felt that he was continuing the topic as he brought up another shooting, this one between gang members. To tell the truth he made the city seem more dangerous and interesting than I had imagined. I remember Uncle Boysie telling me that Canada was so safe the policemen wore nice red outfits and rode on horses but according to Roy the country was like Gotham City with crooks around every corner. When he pushed the *Sun* before another old-timer and said, "Look at the faces of these thugs and see what they have in common," I pictured them as shady Frank Miller characters with bulging muscles and machine guns poking out from trench coats but the photograph from the papers was of a group of boys my age. They kind of resembled some of my friends from Mayaro, too.

I soon realized this was Roy's pet topic as he was regularly grumbling about subsidized housing and criminals who could never be deported and little children running around with guns. All these recent swarms of newcomers were congesting the place and inconveniencing people like himself with their welfare demands. Sometimes, when he went outside for a smoke I would feel that maybe he was a retired policeman who, on the days he didn't show up, was chatting in the station with old friends.

Even though there were no sharks and manatees and smugglers the conversations were always more interesting whenever the group talked of their old-time days. I tried to imagine how Toronto would have looked before all the tall buildings and congested streets were built. Maybe it was like Mayaro with fields of cassava and plantain and coconut trees. Some of the stories were related by a really thin, trembling man whose name I never got. He was from somewhere called Friezeland in the Netherlands and during the war, he hid many Jewish people in his house. He talked sometimes about his move in 1951 to Canada to work as a cheese maker somewhere in Thunder Bay and then to Kitchener, where he had many run-ins with Germans at some annual beer festival. Later, the Germans became his best friends. A truck driver came in now and again to complain about the long waits at the American border and his encounters with policemen in Florida. He considered most Americans as boldfaced braggarts, which was a big shock, because in Trinidad, I always felt they were not too different from Canadians. His name was Jim and although he was as red as a flask of wine, the way he stared crossly from on top of his glasses reminded me of Uncle Boysie dealing with a troublesome customer. Another man, who from a distance looked completely grey, down to his skin, said he had lost two brothers in the war. They spoke about this war quite often, and as though it had been fought just a couple months earlier.

This was new to me: in Trinidad we had no wars (except the ones from our history texts about Captain Jenkins's ear and those with Spanish armadas centuries ago). It felt sort of strange sitting so close to people who had some connection with a war I had seen only in the old movies starring Richard Burton and Clint Eastwood and John Wayne, and sometimes while they were discussing some battle or the other, I would wonder how my Mayaro friends would react if they could see me with all these pale, wrinkly old-timers who were always wrapped-up in thick sweaters with Christmas bells and decorations. I felt they would shake their heads and laugh and make jokes—or *picong*—about my new friends who smelled sometimes like stale milk, and who talked with long gaps and stared outside as if they had forgotten what they were saying and who woke up coughing from little naps. I think they, too, would have been surprised that no arguments broke out between those who had lost family members in the war, and Norbert, who boasted about the fairytale cities his parents once lived in like Bavaria and Dresden. In Trinidad there would have been bottles flying on all sides because everyone there seemed to collect and save all the insults thrown at them. Every now and again, someone would mention Cabbagetown and I would pay extra careful attention as if I was in Mr. Chotolal's history class. Once, Norbert mentioned an Ebenezer Howard fella who had designed something or the other in Cabbagetown. I almost told him that the

Ebenezer name made me think of wrinkly, giraffe-neck men in pyjamas with long sock-hats hanging over their ears but when I glanced around the table, I felt that maybe it was a good thing I kept quiet about this.

The orangeish girl glanced over regularly and I felt she was wondering what I was doing with this pack of old people. I wanted Norbert to call out to her again but all of a sudden he seemed to be more interested in a new topic: the scheminess of doctors who were prescribing all kinds of drugs for healthy people, and these drugs companies that were making tons of money by inventing useless drugs, even for dogs and cats. One day I told him about old Lopi who claimed he could cure diseases with secret Spanish prayers and who prescribed fever grass and aloe vera and hibiscus flowers for this and that sickness. Roy stared at me with his coated eyes and said, "Damn voodoo rubbish," which got me a little mad, not because I disagreed but because he was so quick to criticize. Norbert then began a speech about natural drugs and different types of diets. This topic went on for a week or more, and to tell the truth, I was getting fed up with all this health talk. I believe his friend, judging from her quietness, also didn't like this new direction. She began to go outside with Roy for a smoke whenever he got onto this topic. During those times Norbert complained to me about the chemicals in cigarettes but never to her.

One day I saw him alone in the coffee shop. He was dressed in his usual dark suit and greeted me in another strange language so I didn't make much of his friend's absence. Later, he told Roy that she was on a trip to the States concerning her new business. Roy began to cough and went outside with his western paperback. I waited for Norbert to bring up the cigarette chemicals but he didn't talk much that day, even when Roy later said that if Canadians didn't begin to make more babies in a hurry, the country would be unrecognizable in a couple years. "Where did you say you were from?" Roy glanced over as if he had noticed me sitting at the table for the first time.

Just for spite, I told him Regent Park, instead of Trinidad. He shook his head, doubled a page in his western, and went outside again with his dragging footsteps. He was grumbling under his breath and I wondered how he would have reacted if I had said, "Strange visitor from another planet." Because Norbert was gazing at the cakes on the counter and not saying anything, I asked him, "When is your friend coming back?'

The minute the question popped from my mouth, I regretted it because Norbert took a while before he answered. "She's met some old friends there." He said it in a dry voice that came from high up his throat, which made me think that the meeting had taken place on a dark bridge over a deserted tunnel. That was all he said for the entire evening and I decided to leave him alone. In the days that followed, I noticed that although he was as stylishly dressed as usual, he was no longer greeting me in his different languages. He also stopped talking about Cabbagetown and more about his German places. Once when the old grey man brought up the topic of his two dead brothers from the war, Norbert interrupted him to say that in this Dresden place, many innocent people had also been killed. The other fella hit back by saying that it was the same in London where, early in the battle, there were never any advance warnings of air strikes. Norbert said that the difference was that people were willing to discuss one city while pushing the other under the carpet.

This argument didn't blow up in a big shouting match as it might have done in Trinidad but that day, I felt that something had changed in the Coffee Time. More and more, Norbert took the side of Roy whenever he began his complaints of politicians who were bringing in foreigners just to get more votes, even though these people could barely even speak English. When Roy was listing off the problems in the places these foreigners came from, like Nigeria and Pakistan and Jamaica, I felt relieved that he didn't know more about Trinidad. I noticed, too, that he always used the old-fashioned names like Ceylon and Rhodesia and Dutch Guiana. He felt that Canada was changing into an unfamiliar, dangerous place, with strange people in unusual clothes walking all over Toronto. Talking about Cabbagetown, Roy said they were lucky not to have welfare palaces like the ones along Kingston Road, and then rattled off a list of posh places for refugees from Somalia and Ethiopia. "Guess who's paying for all this?" This became their new topic.

I don't think they were making up this refugee talk but sometimes while they were grumbling, I would think that the Cabbagetown stories of poor families had interested me more because I was in no better condition, and also because these people had turned out so well. I couldn't understand why they were now discussing these new gold-digging foreigners right in front of me and one night, as I was walking to my apartment, I had to laugh when the thought hit me that they had one of these old people diseases that blanked out colour. That same night I decided that I would cut down my visits to the coffee shop because I wasn't making any progress with the orangeish girl who worked there.

The next day I began to explore the area beyond Coffee Time and came across other coffee shops with busy young people staring over their laptops and talking into gadgets hooked up over their ears. I would imagine myself like this, maybe five or six years down the road. I looked through the window of a Starbucks place at a girl facing away from me. She was sitting on a stool and there were tear strips on her tight jeans. I began to wonder if she was waiting on somebody when she turned and saw me gazing. I rushed away; it was not a young girl but an old lady with a stiff smile and a pointed chin. I remembered Pantamoolie saying he could tell the ages of all the Mayaro women by how high up on their waists their dresses were, as they went up half inch each year. He would have real problems here because of these thick coats that could disguise any kind of shape.

I decided to visit this Cabbagetown place that evening instead of Coffee Time. When I crossed Gerrard and Carlton streets I tried to ask directions from a boy my age but he backed away and held up his hands as if I was going to attack him. A man with a long beard and dirty clothes pointed to the north and I walked for ten minutes or so before I realized

I had not marked the buildings for my return trip. I was about to turn back when I spotted a building that could have been drawn by Gene Colan. The steeples and old-fashioned windows and solid brick walls made it look like a castle. Or maybe the Wayne Manor. I wandered around the compound until I came to a plaque that read, Toronto Necropolis. Necropolis: I had come across the word in horror comics and on my way back I imagined that all the old Cabbagetown ghosts were roaming around the place and also complaining about how much the place had changed.

For the next week I, too, roamed around the place, looking for shops with vacancies advertised on their windows but the owners—in all types of accents, some hard to understand—each asked me about my Canadian experience as if they were setting some trap. When next I went to the coffee shop, Roy said, "Look who's here. We thought you had gone back to Mexico."

He laughed in his coughing way and I decided he had made a joke. But that mood didn't last for too long because they soon moved on to their favourite subjects: high taxes to pay for these welfare immigrants, some useless human rights group, young people crime, and old falling-apart army helicopters and tanks. This last topic set off Norbert and the trembling man about the war, and a museum in Ottawa, and Dresden, and the big holocaust. Then Jim, the truck driver, mentioned another of his trips to Carolina and said that Canada was getting too soft and unimportant, and everybody got real quiet as if this was really what they had been arguing about for the last half an hour. To tell the truth that put me at ease, and during the remainder of that session, I felt that maybe these old Canadians liked to throw out all their grievances just to see where they would hook up. Maybe they were like old people everywhere else, always complaining about how things were turning out and how much better they used to be. Uncle Boysie himself used to say the same thing about Mayaro.

The next day on my way to Coffee Time, I made a list of my own grievances, which was easy because that same morning my father had complained about my idleness. Later in the coffee shop, it took about an hour before I got the chance to mention this big wall concerning Canadian qualification, and immediately Roy asked if I had applied for welfare. When I shook my head, he seemed a little surprised so I didn't bother to ask about whether I could qualify or not. For the rest of that evening, the only thing all these old people talked about were their long-time jobs as cheese-makers and ice-cream truck drivers. I don't know if they were throwing out advice but I was sure no one would hire me to make cheese or drive ice cream trucks. Then Norbert said that nowadays people were more interested in money than in happiness, and everyone got quiet for a while.

I let another week skip by before I returned to the coffee shop and when I got there, the old people table was empty. I ordered a coffee and sat by myself. I noticed the orangeish girl staring in my direction but every time I smiled she looked away and I felt I was wasting all these friendly looks on the bare wall. I concentrated on my coffee.

"You by yourself now?"

I jumped and managed to say, "Nobody else is here today."

"The little one, he . . ." I saw her lips moving as if she was searching for a word. "Roy, you know?"

"Yes?'

"He feel very . . . how to say it . . . very dizzy. So they take him?"

"Where?"

"To ambulance." She sat at the nearby table and began refilling the silver napkin holder. "He was nice man. Very friendly."

"To you?"

"Yes, yes. He smile always." She smiled herself and I wanted her to sit right there for the rest of the evening. "I go now." She got up. "I have long-long shift. You work?"

A boldfaced lie formed in my head but I told her, "Nothing so far."

"Yes, but you keep looking."

I couldn't tell from her accent whether she was asking a question or consoling me. "Yes, I keep looking." As she was walking away, I said, "Mum-moon," but softly because I could not remember its meaning.

I was sorry when Norbert walked in a couple minutes later because now I would have to listen to him instead. Straightaway, he asked if I had heard about Roy and before I could reply, said that he had a stroke and was in the Downsview Hospital. I noticed the grey bristles on his face and the coffee stains on one of his cuffs as he gazed around at the customers ordering coffee and doughnuts. Jim the truck driver came in a few minutes later and both of them talked about Roy and his smoking and his unruly grandson and his wife who had died of cancer ten years earlier. Jim said that Roy was never the same after his wife's death, and things only got worse when he moved to his daughter's place. He lived for a while in an old persons' home and, according to Jim, his daughter wasn't happy when he left there to return to her place because he was forever quarrelling with her boys.

As they talked about Roy's younger days—when he owned a cottage near Peterborough and would go drinking and fishing with his friends, could repair all types of engines, and was a smart dresser (which was hard to imagine)—I got the idea they were feeling shaky because they were just a couple years younger than Roy. Then Jim said those days were gone forever and got up.

After Jim left, Norbert's gloomy mood didn't change much. He began to talk about his own young days when he played the piano with an old-time band. He gave performances at fancy clubs where one night he met his wife, who had just come from England. I thought he was talking about the lady who had gone to the States, but he described his wife as tall with red hair and a "loud bubbly laugh." He smiled a bit as if he was remembering something about his wife, and brightened up, even while mentioning how he lost all his money during some real estate crash and how his wife left him to return to England with their son. "What's gone is gone," he told me, using the same stiff voice like Jim a few minutes earlier. "At least we have the memories to sift through."

I couldn't understand if this was a lament because he had been talking for the last twenty minutes about his bad luck with his wife and his money and moving from job to job. And then it hit me that he was really talking about the small smiling lady. Even when he picked up some of Roy's favourite topics about welfare and immigrants, I felt his mind was on this lady. It seemed strange but I believed he was somehow blaming these immigrants for his woman-problem. Because we were alone that day, I felt I should console him but he got up and put on his coat like if he was real tired. Then he left.

"Any luck?" I looked up and saw the orangeish girl. I felt she was referring to a job so I shook my head. She sat and I asked her what her name was. "I don't like to give out name. I am sorry." I said I understood and she smiled as if she knew I was lying. "Okay, I tell you. It is Dilara. Just for you."

"Why just for me?"

I hoped she would say because she knew I would soon be her boyfriend but she told me, speaking slowly as if she would change her mind at any minute, "I get in trouble. I live . . . byself now. I want mother to come here but too far away." She got up. "But we have to look to future. It is all we have."

When she left to serve another customer I realized that she was the exact opposite of the old-timers with their conversations about their younger days and how things were changing so much and getting worse all the time. One week later, I got a job at a gas station on Jarvis Street, just a twenty minute walk from my father's building. At the end of my first day, tired and greasy as I was, I headed for the coffee shop to thank Dilara for her simple advice, which had encouraged me to not give up, but when I got there she was gone.

I wanted to tell her how I had walked from street to street asking all the gas station owners if they needed any help; I wanted to boast about how I eventually told one manager, who seemed fat and oily like if he had just rolled out from an oven, that my father owned a gas station in Trinidad and that me and all my brothers worked there on weekends. Maybe I would have left out the part about the manager—whose pants were unzipped—raising two fingers and saying, "Two weeks' probation. No pay. Any fucking around and you walk. Unnerstan?" I was so happy I didn't even care if he knew I was lying about my father's gas station.

I waited for a while at Coffee Time and wondered whether Dilara had left because she had given me her name or because of the trouble she had hinted at. I hoped, though, she had gotten another, better job. Several days later, I decided to visit on the off chance that Dilara had returned. Another girl was cleaning the table next to the one where Norbert was sitting alone. He seemed older and quieter too. He told me that Jim had returned to Milton but that he often spotted him at the Legion. I was thinking of the Legion of Superheroes when he said Roy had died. We remained quiet for a while and I imagined Roy buried in the Necropolis next to all his old friends. I heard Norbert saying something like, "Jen-kuo-bardso," and adding, "It's Polish. It's all my parents spoke at home."

The foreign language cheered him up a bit and he dropped a couple other strange phrases, so I didn't say what was on my mind: all his references to German cities and to his German parents. I couldn't understand why he had changed his own history and I wondered whether he had also made up all the stories about Cabbagetown.

On my way from work I would pass other rundown coffee shops with groups of old-timers reading the *Sun* and staring at the tight-jeans girls, and I would think of Norbert and Roy gazing back at the good old days, and of Dilara looking forward to getting a good job and bringing her mother to live with her, and I would wonder what, if anything, this knowledge told me about my new country. Maybe the old-timers looked down on newcomers like me because our short airplane trips could not match their long miserable sea voyages during which they had plenty time to remember all their friends who had been killed in some war or the other, while still worrying about how they were going to survive in this new country. I would have liked to throw out this observation to my father but could just imagine how he would react; so instead I settled on the simple idea that all old people were the same, regardless of where they came from. They preferred to sit among their own, polishing their memories and pretending that every change would bring a new set of *bacchanal*.

Chapter Five

TRUDEAU AND THE GOAT PILLS

At the end of my two-week probation at Petrocan I got a
blue overall and a cap. They were both greasy and I had
to wash them twice in the laundry room on the last floor
before the smell of oil disappeared. When I wore it for the
first time I felt a little proud because it was a uniform; not
the same as a fireman's or a cop's but a uniform nevertheless.
I wished my father was at home so he could see me. In the
elevator I saluted a group of little boys with a fast flick of my
finger like in the movies. They broke out laughing and one
said, "What the fuck?" As I was getting off, another stood
upright, saluted me, and almost in the same motion slapped
the palms of the other boys.

I don't think they knew I was joking in the Trinidadian
manner by posing a bit, and later at work when I repeated the
incident to Paul, the tall, greasy-looking wash operator who
had been working at the Petrocan for close to ten years, he got

serious as if I had stained the name of the Petrocan uniform and should be court-martialled. Paul seemed to know all sorts of secrets about the regular taxi drivers who came twice a week to refuel their tanks and sometimes to get an underbody wash.

When I told him that I was from Trinidad he told me he was from Newfoundland and that he knew much of the island I was from, but everything he mentioned—like the word "poo-nanny"—came from Jamaica. Which was why I wasn't sure how I should react to what he called his "inside info." He said that the strapped Sikh had been a wrestler and had developed a special cobra hold, and that the fidgety man with the neat moustache was once an engineer who had to rush out from Iran after some dam he was building washed away a royal palace straight into another kingdom. To listen to Paul, these taxi drivers were all doctors and lawyers and inventors and refugees and terrorists and Nazis and escaped criminals from other countries. Once he told me that a stocky man, whose head seemed to sink into his fleshy body like a *moroccoy* while I was filling his tank, was once the best cook in Poland. "Papa Perogies," Paul called him, and I can't say whether this was the name he was called in Poland or one Paul had given to him.

Now I should say straight off that Paul must have picked up his information from unseen sources because I rarely saw him talking to any of these drivers. It could have been his slack style of walking or all his beads and bracelets or the way his eyes would droop after one of his smokes in the garage, but no one really trusted him. Me, I enjoyed his stories even though they resembled some of the old movies I had seen at the Liberty cinema in Trinidad. Paul reminded me a little of my old school friend Pantamoolie who was always inventing stories about our teachers.

One of Paul's most interesting was of Dr. Bat. According to Paul, his real name was Bharanbose Atambee Tulip and before he came to Canada to drive his taxi he had moved from India to work as a doctor in Nepal. I never asked Paul how he knew that Mr. Tulip was once a doctor and when exactly his name had been shortened to its initials because I knew he would come up with some fancy explanation. Still, I was glad to see these ordinary-looking taxi drivers another way, and on evenings when my hands were freezing and my ears felt like frozen biscuits, for just a little while I would forget the cold.

Sometimes when I was cleaning the windscreen of a fancy van with a pretty woman and her son sitting inside, I would wonder about the kind of house they would return to and try really hard to imagine the fancy furniture surrounding them as they ate from expensive dinner plates while some sort of music played in the living room. I would picture the offices of the men who pulled in for gas with their ties and suits and the boyfriends of the women who fixed their lipstick in the rear-view mirror while I cleaned their windscreens. So close to them while they were doing this personal thing! I even pretended a few times that I was sitting next to these young women, but those pictures couldn't hold, because my mind would be empty about what would happen after they had pulled off. What we would talk about and where we would drive to. Occasionally I imagined that I was driving a red sports car and Dilara, in the passenger seat, was gazing at some other boy filling the tank. But this picture couldn't hold either. Sometimes I felt a trace of sadness, especially when I saw youngish people who I guessed had happy families and nice houses and cottages and who felt at home in this country they were born in. Which could be why I bothered to listen to Paul's stories of those who were not so lucky. People like myself.

Occasionally, I saw faces that may have been famous, although this was again according to Paul. He told me that the plump smiling man who looked like a baker's apprentice happily slapping on flour was from a show called City-TV, and the clean-head fella who resembled some of these old royal families from Trinidad almanacs was a top-class CBC man. "The mother corp," he said as if he was talking about his own mother-in-law. I know it might seem strange but I began to form a picture of Canada from all these people who drove in and out of the gas station. It was Paul who put the idea in my head when he said, "Snapshots, my friend. One hundred little snapshots a day." He claimed that he had serviced the cars of the prime minister and the mayor and hockey stars with names that reminded me of nibbled-down sandwiches.

Me, I just concentrated on the people who seemed average, maybe because I could frame-up their apartments and their jobs in the factories and the arguments with their children about new Canadian habits. The people who quarrelled about Canada but were afraid to return to their own countries. The taxi drivers and haulers and families packed inside big old Dodge cars. People who looked as they were always on the run from this or that. People like Dr. Bat.

I began to pay attention to their clothes and the shape of their cars and the food boxes crumpled in the back seats next to big-eyed children and cardboard containers filled with God knows what. Sometimes they would notice me staring and give me a funny look before they pulled off, and I would see them gazing suspiciously in the rear-view mirrors. One night, almost at the end of my shift, I noticed an old bulky camera in Dr. Bat's car. He caught me peeking and although he said nothing, when he returned later in the week, I tried to be extra careful with my little spying. While I was filling his tank, he picked up the camera and adjusted some small knobs and polished the lenses with the corner of his coat. He pushed the camera into a black leather bag and dusted the flaps.

This was the pattern for the next two or three weeks, and to tell the truth, I began to suspect that Dr. Bat was just showing off with his camera. So I was surprised, when one evening, he told me, "It is for quite notable documentary." I had expected his voice to be small and squeaky but it sounded hollow and flat like if he was rehearsing a speech inside an empty cup.

"What kind of documentary?"

"Yes, yes. Quite so. Notable."

I decided to leave it at that but during his next visit, when he mentioned once more his documentary business, I repeated my question. This time he reflected a bit before he said, "A complete parade of the jiggery pokeries and hul-labaloos."

I didn't know what to say so I remained quiet while he opened his glove compartment and moved around some paper and screwdrivers and little plastic packets. Finally he got out a thick wallet, overflowing with cards and paper peeping out from its flap. He pulled out a card, placed it on the dash, and turned on the interior light. I was able to read his card before he drove off. Dr. Bharanbose Atambee Tulip, exactly as Paul had said. Beneath his name was written "Archivist and Filmmaker," in small gold-plated, playful letters. I knew for sure he had wanted me to read his card. That same evening I walked over to Paul who was smoking at the back of the wash, and before I could ask him about Dr. Bat, he said, "I see you've made a new friend. What he's up to now?"

"I think he is making some film or the other." After a while I added, "He is really a doctor, you know."

"Dr. Bat? I doubt it."

"But what about the place near India you told me about."

Paul threw away his cigarette and pulled out a pair of gloves from his overall pocket. He flapped the gloves before he wriggled his fingers into them. "I think it was a front. He imports spices. Crushed rhino horns and cobra venom and goat pills. Stuff like that." Maybe Paul had also spotted the plastic packets inside Dr. Bat's glove compartment. "Not too sure if there are real universities in those places. Not even sure Nepal is real. Too many fancy stories about the place. So he's making a film, is he?" Paul asked this with a little drag in his voice, like if he was expecting all along that Dr. Bat would make a movie. "What sort of film is it?"

"Something about jiggery-pokeries."

Suddenly this strange word sounded rude and improper and Paul's eyebrows drooped a bit further which was a sign he was thinking. "Don't tell anyone, but he is looking for the Buddha."

"In Canada?"

"According to legend he will be found on a rock covered in ice." He said this in a low voice and I was sure it sprang from a movie. A few minutes later, he came up with a rumour that the fat red taxi driver, who looked like he would one hot day melt right into the seat of his Cutlass, was once a KGB agent whose specialty was toads' poison. I felt that Paul had made up this thing about *crapos* just because of the driver's appearance. This habit of Paul's must have remained in my mind, because during his next stop at the station, Dr. Bat caught me staring boldfaced at his little ears and his thick black glasses and his pushed-out lower lip. To cover up, I asked him quickly, "So how is the film coming along?"

He switched off his engine and pulled his bag onto his lap. "I am engaged in a desperate search for Chinooks and such." I wondered whether this was some strange Nepalese word for China but he added, "It is a notable expedition across Canada, so to say. Serious mapping of landmarks and highlights."

Just to make conversation, I asked, "Like *National Geographic?*"

"Utter bunkum and pooh-bah with willy-nilly pictures galore!"

"Eh?" I almost repeated the swearword the little boy had used in the elevator.

"I am observer and collector of rash views coerced on my people for eons." I thought of the Watcher from *Fantastic Four* but Dr. Bat didn't look the part. "The cloaked-up underbelly of hatched landscape. You follow?" He seemed so stern I nodded. "My observation has told me that we are . . ."

He clicked his fingers, trying to come up with the word. After a while I tried to help him, "Special?"

He shook his head and pointed to the sky. "Other beings."

"Like angels?"

"No such creature in my horoscope. I am a Hindu atheist." His clicking seemed angrier and louder. Finally he gave up and slid forward on his seat, closer to the window. "Pay attention, please. Many years ago I take train, second-class, from Hyderabad straight to Delhi."

"To look for the—?"

He held up a hand for me to be quiet. "On said junket, I jot copious notes of everything. The stations and rails and government buildings. And I say to myself, 'Dr. Tulip, it is quite correct to credit British thugs for rails and civil service and bulky laws but the thugs donated even more important bequest.'" He pushed out his lower lip and I noticed his tongue playing with his teeth. "They teach us to do red-letter taxonomies of copious animal, plants, and minerals. You follow?

Now we are better than said thugs in classification. Best book-keepers, best librarians, best scientists, best mathematicians, best accountants, best stamp collectors, best—"

I felt I had to stop him. "You must be proud of all this."

"But what is to be proud about, gas station boy, tell me please? Who knows what Dr. Tulip knows? Rather we are classified for corner stores and taxis and wife-beating and riotous sidesplitting accents. Now, the ranking is more disagreeable than before because sinister avenge plots is affixed to recipe." He waggled his head as he was complaining and I couldn't say whether this was a sign of his vexation or gloominess. When the driver waiting behind Dr. Bat popped his horn, he said, "That is why hasty chap behind engage in unrefined insults and verbal body blows." He drove off waggling and grumbling.

He continued to come twice a week to refuel his tank and during each visit he would mention some additional information about his expedition. But I soon noticed something strange: he began to sound angrier and angrier as if something was hindering his film. Once he told me, waggling his head one hundred miles a minute, "Everybody require Dr. Tulip to be picture-perfect Indian. 'Oh, sorry, master, it is my fault one hundred percent. It is my heirloom to be so bunglesome. God wills it. Please punish me, sir. I *insist.*'" He also switched back and forth from Canada to India, which made it even more difficult to follow him. Once he asked me, "Where did you spring up?"

"Trinidad. In a little village name Mayaro."

He looked relieved. "These whiskery chaps make it dire for us with their blowing-ups and such. We get hoisted on bloody petards most diabolical. So now Dr. Tulip and his ilk are fair game for questionable looks and third-degrees."

Whenever Dr. Bat stopped to chat, I would notice Paul looking on from the service centre and afterwards he would always ask what we were discussing. I don't know why I bothered to pass on Dr. Bat's speeches about the chaps who were giving his ilk a bad name, and how he had to be extra careful as he would be pressured for the smallest mistake, because Paul always acted as if he already knew all of this. Maybe it was because he always added tiny bits to the stories. All of a sudden, Dr. Bat's search for the Buddha changed into a quest for a baby Dalai Lama who was living, in all places, in Newfoundland. "These quests eat up our souls," Paul said, dragging on his rolled-up cigarette like a movie actor.

Later that week while Dr. Bat was discussing his documentary, he said, "It is unfortunate reality that India is notably eminent for superstitious mumbo jumbo and mystical sleight of hand and every such exotica. Such pigeonholes got soldered on our backs and follow us like leeches even if we profess medical or scientific training, par excellence. No point in Dr. Tulip making grievances public, because before he is finished, the nasty stares are there, the excuses are there, and before you know it, hey presto, the busy signs come up." At the end of my shift, I repeated this to Paul in a bored way because Dr. Bat was now making the same complaints over and over. Maybe what he told me was true but it was depressing to hear, and besides I had my own problems. Paul's talk of soul-eating quests had reminded me of my father, and of Dilara from the coffee shop. I felt I should write off Dr. Bat or maybe just fill his tank and pretend to be too busy to chat.

On a Monday morning, after my weekend off, Paul told me that Dr. Bat had brought in his taxi for an undercoating and wax job, and then real casually, he asked, "Do you know he journeyed to somewhere close to Tibet?"

"Yes, you told me. Nepal."

"No, no. Not Nepal. A glacier or something called Lhotse." He pronounced the word as if he was holding back a sneeze. "One of the highest places on the planet. Home to the fabled mountain kangaroo. And that's not all." For the next fifteen minutes, Paul told me about shy mountain cobras that escaped by drilling holes in the ice with their stiff tails, and snow porcupines with icicles instead of spikes, and ice monkeys that had guided two mountain-men named Hillary and Tenzing up the Himalayas. "Would you believe that he saw these giant rabbits with soft bubbly flesh like cake baking in an oven?"

And yet, no Buddha? I wanted to ask. I didn't believe it for one minute, but all of a sudden Dr. Bat was interesting once more. I began to press him about his time in Nepal and his taxi driving and his documentary and the plotting chaps and even about his ilk. Although he seemed glad I was so interested, he just continued talking about all his hardships. And I was forced to listen. He told me that he had saved up all his money to come to Canada but some doctors' group refused to recognize his degree so he had no choice but to drive this taxi, which he didn't even own and which made just enough money to pay for his apartment in Brampton, where he lived with his wife and two children. But with Paul he was different. Following the weekends when Dr. Bat brought in his taxi for servicing, Paul would fill me up with all the new stories he had heard.

During Dr. Bat's time in this Lhotse place, he had met Madonna and Michael Jackson and Elton John and Deepak Chopra and Marlon Brando. One Monday, I asked Paul what all these famous people were doing up in the mountain and he said they were searching for "the facts of life." He took off his gloves and blew on his fingers and looked so thoughtful, I felt that these facts were some kind of top secret. The same evening during my little conversation with Dr. Bat, I mentioned the facts just to hear what he would say. "Fact, number one, is Dr. Tulip steadfast karma as permanent taxi driver. Fact number two, is abusement by snooty passengers. Fact number three, is ever present whiskery troublemakers who drag Dr. Tulip in their messy ongoing grievance. Fact number four, is that said Dr. Tulip is trapped between two homesteads with no claim to either one." He added many more facts concerning the superintendent at his apartment and his disappointment with his children who no longer respected or obeyed him. Nothing about shy ice cobras and the mysterious facts of life or the Buddha. Every now and again I would drop little titbits from Paul's stories but he would never take the bait.

Meanwhile, Paul continued to claim he had wriggled out all kinds of interesting information from Dr. Bat, who, while he was in Lhotse, had discovered a secret group searching for a good hiding place for the treasures they had stolen over the years. I challenged Paul on this because it sounded like an Indiana Jones movie but he answered me right off the stumps, as if the words were on the tip of his tongue. He told me the group had stolen Beethoven's ear trumpets, which was some kind of hearing aid, and Dr. Freud's couch from a museum in London, and the stuffed remains of Able, a monkey sent into space, and Colonel Sanders' pacemaker, the first in the world ("looked like a small musical box"), and a hubcap from Elvis Presley's Eldorado Biarritz, and Mao's favourite chopsticks, and several unknown books written by famous writers. "*The Dodger's Instrument,*" he told me, thinking deeply. "An erotic novel by Charles Dickens. Used a pseudonym. Julius Babcock. Very few people know of it."

"Just you and Dr. Bat?"

"Believe what you want, buddy. I'm just repeating the facts as I hear them." He pushed his hand into his dirty pants and brought up a crumpled tissue. From this tissue he took out a brown capsule and popped it into his mouth. "Goat pills," he told me, swishing around the capsule. "Got it from Dr. Bat."

"What does it do?"

"Anything you wish it to do?" After a while his eyes looked a little glazed and he began to smile for no reason.

I know it sounds stupid that I would continue to press Dr. Bat about Paul's made-up stories. Maybe I wanted to believe that this sad, quarrelling taxi driver really had all these secrets packed away in the back of his mind, safe from all the bad treatment he claimed everyone was heaping on him. And when Paul said that Marlon Brando was not part of the group of thieves but was there to film a movie in which he played the Buddha, and that when Dr. Bat first saw him in his costume he immediately bowed at his feet, I casually mentioned the Buddha to Dr. Bat. That was a mistake because it opened the pipe to all his anger. "Life is big playground illusion," he told me, wiggling his fingers above his ears to show he was quoting some book or the other. "So all of Dr. Tulip bad luck and harassment is picture perfect hallucination. Just like poofy powder puff ghosts." He wiggled his fingers again. "Be patient, humble seeker of reasonable job and nice apartment, because soon, nirvana will land willy-nilly on your taxi." All this waggling and wiggling made him look like one of these classical Indian dancers I had seen in Trinidad. "Maybe Dr. Tulip conspicuous pigment cover is penance for previous life felonies. When he starve to expiration date, he will reincarnate into stout pink baby with upholstered pram. Then no more hullabaloos and, oh, the inhumanity."

This went on for a couple weeks. I had always listened to Paul's stories; now I decided to tell him in detail those I had picked up. So soon after Paul had reported his last instalment, which upgraded the list of treasure from the Lhotse seekers to include a dog called Owney stolen from the National Postal Museum in America, I gave him my own complete list of all Dr. Bat's worries. He smiled a bit and said he was not

surprised because philosophers like Dr. Bat were usually
tortured and unhappy because of their belief that there must
be some reward for all their suffering. He made the suffering seem like a choice. Before I could say this, he launched
into a story about Brando who had brought with him a big bag
stuffed with butter tarts and marble cakes and frosted raisin
bread and marshmallows (which turned brittle in the cold).
According to Paul, Brando was mistaken for an abominable
snowman by some Sherpas who pelted him with big blocks
of ice. Dr. Bat had rushed to his defence. "Must have been
quite a sight to see Dr. Bat and Brando too rolling down the
mountain with all his cakes behind him." He thought for a
while. "Trudeau was there too. Did I mention him?"

"No. What was he doing there?"

"A walk in the snow. There's no better place than Lhotse
for snowy strolls."

I decided to put a stop to this nonsense once and for all.
During his next stop at the station, I asked Dr. Bat point-blank
if he had ever been to Lhotse. He looked at me like if I was
mad but my mind was made up. Maybe I had mispronounced
the word. I threw out some other names: Owney, Colonel
Sanders, Julius Babcock, Marlon Brando. Trudeau. I can't say
how I expected Dr. Bat to react but the last thing I expected
to hear was, "Yes, quite so. My favourite lizard."

"Which lizard?"

"Trudeau." He wiggled his fingers and laughed, which
I had never seen him do before. "Bloody riotous revenge insti-
gated by Dr. Tulip, no less." He told me that soon after he had

arrived in Canada and was preparing for his family's arrival he had rented a small basement apartment from an old woman in Etobicoke. "Pleasant chatty-chatty woman but Dr. Tulip soon realized that these hammering tête-à-têtes about India were a good Canadian smoke screen and maple syrup." The first clue, according to Dr. Tulip was when the woman renamed her goldfish Krishna, and a new turtle Tagore. Both died shortly afterwards. "A bloody game. Killing out our heroes in deep-rooted instalments. Murder most foul." The last straw was when the old woman revealed she was going to buy a pair of kittens that she would name Gandhi and Nehru. Immediately Dr. Bat went to a pet store and brought the cheapest animal there, which was a little lizard. He named the lizard Trudeau. And each night he would pretend his lizard had escaped and would wail, "Where are you, Trudeau? Why have you deserted me, Trudeau? Don't leave me alone, Trudeau. Dr. Tulip is nothing without you." And Dr. Bat clapped his hand and laughed and laughed and laughed. He laughed so hard that a packet slipped out of his coat pocket. He bent down to get the package from between the brake and accelerator pedals. "Goat pills. Keeps the madam moist, so to say." And he broke into a fresh round of laughter, driving off and doubling over the steering wheel.

From then on, the minute he spotted me he would clap his hands and say, "Oh Trudeau. Why have you deserted me? Please, please come back, Trudeau." I never told this to Paul because I knew he would come up with a bigger story, but I was happy that I had at least brought a little fun and laughter into Dr. Bat's unhappy life.

One rainy night as I was walking home it occurred to me that he and Paul had done the same for me. I felt that all their strange stories had pushed away my worries about my father's mean behaviour. For a few hours every day I was immune. The rain gave the traffic lights at the intersection of Regent Street and Saskville Avenue a washed-out look, as if the city was about to melt so slowly no one would notice. While I waited for the lights to change I remembered my mother, too, making up stories of my father's trips and the gifts he would return with. I was about seven or eight then and I believed every word. During that time, the entire house had been covered with photographs. They hung over doors and windows and vases. Soon after I discovered comics I tried to read the photographs in that manner, panel by panel but I couldn't. They were happy and sad and happy and sad. Then one by one the happy ones were removed.

Chapter Six

THE HEALING ECHO

The following day I was in a quiet mood and when Paul came up with one of his stories, instead of adding to it or displaying any interest I just continued eating the sandwich I had packed earlier in the day. He fished out a crumpled cigarette from his shirt pocket and cupped a hand to light it. After a couple minutes he flicked the cigarette to the back of the garage and took out his gloves from his back pocket. He put them on carefully, opening and closing his fingers slowly, and I felt he was looking at me. During that entire week we were like that: me chewing quietly and Paul smoking in deep puffs.

I was glad he had not asked what was eating me up because I couldn't really explain how miserable I felt whenever I thought of my mother, and I would be too embarrassed to mention anything of my father. For instance, his comment the first time he had spotted me in my uniform: "A gas station boy now. Nice. Plenty ambition. Your uncle will be real proud. Oompa loompa." I was not really immune, after all.

On Thursday night as I was preparing to leave, Paul began to talk about some girl he had broken up with. He said she was a "terrible kisser but a great fiddler." He had accompanied her to rallies across Toronto where she would play the fiddle "like a goddess." One night she had told him that she no longer loved him and moved out. It was beginning to feel like a sad story but he said that a couple weeks later he moved in with her friend, a clarinet player. "Your own orchestra soon," I told him and he nodded as if he had taken my joke seriously. It was only when I was walking home that I realized Paul must have misunderstood my quietness. Yet one thing from that conversation stood out: these rallies all across Toronto. In Mayaro the only rallies were during election time when motorcades rolled though the roads with loudspeakers blaring insults at opposing candidates. Once two motorcades met at the main junction before the police station and bottles began to fly. The police locked up the station, turned off the lights and didn't come out until the next day.

I was sure these Toronto rallies were different. I couldn't picture these people—who walked with their gaze straight ahead, not bothering to smile or anything—cursing and pelting bottles all over the place. On Friday I asked Paul about the rallies. I waited until he was finished boasting about his clarinet player who was "a terrible player but a great kisser" before I inquired about the locations. He mentioned Queen's Park and Nathan Phillips Square and a couple other places.

The next morning I took one look at my father on the balcony and decided to head out but the minute I stepped out of the building I realized I had no idea where Paul's places were. Just outside the lobby a fat boy was tying his shoelaces. He looked a little like a panda and when I asked him about Nathan Square he pointed to the east and then to the west before he resumed his lacing. I stood there for a while until I noticed a stocky man in spectacles staring at us. He was standing next to a skinny old-timer wearing a brimless cap and some kind of white robe with white pants underneath. The old man also had on curling-tip shoes, which made me think of a grandfather genie. As I walked over, the glasses man held his gaze, seeming stricter with each step I made. I almost changed my mind but it was too late so I asked him the direction to Nathan Square. He fixed me with a strict glare and his lips twisted down as if he was about to *bouff* me up like an old schoolmaster.

"Are you going to the protest?" He pronounced his words carefully. Maybe he *was* a schoolmaster with his jacket and tie and thick glasses.

I wasn't sure what he was talking about so I told him, "Maybe."

"If we don't show unity then we shouldn't complain about being neglected."

I couldn't argue with that. "True."

"Take the Dundas streetcar then subway to Queen." He pointed the direction and I noticed the genie mimicking his gestures.

The streetcar was surprisingly packed with old, very well-dressed people. Perhaps the vehicle passed through some area of the city with fancy houses, and as we moved away from the park and into a street congested with buildings as old as those in Port of Spain but with foreign signs I remembered the coffee-shop bunch and I wondered how these streetcar people saw this part of the city. It took less than fifteen minutes to get to the Dundas subway station but the next trip went on and on. I had plenty time to kill but as the train passed beyond College and Rosedale and Summerhill and arrived at stations with unfamiliar names like Lawrence and York Mills and Finch I realized I should have gotten off much earlier. I wondered where exactly I would land up. Then the conductor or whoever made the announcements said we were now southbound and I decided to just enjoy the view. Whenever we pulled into a station I would feel these tunnels were the perfect place for the Lizard or the Morlocks. I could just imagine them leaping and clamping onto the windows with their slimy faces pressed against the glass and people bawling and fainting. But occasionally we emerged from underground into bright bushy valleys.

This time I got off at Queen, and while I was walking to the square I stared at the skyscrapers and tall office towers and noticed how different this part of the city was from Regent Park and the places near the Pape and Coxwell stations. I guess this was how I had pictured Canada when Uncle Boysie had first told me of my move. The people seemed different, too, moving in such a hurry I was surprised they didn't crash into each other. Some of them were staring down at their phones even as they crossed the streets. A pretty girl on a yellow scooter sped by and no one stared or whistled even though a good slice of her leg was exposed. At the entrance to the square some Chinese people were snapping an ugly statue that resembled a plucked, headless chicken. I strolled around for a while until I got to a small group holding up banners with Somalia and Sri Lanka and Palestine written on them. Above them was a statue of Winston Churchill and the sculptor was maybe in a bad mood because Churchill was frowning as if he was going to tell the crowd, "Get the fuck outta here." Maybe in a British accent.

In any case the crowd wasn't interested in the statue. A man with a round whiskery face like Santa Claus was shouting into a microphone about genocide and assassination and racism but the crowd seemed to be in a good mood. Every now and again they would raise their fists at something the Santa Claus man said. I thought of these shows with famous singers I had seen on television because there were so many lively, chanting people my age. I walked around and tried to understand what the meeting or protest was about. Another speaker took the stage and continued the talk about torture. The crowd grew a little quiet. This speaker, a slim man with buttoned-down cuffs was talking about his own experiences. His family had been murdered. He had been jailed for ten years. If he was returned, it would be straight back to prison for him. He mentioned the names of people who had disappeared. His voice got real low and the crowd moved closer to the stage. I wondered if his children were living with him here in Canada or had been killed.

There were many little groups and everyone seemed to know each other. Maybe they attended all of these meetings. I felt a little out of place, like somebody showing up for the wrong *fête*. Perhaps there were all these clubs and secret groups in Toronto new people had to join just to fit in. Then I spotted a woman who looked to be maybe twenty-seven or so, standing by herself. She had a notebook in her hand and she, too, seemed out of place. She was tall and slim and dressed all in black and seemed real quiet and observant. I wondered what she was writing but when I moved closer and peeped at her notebook, I saw only a single sentence: *Pain is an opinion on which we are free to differ.* Beneath was a squiggle of a sun or moon shining down on a few plants and plenty rocks. The eyebrows of the sun or moon were raised as if it was surprised.

I was a little disappointed by her stupid drawing; she had seemed so serious all the time. And that was the look she gave me when she noticed me staring at her notebook. "Are you a refugee?" she asked me.

"Of course." Don't ask me why this lie popped out, because the only explanation I can come up with was the unexpectedness of her question.

"I thought so. Afghanistan?"

At that moment I wished it really was Afghanistan. Then I could mention things I had heard on the television about the Taliban and warlords. A story formed in my mind about a young man running through poppy fields and chased by howling one-legged fanatics on camels and horses but when Dr. Bat popped into the picture I told her instead, "No. From Trinidad."

"Trinidad?"

I tried to make it dangerous. "Near to Jamaica."

"I know where it is." She sounded disappointed.

"I am an orphan."

"I know what you mean." I suspected she knew I was lying but I really felt like an orphan most times. "There's another rally here next weekend." She patted my shoulder lightly and walked away with her long black coat trailing after her like these people from the *Matrix* movies. I left soon after a wild drumming group with colourful clothes began their performance.

On my way to Regent Park I felt a little guilty about lying to the woman. Her question about Afghanistan reminded me of Norbert and the other old-timers who had tried to guess where I was from. In Trinidad my hair and colour marked me as an Indian, different from the black and the white people and the coco-panyols, but here I could be so many people. Nearly anyone I chose. Like Metamorpho who used to hang out with the Outsiders. This was exciting. I tried to think of strange comic book names in case anyone showed any curiosity: Sam Grapula. Ramahoody Moofins. Sookdeo Iggyports. Roti Ramirez. But off course no one asked. In Mayaro they would have stared at me and ask, "Who son you is, boy?"

Maybe it was a good thing no one asked.

On Monday Paul began his talk about his clarinet player. During their lovemaking she always closed her eyes and recited hymns, her voice getting louder and louder until she finally bawled out "Amen." This was a little embarrassing so I told him I had been to a rally. He went on about the clarinet lady and I wondered if she would be mad if she knew Paul was revealing all these secrets about their nights together. The next day he continued with this topic and maybe as a way of shutting him up I said I had met a woman at the rally. He got a little quiet and asked me to describe her. I said she had high cheekbones that matched her broad mouth and that she wore winter clothes even in this normal weather. He said, "Fascinating," just like Mr. Spock and I wondered whether she was his clarinet player. The next day he asked if I planned to meet her again and I nodded. To tell the truth the question got me a little excited and I thought of comic book words like *rendezvous* and *clandestine.*

The crowd was smaller than at the previous rally, and better dressed too. The man on the stage had a tartan hat and he was talking slowly and pausing and smiling at everything that came out of his mouth. He looked like an absent-minded professor reciting from his lecture notes. He said things like, "This world is divided into two groups—those who invoke some cause to varnish their self-delusions and those who sit on the sidelines consumed with doubt and loathing and cowardice." But then he went on to mention many other groups. It seemed as if he wanted to include everyone. The crowd didn't seem bothered by this and I noticed many of them nodding when he said, "We must unshackle ourselves from our delusions. We must act before the window closes on our fingers." He stood before the microphone as if he was trying to remember some other bit of his lecture, then he backed off, placed his hands in his coat pocket and reversed off the stage. The audience applauded.

"Brilliant." It was the woman in the trailing black coat. She had her notebook in her hand and throughout the next boring speech about how all businesses were hooked up in a secret deal, she stood real upright with a sort of secretive smile. At its conclusion, she drew another picture of flowers with big blocky drops of rain. There were faces on the drops. "I am so afraid."

"About what?"

She gave me a surprised look. "You, of all people, should understand." Maybe she was referring to my orphan lie but when I tried to look downcast, she added, "The strong must comfort the weak." She patted my shoulder. "Nearly everyone in this world is walking around with a broken heart."

That entire week I thought of her statement. In Trinidad, mad people usually said things like that but when I repeated the statement to Paul he reacted as if he had expected her to say this all along.

On Saturday, on my way to the Square, I saw the strict man and his grandfather genie on a bench. "We must take a stand," he told me as I walked over. "This is a new world. If we sit on the sidelines then we should not complain about being swept under the carpet."

The genie looked from him to me as if he was expecting a reply. His lips beneath his short beard were very thin. "The strong must comfort the weak," I told them half-heartedly.

"Rubbish! Everyone is equal. We concoct our own weaknesses and parade them as assets. *That* is the problem."

The genie fixed his gaze on me. I felt he could not understand English. "I'm going to a parade," I told them. "At the Square."

The genie cackled and said something like, "Gobble-gooky."

I decided to avoid both of them.

The rally was about global warming. This, at least, was interesting and many of the speakers talked about penguins and polar bears and nasty floods. One of them came with placard drawings of these animals. He smashed the placards one by one and gazed at the junk before him. "This is what will be left." He seemed quite tired with his smashing and collapsed as he was walking off the stage. Everyone applauded. After he was dragged away, a band of musicians came on stage, jumped up and down with their guitars and screamed out some lines. I saw the woman with her notebook, not drawing flowers but swaying with her eyes closed. She seemed to be in a good mood so I walked over. When she opened her eyes she said immediately—as if she had expected I would be there—"The healing echo of music." She closed her eyes once more while a rapper warned that the world was coming to an end. "It's going to burn and shizzle." He crouched and gazed up at the sky like these actors from *Chariots of Fire*.

"The healing echo of extinction." She opened her eyes slowly, flutter by flutter.

From the lights on the stage, I saw a little shower developing. I tried a little joke. "It's going to drizzle and shizzle," but she looked at me like if I was the crazy one. I considered mentioning something about the healing echo of drizzles but said instead, "We concoct our own weaknesses."

"Concoct?" She seemed surprised I had used such a big word. She patted my shoulder and left her hand there. I felt a little shy at this, and as the drizzle grew stronger, also trapped. Finally she told me, "There's a reading at the Art Bar next weekend. I would like you to come."

Although her gesture had made me uncomfortable, during the week I imagined it had led to other invitations, and I tried to imagine what her apartment might look like. I felt there might be pictures of flowers on all the walls and smiley faces on her fridge and fat cats jumping from a plump beige couch to a mysterious chest with strange engravings on its lid.

I had to walk a good little distance from the Christie subway to get to her Art Bar but I didn't mind because there were many interesting old houses on the way. Some resembled Enid Blyton gingerbread cottages with pretty bushes hiding their old-fashioned porches. It was completely different from the ruction of all the red brick boxes in Regent Park. When I got there, I saw a sprinkle of oldish people dressed casually like me, in sneakers and jeans and rumpled T-shirts, seated around long tables. A thin man with a thick, shivering moustache that made his neck seem longer was on the stage. He was telling some sort of story. "And so in this dream, I came upon this village where, with every step, I encountered another sign.

The roads in this village curved and crisscrossed into fields of ice and burning sand and huge sprawling forests. What did this dream signify? What was the true nature of the village?" He stroked his bony neck and gazed at the small audience. I noticed the woman in black hunched forward over a corner table. She seemed to be thinking deeply. The man on stage said, "Each sign was written in a different language."

A woman with sunglasses on top her head shouted out, "A global village."

The man on stage smiled, tapped his paper on the tall table before him and walked off. Everybody clapped. I felt this was going to be an interesting "mystery and riddle solving" night but next, a short woman with glasses almost as big as her pointed face, came to the stage and said, "The mist slithers." She paused and looked over the heads of the crowd. "Slithers like an ethereal slime. Shadows stalk the slopes of the valley." She stopped again. I know it was unfair but I felt that in Trinidad, somebody would have pelted her with a bottle for taking so long. "Tattered clouds are haunted by the ascent of so many spirits." She went on for another ten minutes.

The next speaker or poet, a young man a couple years older than me, was even worse. He started by saying that he had compressed his life into one single poem. "The pain, the bitter pain. The chasm, the unbridgeable chasm. The ideal, the fecund ideal." He repeated himself like that with every line until he reached the end, "The farewell, the final farewell."

I thought it was a mistake to come to this place with so many unhappy people (and to be honest, I wondered whether they were pretending or had genuine problems with their fathers who treated them as if they were parasites). But just when I had written off the night as a complete waste, a small man with patches of stiff, upright grey hair came to the front, held on to the mike tightly as if it was going to escape and began to talk about reincarnation. He said he might have been a coelacanth fish because his family treated him as if he didn't exist. Then he changed his mind and said he might have been a platypus because he had hidden testicles like that animal. I wanted to laugh but everyone around was too serious. Then he began to talk about some lizard he alone had seen. He said this lizard was never attacked by other animals, because whenever it was confronted, it would clasp its hands together and tears would stream down its face. He imitated the lizard by squeezing his hands across his chest and looking pitiful. When he knocked his head against the mike, I felt that he was still imitating the lizard but I soon realized that he was crying. A woman came to the stage and placed her hand around him but he knocked his head a couple more times before he followed her off.

I was still thinking of this strange man and his hidden testicles and his sly lizard when the Matrix woman came up to me and said, "The world is filled with suffering. I am glad you came."

Most of the crowd had left and I was really waiting for her. "Me too."

"Do you drink?" She said this suddenly as if it had just popped in her head. I thought of the five or six times I had gone out with my friends from Mayaro to the dirty rumshop right on the beach. Although I had just two Carib beers during each of these rumshop visits, I always got drunk, and during the last occasion, my mother had said that I was turning out exactly like my father (which was strange because he was not a drinker). I don't know why the woman asked me about drinking because she ordered two coffees instead. She took a little sip and said that she hoped to travel the world someday. Somalia and Ethiopia. From close up, her broad mouth looked dangerous and pretty at the same time. She mentioned a couple of other countries and then became quiet as if it was my turn to talk. But I had nothing to say so we sipped our coffees for another ten minutes or so. Every now and again I would catch her looking seriously at me. She asked again if I had enjoyed the night and said there was another reading (that was the word she used) the following weekend.

The next week Paul chatted a bit about his clarinet player and then asked about the Matrix woman. I told him that she put on her coat with one smooth swirl which for a second made it look like a flowing cape. I think he was disappointed that my description did not match his rude details about the clarinet lady. He asked the location of the Art Bar and I mentioned the Christie subway and the gingerbread cottages. On Saturday as I about to leave my father asked me, "You getting ready to knockabout again? What happen, this apartment get too small for you now?"

"I going to a reading."

He got mad at that. "You couldn't do that in Trinidad? Reading, my ass."

"Oompa loompa," I told him, but beneath my breath. Once I got to the Art Bar I felt that my father might be less grumpy if he went to these events. I never realized there were so many interesting people in Canada. That weekend a man with a safari hat read a poem about his love for rats and weasels. He wished he could have a bacteria as a pet. He would call it, Bachy. And a virus, which he would call, Vivvy. "I feel like a randy marsupial sometimes," he said, grinning and showing some real big teeth. The next week a woman recited a poem she called "But." She started of by saying that the word was one of the most useful in the English language and gave a couple examples. Then midway in her poem, she claimed that she could see these buts. They were tiny, furry animals with glowing eyes and stumpy tails. When she was finished, an old Indian man with a banana drawing on his shirt, got up and said he enjoyed the poem very much. He said his name was Mr. Bhutto. Everyone laughed and applauded and the Indian man looked as if he didn't want to sit down after that.

Finally he took his seat and a fat man with a necktie and a soft baby face told the crowd he had invented a new language. He said, "Writers are propartarions of each other as we possess identical roticles detectable only to a trained psymodist." The crowd applauded which encouraged him to mention places he had visited, like Taposar and Melarou and Scragibad and Dowski and the island of Ascadara. I hoped he would describe these strange places but he shifted to a beautiful woman who worked in his office building. He had never spoken to her even though every night he dreamed that he was, "Gently luftating her twin papyrons."

The Matrix lady nodded and played with the button on her blouse.

I think the real reason I went every weekend was because of my conversations afterwards with her. I wondered sometimes whether her friendliness was because she felt I was an orphan but one night she said that my eyes were filled with pain. It made them beautiful and "soulful," according to her. I wanted to compliment her too and almost mentioned her breasts, which I had recently begun to notice. Instead, I remained quiet. During these times she, too, got quiet, leaning forward and dripping out some small detail of her life. Her name was Canella, and she worked for little periods, as a security guard, a landscaper, a camp instructor and a baker. She liked the time in the bakery because she was "fat and happy then." Once she said she would like to become a cobbler. Because of my school stories, I always placed cobblers in the same category as leprechauns, elves, and gnomes. They were stumpy old men with bumpy noses and white beards. "Just imagine," she told me. "Repairing shoes, which are dusty with miles and miles of travel. Boots, which might have stomped along Mongolia and climbed the foothills of Bhutan. I might pluck out tiny spurs and spotted eggshells and seeds from thousands of miles away." I liked this sort of talk because it made me forget, for a while, my father, and making so little money at the gas station, and seeing so many happy people my age driving around with all their friends. As she described her foreign spots, I would think of the beach and swamp and the mangrove birds in Mayaro. But after a while, my mind would drift to comic book places like the Negative World and the Phantom Zone and parallel universes where superheroes suddenly found themselves—maybe because Mayaro was too familiar and couldn't match up with all her exciting places. Sometimes in the middle of a fancy description, she would begin to talk about wars, famines, floods, and "bug-eyed orphans." Little by little, I started feeling sorry for all these people with their strange poems I had once laughed at. I began to look forward to the weekends; it was my little secret, safe from my father and the genie and his grumpy owner and everyone else who got me annoyed.

But one night at the Art Bar, I had a real shock, because seated right at the front table were Dr. Bat and Paul. While a shorthair woman on stage was explaining why she had changed her name to Mother Man, I glanced over at Dr. Bat and immediately regretted I had mentioned the location to Paul. I couldn't understand why exactly they were in this place for crazy poets and writers. I sat at the last table and when Canella looked back and pointed to an empty seat next to her, I prayed that neither Dr. Bat nor Paul would spot me moving up. Thankfully, it was crowded that night and I soon realized why: some famous writer was going to read from his book and maybe give some advice afterwards.

This famous writer who said his name was Kelvin Raspail looked shy and quiet in his round sunglasses, a little like a cross between Elton John and a fat raccoon but what he read on the stage was not bashful at all. He said, "True progress can only spring from tumult. Consensus just breeds laziness." He coughed into a handkerchief that he flapped right over the head of a woman seated at the front and continued, "I have spent my entire life embalmed in the pleasurable stupor of hatred. I felt a pure rush each time I discovered another hateful person. I prowled the street, turned up to unsolicited interviews, sat in bars just for that one expression." He glanced around and I looked away, just in case he saw his look on my face. Canella's eyes were bright and her nostrils opened and closed a bit like someone tired from climbing stairs. Then the writer finished his reading and asked if there were any questions. To my surprise, Paul got up. He said he had been writing a story for seven years and could never get beyond the opening line. He read this line: "It was on the seventh day of nineteen seventy-seven, when my crippling disease was finally diagnosed as incurable, that my mind turned to murder." The writer suggested that he change this sentence but Paul said it was set in his mind like stone. Next, the writer suggested he change the date or the disease or the diagnosis or his reaction but Paul had a ready answer for all of them. The writer was getting real mad and I think it was this anger which caused him to be so rude to Dr. Bat, who got up next with a pile of paper in his hands. His story, he said, was about ice kangaroos, snow crabs, her father who was dry and evil and her mother who got drunk on wine and imagined that everyone she knew had been replaced with impostors. I ordered two more beers and when mine was finished, two more. I began to feel tipsy and when she asked about Trinidad I told her about my mother waiting all these years for my father to return and pretending to everyone in the village that he was regularly sending her money and gifts. She leaned closer when I revealed that just before she died my mother returned from my uncle's place to our house where she began to dress up like a woman going to a party. Don't ask why I felt so sad and angry at the same time—maybe it was the beer or recalling all these events—but when I reached the point where I met my father at the Pearson airport, I couldn't continue. She reached over and took my hands and stroked my fingers one by one as if she was trying to take off an invisible ring. I looked at her breasts frankly and when she noticed and smiled, I didn't look away. She leaned over and brushed her broad mouth against my cheek and squeezed my fingers and wrists.

Sitting with her on the streetcar, her eyes opening each time the vehicle stopped, I prayed that my father would be away. As we walked towards the apartment, I was suddenly struck by this dangerous thing I was doing. I opened the door nervously and saw an empty plate on the kitchen table and a *Popular Mechanics* magazine on the couch before the television. The balcony door was closed which meant that he was not outside, smoking. Canella went to the washroom and for a moment, I had this dreadful thought that my father

blind terrorists, one-armed dacoits from Bombay, many spicy foods, weeping Bollywood brides, and a superhero named Captain Hindustani. Surprisingly, he was speaking in a Canadian accent and I wondered if he reserved this voice for special occasions. But the writer would have none of it. "Utter offal," he said when Dr. Bat was finally finished. "Nonsense of the highest order. All this exotic stuff is fouling up our bookstores and giving writing a bad name. My one bit of advice to you would be to stop writing immediately. And burn what you already have."

Dr. Bat sat down. He was trembling and I felt he would have many more conversations with his Trudeau lizard. At the end of the function, the writer left immediately and so did most of the crowd. While we were drinking our coffees, Canella asked me, "So what do you think?"

Maybe I wanted to impress her. "I know two of the writers."

"Really? How come?"

"A little group." I felt that mentioning the gas station would somehow lessen my connection. I was relieved neither man had spotted me in the dim light.

After a while, Canella told me, "I met Kelvin once. I was very young. He felt that yeasts were the source of all life. Did you notice the pained expression on his face? It's the look of the premature ejaculator." That night she mentioned many other famous architects, poets and sculptors she had met when she was young. Though she didn't give too many details, I imagined her lying naked in her plump beige couch while her important friends stroked her cat and said weighty things between puffs of their pipes. And every night during that week, I imagined this scene but with me instead of Kelvin Raspail and other old people.

I began to think of her differently and frequently during our conversations, I would glance at her nice breasts and her broad mouth and the way she would bite her lower lip while she was thinking. I can't say whether she noticed this new interest and whether it might have caused her to ask about my first girlfriend and my perfect partner and my thoughts about white women. These questions were really awkward, because in Trinidad, nobody ever talked about these things except in a boastful way. Once she said that I blinked quickly whenever I was ashamed. She looked at my face and said that long eyelashes were a sign of sensitivity. She slid her chair closer and told me about a Lebanese poet who would bury his face in his hands afterwards. "As if he was ashamed of his transgression." Though she did not explain what this transgression was, I had a good idea.

I began to dress differently each Saturday. I bought a striped turtleneck jersey and a grey wool jacket and light brown leather shoes from the Donation Centre. I was tempted by a blue beret, which many of the crowd wore but felt I would look like a perfect fool in it. My father got a fit the first time he spotted me in my new outfit and quarrelled about the rent and groceries and all the other bills. "Less than three months in the place and you already become a little follow-fashion *locho*. Monkey see, monkey do. Typical Trinidadian *locho*."

Maybe he forgot that ever since my first paycheque I had been buying all the groceries.

The genie and his master also noticed. One night as I was about to leave, I met them both in the elevator. The man shook his head and his genie did the same. To tell the truth, that little gesture got me real mad and I wished they would choose some other person to criticize. If the older one was my genie, I would command they both be sent back to wherever they came from. Set them in a field surrounded by one-eye and hook-arm maniacs. However on my way to the Art Bar, my mind returned to Canella.

When I got there, I spotted a brown folder in her hand. There were drawings of animal faces on one of its side. She seemed a little unsettled that night and I soon realized why: soon after an old woman with plenty beads read a poem filled with unusual recipes like baked babies and scrotum soup, the host called Canella's name and she walked to the stage in her Matrix manner. I thought she would recite a poem about shoes or the healing echoes of this and that but instead she read a story. The woman in the story worked at a museum and was "fixated on slender men with childlike features." She had affairs with a couple of sick and dying people and once with a dwarf from Florence who drew only the "corpses of birds with live intense eyes."

It was an interesting story and I told her this at the end of the session. That night she ordered two beers and she seemed more in motion than usual, waving her hands and crossing her legs and playing with her hair. She talked about

might be in there. When she returned, she took off her coat, placed it on the kitchen table, and walked over to the couch. She laid back her head and closed her eyes. As I sat next to her I noticed her breasts poking out from behind her shirt. She made a little tired sound and slid her head onto my shoulder. Some of my tipsiness returned—or maybe it was nervousness—and I played with the collar of her shirt and its top button. She placed her hand over mine and once more squeezed my fingers. But I was determined to get to her breasts and I loosened the button and slipped my hand down. I felt her hands over mine guiding me. Her skin felt soft and slightly oily, or maybe silky and from the dim balcony light, it seemed really pale. It was strange then that I should remember Paula who was two years older than everyone from our fourth form. She had showed me her breasts while we were walking home from a school bazaar but laughed and ran away when I tried to stroke them.

When Canella suddenly stiffened, I thought I had reached that point with her, too. "Stop," she told me in a quiet voice and when I glanced up at her I saw her staring at the door. I turned around. The door was open and it took a while before I saw the shadow of my father framed against the doorway. I froze. Canella buttoned her blouse and slid upright. I wondered how long he had been standing there, gazing at us. Without saying a word, he went to his room.

Canella got her coat and in the hall she walked with long strides. On our way to the streetcar, I spotted the old man and his genie sitting together on a bench in the park.

Canella didn't speak for the entire five minutes it took for us to get to the streetcar but at its entrance she held my hands, looked at my face, and pulled me towards her. She told me softly, "We are always hostile to those who reflect our weaknesses." Then she walked away. On my way back, I wondered if she was talking about my father, or me, or her dwarf from Florence or her Lebanese poet. Or herself. On my way back, as I passed the genie, I heard his handler saying in his mocking voice, "This is the new way. Always games and foolishness," and the genie cackling and saying, "*Phoolish-ness.*"

My father never said a word about what he had seen; not that night, not even during his bad moments. But his attitude towards me changed. Rather than his usual quarrels, he would now stare at me as if I was an enemy in his apartment. He crashed plates against the kitchen walls and slammed his bedroom door and I would hear him swearing in his room and banging against the wall if the television was too loud. Once, the genie and his master got into the elevator from the floor beneath ours and they both gazed disapprovingly at me. I couldn't say whether this was because they had spotted me with Canella or because they heard all the commotion from their balcony beneath ours.

Even though I finally had some spicy details to share with Paul my mind was more on my father and on the genie and his master. For the first time I wished I lived in a place far from Regent Park without a father who would suddenly walk in and catch me stroking a woman's breast. During my weekends, instead of going to the Art Bar, I began to stroll around these little streets with their old houses half-covered with vines and plants, and pretending I would one day live in one of these buildings. I thought of them as villas and wished I knew what their insides looked like. I ventured further and further each trip and—as the weather was now warmish with people dressed in shorts and light shirts—I walked for an hour or so before I took a streetcar.

During some of these walks I would recall the Art Bar people and what I would have said if I was asked to read out a poem or something. I played around with a story of a boy who walked around some strange city touching all sorts of objects and immediately getting a vision of other people grazing their hands on these same objects. I believe the boy could also gauge the thoughts of the touchers during the exact moment of contact. Maybe his name was the Astonishing Connection Boy or Memory Lad or something like that. One night the beginning of another story—but with the same boy—formed, just like that:

When my mother died, I felt I had already received glimpses of all that would follow. Like if I was once again sitting on a dusty, silvery asteroid and could see through lanes of swirling space dust and dark, puffed-up clouds and even the samaan tree in our front yard where the shadows of our Mayaro neighbours cast a crooked picket fence on the coffin. I could even make out Uncle Boysie still looking funny in his black suit, staring again at the road as if in this replay my father would suddenly appear in a big puff of sulphurous smoke.

Chapter Seven

AUNTIE UMBRELLA

I t was Auntie Umbrella who appeared like a puff of sulphurous smoke. I was making my way to our apartment after work and when I spotted her outside the door I thought at first it was my imagination because I had been thinking so much of Mayaro but there was no mistaking Auntie Umbrella. Although she was my father's sister she was the total opposite of him in looks. She was black like tar and had stumpy bandy legs that made her resemble one of these evil Dalek robots from *Doctor Who*. When I noticed an umbrella reinforced with bicycle spokes parked right next to a scrape-up brown suitcase, I knew for sure it was my auntie. She was trembling like mad either from vexation or the nightcoldness and when she spotted me instead of giving a hug she said, "Open the door fast, boy. This is not weather for man nor beast." Then she pushed me aside, dragged her suitcase inside, took a long look at the apartment, and headed for my father's bedroom.

"What you doing here, auntie?" I asked when she came out.

"What?" She had the habit of closing one eye whenever she was about to quote some criticizing verse from her Bible. Instead she launched into a long speech about my father; it seemed he was supposed to meet her at the airport.

"So he knew you was coming?"

"You hard of hearing, boy?" She glared at me with one eye.

"So how you find this place?"

"The Lord always protect his shepherd." But what she said next had little to do with the Lord. She had been dragging her suitcase and her umbrella around for the last two hours, asking directions from people who pretended they couldn't understand her accent. I felt they might have been afraid of her, especially as she mentioned the customs people in the airport making a big fuss about her reinforced umbrella.

That night for the first time since I came to Canada I wished my father was at home. While she was sweeping and cleaning and packing away, she was shooting questions at me like if I was on the witness box. Where was my father? Did he still chain smoke? What nonsense was he pretending to invent now? Why was the place so messy? Did I have a girl-friend? Why was my hair so long? How much effort would it take to simply put up a few pictures of the Lord? Was there a Presbyterian Church nearby? She didn't wait for any answers either, because after every question, she would sing, *Jesus loves me, this, I know,* in her scratch-up voice.

When I was about seven, she had dragged me to the tall, whitewashed Presbyterian Church next to a rumshop, and although I had put on my best manners while the preacher, who was also the principal of the Canadian Missionary school, talked about angels and ladders and locusts, and once, about a picture of Moses imprinted on a thick round cassava *pone*, when we got home Auntie Umbrella complained to my mother about my behaviour. "The little boy like a top," she had said. "He can't hold still for a single minute. Good material for the devil." To tell the truth, while all this was going on I was wondering how everybody in the church excepting me could spot old-man Moses on the cake. My mother always listened quietly to all of auntie's proverbs but once I heard Uncle Boysie telling her in a lighthearted way, "The damn woman like a bat that get hit with lightning. Feel she so special with all this fire and brimstone talk."

She had never married and even though she lived in Rio Claro, close to an hour away from Mayaro, some nasty rumours had sprung up about her. I had overheard Latchmin, the sign lady, telling another woman from the church that Auntie Umbrella was once engaged to be married to a bus driver who on the day of the wedding disappeared completely, bus and all. According to her story, Auntie went up and down the island searching for him but all in vain. Another story was that she was engaged to a musician who disappeared too. Auntie would stop the taxi or whatever else she was travelling in whenever she heard ballroom music streaming out from a house and rush up the stairs like a madwoman. All the stories were about her *almost* getting married, maybe because she could frighten anybody.

Even though I never believed these stories—that always seemed to be about stumpy, quarrelsome people like Auntie— the musician story may have had some little truth because her house, which was boxy like her, was filled with music instruments such as a one-string guitar and a piano that I never saw open.

"Where all the furniture in this place, boy?" She had hooked up thick glasses that doubled the size of her criticizing eyes.

"This is all it have."

"Where you does sleep?"

I pointed to the foam.

She let out a long sigh that halfway through changed into a belch. After a while she said, "Foam-poam," and I remembered her habit of rhyming words whenever she disapproved of something. That night it was strange hearing hymns coming out from my father's bedroom.

When I awoke the next morning she was sitting at the kitchen table, dressed in going-out clothes. For a minute I had the horrible idea that she was planning to accompany me to the gas station but she asked, "You have a key for this place?"

I held out the key. "Where you going?"

"The Lord don't make mistake. He send me here."

All day at work I wondered what Auntie Umbrella was doing. I prayed that she was not going from apartment to apartment like these Jehovah pests, harassing busy people with *Watchtower* magazines. I didn't know what to expect so I was relieved when I got home and saw her by the kitchen table wearing one of my father's old sweaters. She had a red marker in her hand and scattered before her on the table were copies of the *Star* and *Metro* and Caribbean and Indian newspapers. There were even a couple in Chinese writing. "Where you get these, Auntie?"

"From these boxes by the street corner." She patted the nearby chair. "Come here and tell me about Canada."

"I really don't know much about the place. I here barely three months." I tried to think of some excuse to leave. "What exactly you want to know?"

"Describe Canada for me, Sam." She closed her eyes.

"It like a mall."

One eye opened. "That is all? Describe the people and take your time."

I thought deeply. "It don't have any albino people here."

Which was true. There were four in Mayaro, and a couple in Rio Claro but auntie didn't seem impressed. "How you could tell for sure?"

I chose a safer observation. "If you cross the road you could come to a different country."

"America?"

"No, no. Batches of people from some country or the other sticking together."

"Like in Trinidad with all the Indian in the central, the Creole in Laventille and the white and them in St Clair?"

I didn't even know that but I nodded. She thought for a while before she asked, "Where you working?"

"At a gas station."

I thought she was going to criticize because in Trinidad that sort of work was only done by uneducated people. Instead she asked, "And you father? Boysie say that he involve in some workman compensation scheme. Scheme, in truth."

"I really don't know, Auntie. We don't . . ."

I felt embarrassed to go further but she said in a suddenly cheerful voice, "He will land straight in hell. With he foot in the air like a dead cockroach." She burst out in a hymn before she asked, "It true that everybody in this place could get free treatment for any disease?"

I wondered whether she was sent here because of some horrible disease like leper or Ebola but she then asked about the lottery winners who were pictured in the *Star,* praising their luck and thanking their gods from Guyana and Hungary and Russia for guiding them to Canada. I knew she was not interested in gambling because in Trinidad she always complained about betting and drinking. Next, she asked about a woman from some electric company who got a million dollars after she was fired. I think she was a little angry that I could not answer any of her questions.

Early the next morning as I was coming out from the bathroom she glanced at my towel and told me, "I hope you not involve still with this comic book nonsense. Tying your mother good towel on some mangy *pothound.*" I was surprised she could still remember when I had brought home a stray puppy and tied a red towel around its neck so it would look like Krypto. I was eight or nine then. "Superman-pooperman." She almost cracked a smile. "Now tell me about these senior bus tours."

So it went every day. By the end of the first week, the blue recycling box was completely filled with newspapers, and during that time, Auntie Umbrella had discovered there was a zoo with animals from around the world, an Exhibition place with many activities, a science centre with all sorts of fancy gadgets, ballrooms packed with rich women in fancy clothes dancing, and all sorts of art galleries. In the nights, while I was sleeping on my foam, I would spot her on the balcony gazing at the lights from the CN tower shining in our patch of the city. "It look as if somebody sprinkle jewels all over the place," she told me one night. "The Lord take his time when he was making Canada."

I was sleepy but still alert enough to tell her, "And it is a real safe place in the night too. Old people does be walking around in the parks all the time." I was tempted to mention the Coffee Time in Parliament Street.

She took my advice but went out in the days instead, and from then, I heard about the squirrels walking around as if they were not afraid of a single soul, and ducks that were not muddy and nasty like the Trinidadian variety but green and white, and flowers which were a perfect shade of red, and no miserable vines and stray dogs and rubbish all over. I never liked the area close to Regent Park but she seemed to see a balance between the lanes and the boxy apartment buildings and the little parks. "Everything design so nice.

A place for everybody." She made Regent Park seem like one big playground, and I have to admit that on my way to and from work, I started to notice all the things that I didn't have time to study before. The big greenhouse for flowers in Allan Gardens and all the grassy areas with benches for sleeping people and old people with no shoes. I sometimes varied my route and saw some pretty old houses that where not *mashed up* and haunted looking and hiding in the back of junked cars and bushes, but well kept like those cartoon ginger-bread cottages. I observed how all the buildings in some areas were alike and matching, and that there were no *macco* big mansion right next to rundown shacks like in Trinidad.

Eight days after she materialized I felt a rough hand on my shoulder. I was returning from work and when I turned, I saw my father with an old plaid hat and little grey stubbles all over his long face. "She went back as yet?"

I knew who he was talking about but he made me so nervous that I asked him, "Who?"

"Who? Who the hell you think I talking about? The *Dolly* Lama? Or that blasted woman you bring in my apartment without asking for permission? Eh? Your damn hypocrite aunt, that is who."

"No. She still there."

"When she intend to leave?"

"I don't know. She didn't say anything about that."

I saw him thinking. He looked a little like a dangerous spy in his hat and long coat. "She brought a lot of luggage?"

Just for spite I told him, "A lot."

"The bitch! What she does be doing all day?"

"Cleaning the place. Singing. And walking about in the park and watching the squirrels and flowers and ducks. She like the place."

He looked at me like if I was mad. After a while he said, "And with that damn umbrella stick up on her head, I sure."

Because he didn't say anything else I asked him, "When you coming back?"

"When that miserable old Presbyterian leave."

"Where you staying?"

"You is a blasted police inspector or something now?" He walked away with his coat flapping around his legs. I wondered if he was returning to a shelter. Surrounded by chanting molemen.

If my father was upset about Aunt Umbrella's visit to Canada, I think the place had the opposite effect on her. She stopped peppering me with questions and even her voice seemed to soften from its flat, criticizing scratch-bottle tone. She bought a broad straw hat and one evening, I noticed a brand-new red umbrella parked next to the couch. I started to get used to her and to tell the truth, I really enjoyed all the cakes and pies and cookies she baked. In Trinidad she would mention bake sales at the church to my mother but I thought this was just a Presbyterian habit. Now, she baked every single day, experimenting with the recipes she cut out from the newspapers. Fish, chicken, eggplant, sweet potatoes, apples, and pears—everything landed up in the oven. It seemed she had come with a good stock of money.

While the food was baking, she would sit before the television and switch from channel to channel. I thought she might not have approved of all the kissing and cursing and the rude boys and girls on television but while she was watching, she would pull the couch forward until she was just a few inches from the screen. One night she told me, "Look how friendly this politician mister is." I noticed a fat smiling man making chopping gestures with his hands as he spoke. He looked as if he was wringing a baby's neck. "And his cheeks so fat and nice. Just like a little child." The politician was saying something about clamping down on immigrants. "I feel I could just reach over and pinch them up good and proper." Another night, she frightened me when she mentioned that old people here didn't hideaway in rockers and settees but went about climbing and exercising and roller-skating. I had this picture of Auntie Umbrella with roller skates on her feet and umbrella on her head, scattering people on all sides. But she was interested in another type of show: those where people were selected to have their houses fixed up for free.

Listening to her, you would think there were packs of renovating people roaming all over Toronto just looking for people with old houses. "Who would believe that?" She would say over and over as old carpets and cabinets were ripped out and mildewed walls repainted and couches and tables replaced in fast motion. When there were advertisements, she would sing one of her hymns and I had this idea she was picturing the grey Presbyterian Church in Mayaro getting spruced up by muscular men and pretty women with tight jerseys.

I think these shows encouraged her to fix up the apartment in Regent Park because she bought doilies and vases and glass angels and wire flowers from a dollar store and I would see her sometimes glancing around and scratching her head before she shifted this or that. One night she discovered a channel that fixed up not old houses but ugly people. This show starred a woman who looked like she could frighten away bats but by the time the doctors had scraped her face and dug out a piece of her nose and siphoned out a bucket of nasty fat and capped her teeth, she resembled a movie star. Her boyfriend and family were waiting for her in a big hotel room and when she walked down the steps, everybody began to cry, don't ask me why.

"Look at that, eh. Look at that," Auntie Umbrella said, and I felt she was imagining her church people in Trinidad clapping and bawling as she entered the church fixed up, good and proper, from the top of her flat head straight down to her bandy legs. I don't think this thought was far off the mark because I soon noticed she began to wear colourful bow clips and would constantly tap back her teeth, which to tell the truth, were sort of pushed out. Whenever she did that, I would remember Mothski the moleman who could fix her up for only forty dollars. But it seemed she had come to Canada with a tidy sum of money because she bought new dresses and shoes and grassy green purses and frilly shawls. "Who would ever know," she told me one night. "That old people could get such special treatment. Discounts on every side." She thought for a while and added, "Is the small things that add up to the big picture." She was happier than I had ever seen her, and one day she surprised me by saying, "Your mother would have liked this place."

That sentence remained with me and while she was baking some pecan pies, I asked why she believed this. "Listen, boy. Who in their right mind would prefer to live in an old house doing the same thing day after day after day? Wearing the same clothes. Cooking the same food. Thinking the same thoughts. Day after day. Nothing nice to remember and nothing nice to look forward to. What sort of life is that? Always waiting, always waiting." She sounded a bit like the stern old Auntie but a few minutes later, she added, "She would have been happy to know that you living here now. God bless her soul." That sparked out a couple of hymns. It sounded as if she was praising God for giving her this opportunity in her old age.

A couple years ago I had heard her telling my mother, the Lord giveth and the Lord taketh, and about thirteen days after she appeared outside the door, I felt she had reached the end of the giveth phase. Out of the blue, my father popped up. They began to quarrel ten minutes later, as if they were picking up from where they had left off in Trinidad. It started when Auntie asked him if he was still sinning or had found it in his heart to repent. He replied that he must be still sinning because her visit was a heavy punishment. Then she started to complain about the condition she found the house in and he told her she was free to leave if she didn't like it. They went on for close to half an hour like that. Finally Auntie walked away and turned on the television. That night though, she didn't look at her makeover shows but kept moving from channel to channel. And when my father stormed past her to the balcony for his smoke, she got up and went into the bedroom. I saw my father flicking his butt over the railing and then peeping inside. "Where she went?"

"To sleep."

"The damn nastiness. In my own bed. What happen to all the generosity and sacrifice she always quacking about? Hypocrite."

I didn't tell him that, in spite of all of Auntie's faults, she was still far better company than him.

From the room came the sound of *Jesus loves me, this I know.* That night I had to coil up on a corner of the foam because my father was sleeping next to me. I fell asleep with him grumbling and cursing about hypocrites.

That was the pattern every single day. In a way, it reminded me of some of the Mayaro families and I wondered if the neighbours were able to hear Auntie telling my father he was the cause of my mother's death, and he saying that he now figured out that she used her umbrella to hide from God, and she hitting back with a parable about Joshua and Jericho and tumbling-down walls and fake illnesses. On and on and on. Once she picked up her umbrella and pointed it at him like the Penguin. "This workman-pokeman scheme going to give you a seat right next to the devil. Mark my word!" I would like to say that the situation was better when my father was away but during these periods

Auntie would now warn me about idleness and worthless-
ness. "Philandering" was a word she used all the time. Her
old scratch-up, complaining voice came back too.

One evening I tried to cheer her up. "These lights on the
buildings outside really look like jewels."

"Souls burning up," she said flatly.

And this was the start. From then, all the *sweetmouth*
about Canada came to an end. She still collected all her
newspapers but instead of talking about the cleanness or the
flowers and squirrels in the park, she would ask me, "You ever
notice that all the people who get in accident or fall from
building or get burn up or drown in some lake, have foreign
names?" Or "You ever notice how nobody willing to smile
back at you? Some of these people in the park can't recognize
a blessing if it run up and bite them." I couldn't understand
why she was turning against the country just because things
weren't working out between her and my father. It was almost
like she was taking out all her vexation on this place, which
less than a week earlier, she could find nothing bad about.
Now nothing could please her. She complained about the
urine smell in the hallway and children smoking on the stairs
and one night, with a heap of clothes in her hand, she asked
if the basement laundry room also doubled as a drugstore.
"Smoking-poking all over the place." Even the television
shows she had enjoyed so much began to eat her up.

"Look at these girls," she told me one evening. "Stooping
to any level just to win a little prize. Fighting and complaining and backbiting just like . . . I better bite my tongue, yes. "

She took off her hat and fanned her face tiredly. "Everything is always a big competition. Fight-fight win-win." Another day she was flipping channels idly when she said, "In some countries, people have respect for their elders but not here. Not here at all." I remembered her earlier statement about old people but said nothing. "Hello. I don't think so. Talk to the finger." I had to laugh at her imitation and the way she pushed out her hand and waggled her head like one of the black girls on the show. She gave me a hard look like if I was somehow involved with the group of teenagers who were criticizing their parents with a tall glasses-woman who looked like a lonely bird.

I can't pick out the exact moment when she turned against me but I soon noticed that she began to lump my father, Canada, the people in the park and on TV, the condition of the Regent Park buildings, and me, into one big frustrating ball. One night soon after an argument with my father, she screamed out, "Oh Lord Jesus! I could feel this cold seeping inside my bones. Eating me out from the inside." I jumped and wished I could follow my father out of the apartment but felt it would be disrespectful to leave her alone. That night she baked for hours. From my foam, I heard her slapping the flour and singing her hymns so angrily, I felt she was chasing out all the bad spirits from around her. When my father got back late in the night, she was still bawling out her hymns. To tell the truth, I think this got him a little frightened because he went quietly to the television instead of putting up an argument. When Auntie saw him there, she said in the same tune with her singing, "He sitteth alone and keepeth silence, because he hath borne it upon him. Gadarene swine!"

The next night when I returned from work, she was gone. The place smelled of cinnamon and on the cupboard were all kinds of cakes and pies and buns. The bottom shelf of the fridge was also filled with baked potatoes and eggplant, and when I closed the door the letter she had stuck there with a dollar store magnet fell to the ground.

When my father returned in the night, he noticed all the baked stuff and asked me about my aunt. I told him she had returned to Trinidad. "Why? She used up all her bad-mindness?" He went on like that for close to half an hour, talking about how all these old miserable Presbyterians from Trinidad always thought they were one step away from the white people just because they had learned a couple hymns and could eat with knife and fork. I don't know what these Presbyterians ever did to him because he continued on about how they were always with their hats and umbrellas just like these old missionaries they admired so much even though the sun only bounced off people like my auntie. "Sun don't have any effect on tar," he said nastily. "The blacker people is, the more they does run from the sun." While he was carrying on, I thought of showing him the sheet Auntie had left on the fridge that had stated simply: They have sown the wind and they shall reap the whirlwind. And beneath, in smaller letters: But if we hope for that we see not, then do we with patience wait for it.

I didn't know if it was a question or some Bible proverb or meant for my father or me or something she had dug up after the bus driver and then her musician disappeared.

I have to say I missed her more than I could have imagined. I don't know if it was her baking or whether she reminded me of Trinidad and my mother, or just for spite, because my father hated her so much. Sometimes I would look at her old *mash-up* umbrella she had left behind and remember how all her *sweetmouth* about Canada had changed the minute my father returned to the apartment.

It took less than a week for my father to get back to his old self. During the last days of Auntie Umbrella's visit he had acted a little frightened of her loud hymns but now he would constantly complain about hypocrites. I wondered if there was anyone who ever pleased him. He couldn't stand Auntie Umbrella who was his own sister, he hated Uncle Boysie, and he acted as if he wished I was not around. Which left just my mother.

At Petrocan I began to pay attention to the middle-aged couples. While I was filling their gas tanks I watched their gestures and sometimes when they slid closer, even though I could not hear their words I felt they were saying kind things to each other. Two weeks after Auntie Umbrella left, I asked my father, "Did you like Mummy at all?"

He was before the television and I saw him stiffening. "What you say?"

I had rushed home and asked the question quickly before I could change my mind. Even though I was sure he had heard me, I repeated the question.

He pulled up a leg and adjusted a sock. "That is what you and the Presbyterian use to be discussing all day? That is the assness she put in your head?" He asked his questions in a stupid drawl. I noticed a hole in the sock's heel.

From that point I felt I couldn't stand him. I hated the slurping sound he made at the kitchen table, his slippers dragging on the kitchen tiles, his foolish advice to the television characters, the constant coughing in the nights, hawking and spitting over the balcony, grumbling about every single thing. I wondered if my mother had also hated these disgusting sounds or if he was more courteous in those days. Maybe if he had lived with us in Mayaro I would have grown accustomed and it would not have upset me so much. But not now. Not now.

There were times when I felt I should slide out of my Trinidadian habit to become more like these television teenagers. Put him in his place good and proper. Loose some good curses on him. But I remembered all my mother's lectures about respecting older people, even those she hated, like the fisherman, Matapal. For her part, she always stepped out of the kitchen when the fisherman was around. I decided to do the same thing—but I would go one step further. I knew my father hated the genie and his handler for I would often hear him grumbling whenever he spotted them from the balcony. So on my way from work, whenever I spotted the couple on a bench and noticed my father's cigarette glinting on the balcony, I would stop to chat. I didn't care that he would later scream, "Cult! Cult. I surrounded by cultist."

Chapter Eight

DILARA AND PETROMAN

My father's talk of cultists actually made the genie and his handler more interesting, and during our nightly chats outside the apartment I would ignore the handler's boring comments and think instead of Ra's al Ghul, Batman's nemesis who slept in a Lazarus Pit that made him live forever. Both men resembled the villain too.

"Before we didn't exist. Now we are everywhere, you understand . . ." Ah, but I have discovered that your pit is in a dungeon below the Toronto Necropolis.

"We cannot be ignored anymore . . ." Batman can still beat you any day.

"Hatred is no worse than indifference . . ." Your own daughter Talia hates you.

"Young people such as yourself must resist the temptations that are all around . . ." Resist? Ha ha ha. Release the hounds!

"Gobble-gooky." Gobble-gooky to you, buddy.

I knew all of this was childish: at Petrocan I had seen
boys who seemed my age smoking and driving and confi-
dently hugging their girlfriends but the minute I entered my
father's apartment and heard him grumbling about cults
and (of all things) no-good foreigners, I felt the little chats
were worth it. "They will reel you in like a catfish." For a second I felt there was a tiny bit of concern, then he added, "They
looking especially for green jackasses like you."

This was so interesting I carried the game to the gas
station. One evening I asked Paul, "You ever heard of the
Lazarus Pit?"

He thought for an instant. "It's somewhere on the north
coast of Newfoundland."

"I think it's below the Necropolis."

"Could be a decoy."

And another evening: "Have you ever seen a genie?"

I never knew there were so many mysterious lamps
and corked bottles strewn all over Newfoundland's coast.
While I was walking home I wondered what I would demand
if I was given three wishes by a genie. When I was younger,
I always wished for the power to fly or super strength or
coming out first in my class at Mayaro Composite but now
I felt that my first wish would be for my mother to still be
alive. My second would be for my father to suddenly take an
interest in me and notice my Timex and talk about his time
alone in Canada and take me to hockey games and wrestling
matches. These two concerns were always on my mind so it
took a while before I could come up with a third wish.

Finally, I decided that I would ask for an opportunity to meet Dilara from the Coffee Time.

Three days later, I saw her. Seriously. She was in the back seat of a car driven by a man in clothing like the genie's. At first, I couldn't be sure but when the genie and his handler walked over to the car, opened the door and went in I got a good look at the frightened face in the back seat. There was no doubt. In the apartment my father said, "Reel you ass in good and proper." I couldn't play the game that night. What was Dilara doing here? When she had disappeared from the coffee shop, I felt I would never see her again as this city was so big. My father was still grumbling about cults and catfish then it hit me: the Coffee Time was just a few minutes from here so she must live nearby. Why hadn't I thought of this before?

The next night I rushed home, running part of the way, but the bench was empty. I hung around for a while before I sat. A couple teenagers in hoodies and slack pants were smoking next to the big garbage unit. I saw them glancing at me sitting alone. One of the group, a young woman with a nose ring and a sweater with the name of some basketball team on it walked over and asked for a light. I told her I did not smoke and she pushed her hands in her pocket and stared at me for a while before she walked away with a bouncy, wide-apart stride like a boy. A cigarette was tossed from our balcony, its glowing end sprinkling in tiny sparks as it landed on the curb. I was about to leave when the black car pulled up. Dilara was sitting in the back seat as before. The genie got out and walked to the lobby's door but his handler stood by the car for a while, talking with the driver. I walked over to the curb but the car pulled off, taking Dilara away, and I couldn't say whether she had noticed me. I held open the building door while the handler guided the genie to the elevator. Both men spoke in a strange language before the elevator stopped at the third floor.

Later: "Bait. Bait! You little jackass." I didn't have time for my father as I was wondering why the pair had chosen a foreign language. What secrets were they hiding?

The following night I waited by the curb instead. A cigarette almost landed on my head. I didn't know what my next move would be when I spotted the black car. The genie got out and held out his hand. I helped him up the curb and to the door while his handler chatted with the driver. He held on to my hand and I wanted to shrug him off and wave to Dilara. Another cigarette floated down. I wondered if my father was really trying to burn me of just wanted me to know he was watching my every move from the balcony.

That night the handler invited me into his apartment. Or rather, he held the elevator's door open after the genie had exited and I followed the pair. The apartment was really tidy and packed with frilly hooked mats on the wall and different types of lamps near to the sofa and the bookcase and the computer table. Behind the lamps were nice plants with jumbled vines and small scattered leaves that looked like dried coins. The genie was grinning at me as if my presence in his apartment was a big joke. His handler pointed to the couch and when I sat, he pulled the chair from the computer table.

He told me his name. It sounded like Bungavalla or Bunglevalley or something. Then he said it was good that I didn't hang out with the teenagers loitering around the compound and I recalled how he had fixed me with a strict look when Canella and I were leaving the compound. These teenagers were rude and disrespectful, he continued, even though many of their parents had come from "good countries." This place we were living in was a trap because there were too many temptations. I didn't know if he was talking about Regent Park or Canada. He pulled out a book from the nearby shelf and stared at its spine. From the corner of my eyes, I saw a woman walking to the kitchen, which surprised me because I had never ever seen her before. I think my mind was on the woman when Mr. Bunglevalley began a story. It was about a family of immigrants. They had come to Canada many years ago and had a hard time because of all the unfriendly customs and also because no one would hire the husband. They lived with their three children in a tiny one-bedroom apartment. Finally, the husband got a night job five or six buses away. He was a hard worker and when other people in the factory were at home, he would stay for extra shifts. Mr. Bunglevalley told me as if he was delivering a lecture, "Everything he did, you understand, was for the sake of his children. All the sacrifices."

The genie nodded as if he understood and I did the same. "Years passed." Mr. Bunglevalley gestured to the window as if this family was just outside, peeping in. "The sacrifice began to pay off. The children did well at school and were accepted at prestigious universities. Then they began to weaken."

The woman came over and placed a tray on the coffee table. I felt I should tell her hello or something but she did not look at me and walked back quickly to the kitchen. Mr. Bunglevalley went over and brought the tray to me and I took a small fancy teacup. The tea was bitter and yet sweet with an aftertaste of some spice. "How does it taste?"

"Very nice," I lied. I wondered whether it was some kind of medicinal tea like the fever-grass brew my mother used to force me to drink.

He waited till I had a couple more sips before he continued his story. "The family forgot why they had come to Canada. The two daughters went to clubs and got boyfriends and the son began to drink and smoke. And what did the parents do?" The genie drew closer and pulled his feet up on the couch as if this was the good part of the story. "They encouraged it because they thought it was sign of progress. One weekend the entire family packed into their minivan for a trip. A vacation, you understand. Somewhere between Barrie and Sudbury, the minivan hit a tractor-trailer. No one survived."

The genie began to clap. Mr. Bunglevalley returned the book to the shelf. And I remembered Auntie Umbrella's observation about how all the victims of vehicle accidents and fires and drowning were immigrants. I felt this was the point of Mr. Bunglevalley's story but he said, "There is a price to be paid for living such a life, you understand? When you forget the rules, there are always these reminders." He pointed to the ceiling and the genie looked up.

I don't know if he was throwing words at me because of Canella but in any case, it was a horrible story. I told them I had to get to work early the next day and I hurried out from their apartment. I became worried for Dilara. I was more determined than ever to make contact. Make contact. I liked the phrase and it made me feel like a shadowy hero with a secret identity. Shy and often puzzled on the surface but understanding everything, all the confusing Canadian customs and laws, in my hero identity. Maybe something like Dr. Bat's Captain Hindustani. In the gas station, I hit on the name, Petroman, and I had to smile before I got back to the serious business of planning to actually meet Dilara.

Each night I waited by the curb and ducked away from cigarette butts. I hoped Dilara would see me and get out from the black car. She never did but the smoking teenagers became a bit friendlier, and once one of them bounced a basketball in my direction and shouted out, "Over here, man." I threw the ball, and at that same instant, the black car pulled up. That night Dilara was in the front seat and before the car drove off, I saw her fingers tapping the window. In Trinidad we called that gesture a bye-bye, and there it was flirty temporary goodbye that a girl might give to her boyfriend. I had no idea if it was the same in Dilara's culture, whatever that was.

I took the genie's arm. Once again, I was invited into Mr. Bunglevalley's apartment. Once again, the woman brought a tray of tea but not directly to us. There was another story about an immigrant family. They didn't get into an accident like the last family but ended up fighting among themselves and living like cats and dogs. "They forgot the rules, you understand," he said again. "They forgot who they were and where they had come from."

The genie lapped his tea and I saw his tongue moving around in his mouth like a macaw.

That night my father added to his catfish and bait parable. "These people next door, you know anything about them? You know exactly who they could be hooked-up with? When you ass get bag up good and proper don't drag me in it because I will say I don't know nothing about you." I didn't say anything but all the while I was thinking that in Canada, foreigners always seemed to hate other foreigners. It was the sort of insight that Petroman might have and when I smiled at that, my father got even angrier.

Over the next few days, I realized I had to find some other way to make contact with Dilara. I began to plan but knew that none of the plots would work: they were the sort of fantastic ideas only Petroman would come up with. It was frustrating because I had wasted about three weeks and the only results were these lectures about doomed families from Mr. Bunglevalley. Then one night the black car had two extra passengers. They were younger than the genie but were dressed in the same white robes. They got out of the car. One held the genie's arm and the other beckoned to the driver. All four went into the building. Dilara was alone.

I stood at the curb until they went inside before I walked over and told Dilara hello. She appeared a little nervous, staring up at the balcony, but I had waited too long. I told her I had missed her at the coffee shop and asked if she was working elsewhere. After a while, she shook her head. Then she told me point-blank that I should leave. Maybe it was the Petroman stupidness in my head that gave me the courage to ask if she was in college or just waiting for another job. I almost added, "Or trapped."

She reached by the door and began to wind up the glass but just before I was completely shut out she whispered, "The reference library."

I had to wait until the weekend before I headed for the place. I loitered on all the floors—a little surprised there were so many people sitting before computers—before I settled in the little eating section on the first floor. Two Saturdays later, I saw her. She was talking to the girl who sold the coffee and I noticed how alike they seemed. The same orangeish colour and the same pointed features and big eyes. Except that the other girl was wearing a stylish veil. When Dilara spotted me, she leaned over the counter and whispered to the girl. I went to an empty table and took the newspaper lying in its top. There were a few articles about architecture and other boring things but in any case I was using the newspaper just as a cover. Like a shadowy rescuer would.

"So you are here, in library." Gone was her impatience. Now she was smiling mischievously.

"Yes, I am here."

"Can I sit near with you?" she asked me. I pulled the empty chair a little closer to me and she placed her purse on the table and sat. "So for what purpose you come to library?" She glanced back at the coffee girl, who seemed to be giggling. This was not how I had expected our meeting to be.

"What is *your* purpose?"

"I ask question first, but I tell you, still." She reached for her purse and took out a necklace with small green stones leading to a crystal butterfly. "These I make. Sometimes bird, sometimes flowers. And my friend sell for me." She waved to the coffee girl. "So I make a little money. Not much, only little. And what about you?"

"I work at a gas station."

"Ooh. Gas station." She made it seem like an important job. "What trade . . . no that is not word . . . what task do you have at station?"

As I recited the list of tasks—pumping gas, cleaning windscreens, checking oil, sweeping the service area at the end of my shift—I realized how boring it sounded. Her jewellery job was far more interesting, and after our short conversation, while I was walking to Regent Park, I imagined Dilara in a room bright with dancing, flickering light, and gold and silver dust swirling around in rainbow patterns over her head. And some of the dust settling on her hair and shoulders and fingers. This was the sort of room where someone could easily fly or make magical wishes or talk with sprites. Thinking of her like this, in such a setting, gave me my own butterflies, chasing around in my stomach. I could barely wait till our next meeting.

It was a Saturday again and when I got to the library she was chatting once more with the coffee girl. When she spotted me she waved in her flirty way, and after a couple minutes, came over to my table. "And so, you come to library again?"

"Yes, I am doing some research on jewels."

"Is this true?" Her eyes widened. It was a little joke that a boy who was putting the moves on a girl might make but I let it rest. And I was glad that I did because she told me that in her country—whose name she never mentioned—women wore gems instead of makeup, and little girls were taught by their mothers to make insect jewellery with corals and jade and jasper and other magical-sounding gems. She told me that in her homeland, young men proposed to their girlfriends with these homemade necklaces instead of rings. "I say enough for time," she told me. "Now you say."

What could I say to match her jade and jasper and engagement revelations? The only thing I knew about marriage was from my mother who complained that it was it was "only icing and no cake" and a trap for foolish people to fall into. Not even Petroman could transform this dreary view into something magical. "What do you want me to say?" I told her at last.

She too got quiet and I felt I was losing her. I saw her playing with the strap of her purse and assumed she was getting ready to leave. "Do you want to see?" She was looking over my head in the direction of the glass elevator. She took out a necklace with speckled beads, which looked like hummingbird eggs. "I call it Caribbing island dream."

"Caribbean?"

"Yes. Say again, please."

I repeated the word a couple times and for some reason it broke down my shyness. I told her I was from there and I began to talk about the night lights over the sea and the corals washed ashore from the reef and the gold-coloured sand and the cool morning mist on the mountains and fruits and berries which were found only deep in the forest. I told her of the howler monkeys and macaws and leatherback turtles and the pitch lake and the old castles in Port of Spain and the wrecks where I had heard there might be treasure left behind by Bluebeard and Sir Henry Morgan. I was really surprised that I remembered so much and that I was able to push aside all the other bad things I had heard from Uncle Boysie and my mother.

"I love to live in Caribbing island. Why for you leave?"

"My mother died. My father lives here."

"Oh, it is too sad. My mother, she is sick too. So far, far away. But what it is to do? I have to make best. So I make jewels and wait for papers. You have?" I didn't know what she was talking about so I shook my head. "It is good to have. My mother, she thinks I have. Yes, I write and tell her so. Some people they help but . . ."

I was even more confused. I felt she was referring to Mr. Bunglevalley and his gang but I didn't know what papers she was talking about and how they were helping her. "But what?"

"It is not good for me to say."

She seemed a little disturbed so I changed the topic somewhat. "What will happen when you get the papers?"

"Oh. I go to school and get regular jobs. And then I send for mother to come live with me. It is my dream all the time for such a thing."

I recalled her mentioning her mother at the coffee shop. "The papers will do all that?"

"You don't know?" She seemed surprised by this, and for the next half an hour or so she explained all these complicated facts about landed immigrants and student visas and work permits and citizenship and refugee status. As I listened, some of my father's threats began to make more sense and Dilara clarified his most common threat when she asked if I was here in Canada illegally. She seemed so shocked by my status that I began to feel nervous and frightened, to tell the truth. She told me that I should apply to be a refugee and I remembered Roy and Norbert bad-mouthing all these refugees who were living in palaces and "milking the system."

When I left her that night, there were no visions of swirling gold dust and jewels. I didn't know how I would approach this topic with my father because I could just imagine how vexed he would be.

It was worse than that! "Status eh. You think that all you have to do is walk inside a office like Lord Laloo and say, 'Give me status right now,' and somebody will type it out in a hurry and push it in your pocket? Where the hell you getting these ideas from? From them cultist downstairs? Then why the ass you don't ask them to help you?" On and on he went. That night I was awakened a few times by his door slamming.

At work, I wondered if I should discuss this papers-complication business with Paul or Dr. Bat but I knew that instead of explaining they would most likely come up with some stupid story. I couldn't ask Mr. Bunglevalley either, because he was so critical of all immigrants. In the end, I turned to Dilara. And I was glad that I did because she didn't act as if I was stupid or childish for not knowing all these important things. She told me that illegal people had to live in the shadows always because they could be deported at any time. The employers knew this so they hired these people to work for them for next to nothing. There were many such people who had to do these jobs even though they were educated. Although I was not educated, I wondered whether this was why my boss at Petrocan always paid me in cash. Dilara then explained that parents could sponsor their children and paused as if she was wondering why I couldn't use that route. She told me that she was here on a student visa, which would expire in half a year. The coffee girl was also on a student visa and both of them had applied for extensions. "School . . . it is very hard to pay so many fees. My friend, she say we should teach making jewellery. But it is only joke she make." She glanced over to the girl who cupped her hand to her mouth and whispered something that neither I nor Dilara could hear. "My friend is . . . how to say it . . . plenty mischief. She say last week that you are cute boy."

I felt a little ashamed to be so close to her while she was saying this and tried to pass it off with a joke. "You are cute girl, too."

I expected she would blush or blink quickly and stammer or make her own joke but she asked me seriously, "What cute in me you find?"

I looked quickly at her long black hair and her thin nose and her full lower lip and her round eyes that made her look as if she was always surprised. To tell the truth she looked a little like an orange bird. I had never noticed that before. I chose the safest feature, the one she must have been complimented on many times before. "Your eyes. They are always asking so many questions."

"And sad, sometimes, you find?"

I shook my head.

"It is good that my eyes show all these things." But she was sounding sad rather than satisfied, and for some reason I thought of the woman in Mr. Bunglevalley's apartment. "Soon it will be all."

She got quiet and I asked her, "These people who live in my apartment complex . . . are they helping you to get your student visa?"

"It is not a good topic for me to talk."

"I went to their place. There is a woman there. And an old"—I almost said genie—"man."

She seemed surprised that I had been there. "They are friends to you?"

"I help the old man up the stairs."

"Yes, I see." She looked to the coffee girl who was bent beneath the counter, wiping the glass. Finally, she told me, "The man, he get me and friend into his school. It is small school but too many rules. Maybe he get you into school, too."

I remembered my strict principal from Mayaro Composite and told her, "Too many rules."

She replied immediately as if she had anticipated my reply. "Oh, with boy it is not same. They get all the freedoms."

I wondered why she had been so reluctant to talk about Mr. Bunglevalley and this simple school matter. The Petroman thoughts of rescuing her suddenly seemed more silly than usual. In a way, she was luckier than me, making her jewellery and having a close friend and going to school and getting this help from Mr. Bunglevalley. So the following Saturday we chatted mostly about her jewellery, which got her pleased and talkative, and as they were closing up, I bought a butterfly necklace for ten dollars. While we were leaving the library her friend asked me, "You give back this to girlfriend?" She leaned over and said something in another language and Dilara bent her head and walked faster. At the Bloor subway, she told me that jewellery had great powers and I thought of Green Lantern's ring and felt we were so alike. That night I was in as good a mood as I had ever been since I came to Canada.

But I never saw her again.

For three Saturdays, I waited in the library, hoping she would show up. In the meantime, Mr. Bunglevalley and his genie disappeared from their apartment, just like that. It was strange because it was not even the end of the month so they had lost their deposit. I wanted to ask the coffee girl about all of this but every time I glanced at her, she would look away. I felt she did not want any questions but on the third Saturday

I was so desperate I didn't care any longer. I asked her point-blank and she frowned as if she didn't want to say anything to me. I asked her again. She had a damp sponge in her hand, which she was squeezing. She told me that there was "a big trouble." I tried to follow her as best I could, because she was grasping for the proper English words. There was some sort of problem with Mr. Bunglevalley's school. It had never been licensed. Many of the students were under investigation. Mr. Bunglevalley himself was under some type of probe. "The school . . . it is not legal," she told me and then as if she had said too much, she clammed up. I asked about Dilara. She pressed her palms against the sponge as if she was creating some new shape. "Now she must start over."

A sinking thought hit me. "Is she in Canada?"

"You have necklace still?" The question surprised me and I told her that I had carried it in my pocket ever since. For some reason she brightened up a bit and she said, "She is best at making butterflies. Yes, and flowers. Her fingers, they know everything."

I took out the necklace. "Please give this to her."

"No, you keep."

I left the necklace there on the counter. On my way to the subway, I nearly changed my mind and returned for it, but when I though that Dilari might be happy to see it again, I continued on my way.

In the weeks that followed, while I was cleaning some woman's windscreen at Petrocan I would catch some gesture, maybe slim fingers clasping the steering wheel or pushing back a strand of hair, and I would be reminded of Dilara, who would never know she had encouraged me to get this job more than four months earlier or that she had got me thinking of signing up at some college so that I could get a student visa. And when the woman drove off, I would feel that some little bit of Dilara had remained there in the gas station, and I would imagine her in a room made bright with dancing, flickering dust as she carefully carved out her birds and butterflies and flowers.

I continued going to the library on Saturdays—still nursing the frail hope of meeting Dilara. One Saturday I joined a group of people who looked like foreigners. They were sitting on chairs arranged on the first floor. An Indian woman was talking about job banks and resumés and college diplomas. At the end of her speech, she handed out some slim booklets. On the last two pages were the lists of community colleges in Toronto. The following Saturday another woman lectured on illegal immigrants. She said they were forced to live like ghosts. Her speech got me frightened and I did not take her booklet even though she ended by saying that "illegal immigrant" was the wrong term and should be replaced instead by "non-status individuals."

Following that meeting, I wandered up to the third floor, where there was a Caribbean section, and there I met the chimera.

Chapter Nine

THE CHIMERA IN THE LIBRARY

S ometimes when I was sitting on the third floor of the library, gazing down at the street, I would imagine what my friends at Mayaro Composite might think if they could see me here. At that school, the library doubled as a detention centre where delinquents had to spend an hour after dismissal doing nothing in particular while one of the male teachers chatted up the librarian, Miss Garcia. A mobile library came once a month at the Mayaro junction but there was usually a line of drunkards demanding picture books on diseases and witchcraft and outer space. In any case, Uncle Boysie's shop was always stocked with comics so I had little use for libraries.

This place, though, was different. There was an elevator with glass sides that went straight up to the fourth floor where a host of people sat before computers. It wasn't long before I would head straight for the third floor where I had discovered there were Caribbean storybooks, comics, movies, thick old books with mostly pictures, and, here, too, computers all over the place. I sampled all, moving from place to place, watching boys my age concentrating on their monitors. I wondered how many of them were here on a six-month visitor's visa that would expire in twenty-one days. That always brought me back to earth; and I hung around the weekend seminars on the first floor before I got too distressed and bolted to some other spot. During those times, I wished Dilara was still around so I could share my concern.

One Saturday there was a seminar on family sponsorship. The seats were filled with grandfather Sikhs who with their white beards looked like corralled lions. The speaker who had brownish-reddish hair that matched her jacket repeated all her sentences and spoke very slowly so what she said was easy to understand: I was in real trouble. I rushed up the steps nearly tumbling a fat man in an old cream jacket.

The next day I changed my mind several times about whether I should go to the library and when I eventually decided to go I ignored the seminar—this one mostly of women in veils—and headed for the third floor. I plucked out a Trinidad storybook and flipped through its pages searching for some reference to Mayaro. "A mediocre little island." I glanced up and saw the man I had almost tumbled the previous day. "Think they are smarter than everyone else. The presumptuousness of silly little islanders. Mud-hut folks."

And who ask you that? I thought. But I said nothing because this fella looked as if he was working here. After a minute or so, I got a little uncomfortable because he was still looking over my shoulder. When I went to replace the book on the shelf, I saw him staring at me. During the week, I forgot about him as I had other things to occupy my mind but on Saturday, he appeared once more. "I have seen you hanging around the seminars," he told me. "You always leave halfway."

Could he be some sort of library police? I looked up for a good glance and to be honest, he was one of the ugliest persons I had ever set eyes on. There was nothing wrong with any particular feature but the way everything was patched together gave the idea of a man who had no use for friends. Without any invitation, he boldfacedly pulled a chair next to mine. "Yesterday a boy jumped off the fourth floor. He landed right there." He pointed in the direction of a square enclosure filled with plants.

"What happened to him?"

"Exactly what one would expect when a body lands on its head. Every month someone tries to commit suicide here."

"You mean the books so boring?" The minute the words left my mouth, I regretted saying them. This fella didn't look as if he approved of jokes, particularly of tragic topics. I tried to cover up. "Why here?"

"One does not know. One can only speculate. Perhaps there is a special gravitas to expiring in a place like this. In the case in question, the victim was a refugee claimant who received news that his parents had been murdered in Pakistan." He daubed away some hair oil that had leaked on his huge forehead and wiped his hand on his jacket. "I am leaving in two months."

"To go where?"

"One goes where life takes one." He paused a bit. "And you?"

I had the sudden suspicion that he was some kind of undercover agent to smoke out illegal immigrants. "One will stay here."

"Will you allow me to indulge a bit in a favourite pastime?"

"Go ahead."

"You are in some kind of trouble. There is a decision to be made." He brought his hands before him like if he was praying and I noticed the caterpillar bumps on his wrist veins. "See those people walking along Bloor Street? They arrive here from every corner of the globe. A huge conference of nomads. Do you know there are Gurkhas and Bedouins and Shullaks and Mongols and Kushites squeezed together in the streets?"

Whoever they were. I felt I had to say, "No, I didn't know that."

"Have you ever wondered where they disappear to?"

"To their homes, I would say."

"In the nights when everyone else in the city is asleep, their lights are still on. What mysteries are they poring over?" When he said the word "mysteries" he smacked his lips and sniffed as if it was the last piece of a buttery cake. "What are they doing up so late? What are they reading, and eating? Who really knows?"

I know it might sound disrespectful but the words popped out of my mouth. "Why you telling me all this?"

"One simply throws out observations. One has no control over their interpretations."

The next weekend I decided to avoid him so I sat in a seminar and listened to a strict-looking lady talk about nannies. In Trinidad, nannies were grandmothers but here it seemed that they were servants of some kind. These nannies, the lady explained, had to take care of a pack of children all day, while cooking and washing at the same time. Just like Trinidad nannies. Then a man with his glasses pushed over his bald head said that one group from the Philippines ended up working in an apple farm. When he was finished the woman asked for questions and a Philippines lady said she had been a registered nurse in her old country and many in the audience nodded. One by one, they got up and listed their previous professions. Finally, a youngish girl asked what could be done. The strict woman talked about agencies and sponsorship and some women's group. When I left, I saw the ugly man staring at me from the third-floor railing.

All week at work I tried to think of some way I could get my father to understand my problem. I rehearsed questions on my way home, ranging from pleading to threatening to patiently explaining but each time I imagined my father's reaction to be the same: *What assness you talking about?*

On the day my visitor's visa finally expired, I chose a quiet spot in the library to consider all my options. I decided to write a letter to Uncle Boysie. I got out a pen and began to write:

Dear Uncle Boysie,

My visa ran out today.

I tried to think of the next sentence but was stuck. I didn't want him to think I was being ungrateful or too complaining.

" . . . and I have discovered this booming city withholds its generosity from the disenfranchised," said a voice. I looked up and saw the ugly man. "Consequently I am trapped on a bridge with no destination in sight," he said, and added, "Continue writing, please."

"Why?"

"One couldn't help but notice—"

"Because one was right over my shoulder peeping at my letter."

He sat. "You're right, of course." He brought his hands before him and made a triangle with his fingers. "This library has changed over the years. Once it was a nesting place for privileged folks researching some arcane topic but now . . . now there's a whiff of desperation about the people you see." He broke his triangle and waved at a line of Indians before computers. "They are all e-mailing their folks back home pleading for money and understanding. You, on the other hand, have chosen the old-fashioned route. A letter. It's more poignant, I believe. Each word is stamped with pain." He got up. "My time is almost up, too."

I completed the letter the next day at home. I ended it with this line: *I feel I have reached a bridge with no end in sight.*

In a strange way, I was grateful to the library fella. I searched him out the following weekend. He was sitting before a desk gazing at a book and smacking his lips. "Yes," he asked without looking up.

"I wrote the letter."

"Ah." He glanced at his watch. "I will be with you forthwith. My shift finishes at six."

I sat by a window table and gazed down. I wondered how long it would take the letter to reach Mayaro. I remembered my plane ride to Canada, imagining that I was flying over big blocks of ice to a Fortress of Solitude place that was cool and quiet and windswept. I recalled the bus trip with my father from the airport, gazing at the rows of similar houses. And for no reason at all, I felt afraid of returning to Trinidad. It wasn't like a fear of *jumbies* or anything but a deep cold fear as if a block of ice had lodged somewhere in my chest and was making its ways down, numbing and then eating away all my joy. I remembered a comic book word: contagion.

"One feels that one is trapped." He sat.

"One too."

We sat side by side for a few minutes. I tried to understand my fear of returning to a place I missed so much. I wondered whether I was afraid of disappointing Uncle Boysie, or because Auntie Umbrella had mentioned my mother would have been happy to know I was here, or just because my departure would be a victory for my father. In Mayaro, people who returned suddenly from what we called "the cold" were always laughed at. Like Mister Dana who walked around the street in winter boots and shorts, telling everyone "Hi" and saying "Wow" whenever he spotted a ripe mango or *pommecythere* on a tree.

I noticed the library fella looking at me as he reached for a book on the table. He pressed it to his nose. "For years I lived in the Beaches. One morning I woke up and discovered that all my neighbours were missing. There were new people managing the shops and sitting in the pubs and staring at me in the bistros. Who were these people, I wondered? How long have they been my neighbours? What did I miss?" He glanced at the jacket photograph on the book. "I met him once, you know. He was chatting up some women who had no idea who he was."

"The writer?"

"Poet. He had come to do a reading and was quite distressed by the women's mistake. He didn't come here for anonymity, you see."

"Where was he from?"

"The Caribbean."

"And you?"

"One lives between . . ." He seemed to be searching for a word.

"Bridges?"

"Yes," he said finally. "But they are quite shaky at this point." He got up and walked unsteadily to his desk.

I liked talking to this library man. He appeared more educated than everyone I had met so far, but I believe it was really the idea that he was at some kind of crossroad. Just like me. The next day I was waiting by a glass case that enclosed some books by an Iranian writer when I saw the reflection of a woman in a long Matrix coat.

"Canella?" I turned to face her.

"It's Ginny. And you?"

"Kelvin Raspail." I saw her pretty broad mouth opening a bit before she turned and walked away, her coat swirling.

"A friend?" The library man had a book clasped against his chest.

"Maybe. I was waiting for your shift to finish."

"Come." I followed him to a corner table and when he sat, I did the same.

After a minute or so of silence I asked him, "What's up?"

He spent another minute passing his tongue over his thick lower lip before he said, "One feels sometimes like a chimera." It was an interesting comic book word and I tried to picture him with horns and scales. It was surprisingly easy. "It may be difficult to conceive but there was a time when I actually enjoyed my work. This place was my home."

"Is that why you are leaving?"

He shook his head. "Everything has changed. Now the entire staff is beholden to lists. Horrible memoirs bursting with frivolous grief. I feel sometimes as if I am a custodian of misery. But to answer your question, I am leaving because I have been pushed out."

"By who?"

"By my advancing years. In two weeks, I will have reached my retirement age. There is just one regret. Just one." He didn't seem willing to continue but I just had to ask. When I did, he brought up his hands, made his triangle, and peered through. "I began a poem on August sixteenth, 1984. It was my first day at the library."

"It must be very long."

"It's two lines." I would have laughed if he wasn't so serious. "The first line is 'The snow piffles.' The second line, written the following year, is 'Like orphaned kittens.' For twenty-three years, I have been searching for the third line. It's inconsequential now." His triangle collapsed and he looked down at the table. "One had reached an impasse, you see." He got up suddenly and leaned across the table as if he was about to make a speech. I saw him looking through the window at the people walking along Bloor Street. "One could no longer be inspired. The magic . . ." He sat once more.

Magic? I wasn't going to let him stop here. But what he said, pausing to stare at the table, was the last thing from magic. He said that his inspiration had dried up because his poem was supposed to capture the city but each time he had nailed the place, some change or the other made his line irrelevant. "One was always too late, you see. Not unlike a guest who had arrived at a dinner after the festivities, gazing at the drawn curtain and the darkened house." Then he said something real unusual. "I have been watching you ever since you first entered this place. Chatting with the jewellery girl, taking the elevators to all the floors, sitting uneasily in the seminars, hiding in a corner to read your book, gazing at the street beneath, writing the letter to your uncle." He went on with some more observations that got me real uncomfortable, as I had no idea I was under this kind of surveillance. But his little speech seemed to have the opposite effect on him as with each new observation his voice got livelier. The way he was pronouncing his words made me think of plump fishes that had jumped from an aquarium to land on the hard tile. I even told him that. He smiled broadly, which made him look like his chimera creature.

The following Saturday I hurried out of the Bloor and Yonge station and the minute I got to the library I ran up the stairs. I searched from floor to floor until I eventually walked up to a woman at the desk. I didn't know the chimera's name so I described him as honestly as I could. The woman frowned a bit as if she didn't like him. Eventually she told me that he had retired.

I took the stairs to the seminar on the first floor: perhaps he would soon return to clear up his desk or take home some personal effects or something. The speaker before the podium was a young man with a real stylish haircut. He was saying, "If we want to capitalize our assets we need to action-ize in a robust manner." I gazed around at the group of oldish Philippine and Somalian people glancing at each other rather than focusing on the speaker. "We must think outside the box," he said as he connected his laptop to a machine. Words appeared on a screen behind him. He tapped the heading *Incentivizing Your Resumé.* The words scrolled up and he tapped other words: *ballpark figure, winningest,* and a series of abbreviations. When the man next to me began to snore, I got out the letter I had received the previous day and pretended I was reading it to the chimera.

Dear Sammy,

Is about time that you decide to further you educa-
tion. My head was always too hard for studies but
I always believe that you had it in you. Don't mind
the comic books and them. I sending one thousand
with this letter, which will help you to register. Make
sure that you don't waste it on any foolishness. If ever
you need any help don't feel shame to write me and
let me know. I going to write a letter to you father too
just to make sure that he play his part. He not going
to get away from this one.

> *Righto Pappyo.*
> *Uncle Boysie*

I imagined the chimera listening to me and saying
something about "One should do this" or "One should do
that." Just like his last words to me as he was talking about his
poem and this magic business: Presumptuousness and inno-
cence must be poured in equal parts into the same container.
It is only then that one can discover magic. The way he went
on it had seemed that magic for him was not spells and frogs
and Ra's al Ghul, but a new way of looking at some old thing.

Chapter Ten

A THOUSAND LITTLE SECRETS

I continued going to the library on weekends, collecting booklets and trying to understand this whole college system. In Trinidad, high schools were called colleges but it seemed that here they were almost like universities. That almost made me put the whole picture out of my mind, especially when I realized that I also had to do preparatory courses just to qualify for acceptance. One Sunday, a shaved-head black boy showed me how to use the computer to get more information. While he was scrolling through the different sites I asked him if he was from Regent Park and he asked why I would conclude that. I felt he might be displeased by my explanation so I said someone like him was walking up the stairs a couple weeks earlier. He seemed to believe the lie and mentioned he was from the Beaches and that he felt Regent Park was a rathole.

He himself was in a college doing some cooking course.

He had dropped out of high school after his parents split up and his mother moved briefly to a neighbourhood called Malvern. After a year of fooling around he signed up with a programme run by the Scarborough School Board that fast-tracked him to a high school diploma. It was at some alternative centre at the Centennial College campus. He boasted a bit of his cooking classes. I mentioned that in Trinidad, there were only girls in the home economic class, and that got him more offended than my Regent Park mistake. After he left I felt I should have kept my mouth shut, as he was quite helpful. I tried to picture myself in the kitchen of a Canadian restaurant; however, that place was too unfamiliar so I shifted first to a Mayaro bakery where I was punching balls of flour, and then in Rio Claro where I was a *doubles* vendor slapping *channa* into a *barra*. Vendors in Trinidad were usually fat and sweaty and every week someone claimed they had found a rotten tooth or a couple pubic hairs, which we called *jhat,* in some purchased food. I decided to write off that profession.

In any case there were so many other interesting courses. Design and fashion and film and computer stuff and everything under the sun. It was exciting just to read about them. Once I saw a course on dentistry and remembered something so vague I couldn't be sure if it was just a memory. It must have been a year or so before my father left Mayaro for good and in my recollection he was bent over a tray with some white powder. Next to the tray was a *flambeau* shining on a skull. There may have been knives and icepicks on the table too. He was making a set of teeth and not once did he quarrel with me.

The next day I wished he was still as peaceful because I discovered that for me to be admitted to the college I needed him to sign my admission form, as I was still a minor. This was a funny word. I had never considered myself a minor in any way. A few weeks earlier, a group of Sri Lankan men in the laundry room of our building were talking about minorities. One of the men, a real dark fella with jacket and tie was saying that everybody pushed them to the side and yet complained because they didn't mingle. After that they broke into their own language talking real fast and rolling their tongues. I guess they were chatting about a zoo as another fella mentioned something about a tiger.

Anyways back to my own problem. For close to two weeks I tried to think of some way to approach my father. Should I suggest that we move to a two-bedroom apartment using a portion of Uncle Boysie's money? However, I didn't know how he would react to the news that money had been sent to me. Perhaps I could redecorate the apartment or buy him some present like teeth-making equipment. Other ideas came but I had to throw them out them one after the other.

At work I told Paul that a friend was worried as his visitor's visa was up. He said that half the taxi drivers were in the same position and they regularly used each other's identity papers and driving permits. Same with the Chinese people in Markham. He made it sound like an exciting game, and after that conversation I pretended I was part of a shadowy group, like Professor Xavier's mutants, that only came out at nights. This fantasy disappeared by the time I got home.

Once Uncle Boysie had told me that the fella upstairs knew exactly how much weight we could carry on our shoulders and he always increased and lightened the burden to suit. I think maybe he forgot about the rules in my case because the same time I was worrying about my status I learned that I would be laid off from the gas station at the end of the month. For a while I suspected that Paul had reported my question about visitor's visas to the boss but Paul seemed genuinely sad to see me leave. On my last day he took off a beaded necklace and held it before me. He said it had been left by the Vikings at Pistolet Bay (which I guessed was somewhere in Newfoundland) and that it would bring me good luck.

That night I decided to test its powers on my father.

This is how it went. First he said that every day he was discovering that sending for me was a big mistake, then he shifted to some trap he felt I was laying for him and finally he shouted, "You start back with this status nonsense again? You think anybody was rushing to help me when I come to this place? Laying out the red carpet? If is kissmeass school you wanted to go to, then why the hell you didn't stay in Trinidad? You know anything about the rules and regulations here? I don't know why I ever listen to that fat, lazy uncle of yours," he shouted. "I wring my ears. I wring it a thousand times!"

While he was wringing his ears I was stroking my necklace, which got him in a worse mood. "Dressing up like a damn rasta *locho*."

I had to say something. I told him, "Is no damn rasta jewellery. Is a damn charm!" I don't know if it was because

I had raised my voice to him for the first time or because he was afraid of magic, but he backed away and I felt for just a second or so his eyes went blank as if he didn't know what to say.

By the end of the week I felt it was fear. It was a rainy evening and I was returning from the library when I saw him talking to a woman outside our building. He was wearing a yellow raincoat and was shifting from one leg to the other as if he was impatient to get out from the rain but the woman, who had no coat and was completely drenched, didn't look as if she was in a hurry. She had frizzled red hair like a troll and high heel shoes that made her legs look even stumpier. The next day when I returned from the library I saw her in our apartment.

She and my father were sitting on opposite ends of the kitchen table and between them was some sort of Chinese checkers board but instead of marbles there were pointed little crystals in the holes. The woman was stroking the crystals and saying "Woo woo" like a mother petting a baby. She kept her eyes closed as I walked to the balcony but I caught a glimpse of my father frowning as if I had broken the spell or trance or whatever they were doing. I remained on the balcony for maybe fifteen minutes peeking at them. When they both left, I walked into the kitchen and caught a whiff of a strong smell like ground-up garlic and clove.

The next day it was the same but instead of a Chinese checkers board, on the table was a row of little vials, each a different colour. From the balcony I saw the woman picking up some of the vials and puffing out her cheeks as she blew over the fridge and stove and cupboard. My first thought was that she was getting rid of the cockroaches and rats my father often complained about but then she began her wailing sound again. From the balcony I heard her murmuring as she sprinkled: "We must fumigate the soul. We must bleach the spirits. We must scrub the mind." I felt maybe she had been a cleaning lady before she picked up this hocus-pocus business. After they had left together, I noticed a vial on the table. I shook it a bit and almost dropped it—I don't think I had ever smelled anything nastier. It reeked of cat shit and oil and ginger. I put it back on the table just as my father returned. He glanced at me suspiciously for a couple seconds before he said, "You trying to cancel out the blasted thing or what?"

"Cancel out what?"

"You wouldn't understand."

It seemed like an opening to some explanation but his face got hard as usual. However, he was wrong. I *did* understand. In Mayaro, people only went to real doctors in emergencies, after they had visited wrinkly old ladies for scented oils and special herbs and secret prayers and a load of other nonsense. The most popular quack was not a wrinkly old lady though. His name was Amos and he made concoctions from vines and barks and roots he claimed he got from secret trees in the Guayaguayare forest. Once I heard one of our neighbours, a woman who could balance a basket of plantain on her head with no trouble at all, telling my mother she should see Amos. As far as I can tell, my mother never took the woman's advice.

Me and a couple of my friends from Mayaro Composite went to his board house one evening. We were curious because that day, our history teacher, Mr. Chotolal, had shifted from his slavery topic to a discussion of voodoo and *obeah*. First, we pelted a few stones on top of Amos's roof to make sure he was not around before we entered the building. I have to say that it was exactly as we had pictured it, with the junk he sometimes collected from people as payment scattered all around a long table. On the table were also little heaps of crushed-up herbs. We noticed some mildewed copybook pages at the side of each pile. It took a while to read the *crapo-foot* handwriting on the pages but we were able to decipher a couple instructions like, "For woman who man leave them," and "For ugly *squingy* man," and "To stop *horning*," and "Getting rid of *ownway* children." We left Amos's house laughing because we had rearranged all the pages.

This memory must have caused me to smile because my father glanced at me, uttered something about traps and went to the television. There, he settled on a channel where a man with a big puff of hair was talking about magnetic charm bracelets. This was the first time he had chosen a show other than *MacGyver* or *The Mythbusters,* and as he leaned forward to place his hands on his lap I felt that after all his years in Canada he was no better than these people from the Guayaguayare forest.

I got more curious about this woman's sudden appearance in our apartment. It couldn't simply be because my father was afraid of my necklace.

Five nights after I first saw her, I woke up from a sudden noise and as my eyes adjusted to the dark I saw that the balcony door was open a crack and the wind was whistling through. I closed the door and returned to my foam but before I fell asleep I wondered if my father was trying to exorcise me from his apartment. In Trinidad "putting a light" on an enemy's head was a common enough practice, and everybody knew that all the mad people who roamed about the streets in Rio Claro had been "lighted." Maybe I was pushing my father too hard with my college talk. The next evening, I waited by the curb until the lights were off in our apartment before I entered the building. I speculated about what they were doing in the dark, my father and this strange woman with her red hair and her high heels. All of a sudden I thought of my mother. The elevator stopped at the third floor for a woman who was holding a cat in one hand and a shopping bag in the other. I moved to the corner.

"Thanks for holding open the door for me, asshole."

I was the only other person on the elevator. I looked at her. The cat was scratching at a red boil on her arm, maybe to escape from her clutch. "I look like a blasted slave to you?" The minute the words left my mouth I was sorry. I bolted out of the elevator at our floor and before its door closed the woman shouted out some nasty curses in a whining but musical voice. When I entered our apartment the lights were still off so I coughed a couple times to alert my father and the woman, if she was still here.

"You just break the kissmeass rainbow."

I turned on the kitchen light. "Which rainbow?"

"It not visible to jackasses."

My annoyance returned and I tried to pack all the mockery I could muster up into my voice. "Only to you? Nice. Very nice."

"Yes, only to me, you little bitch. Only to people with a clean heart." I swear he said that.

The next day I felt really awkward and out of place in the library. I looked at all the boys bent so seriously over their books and computers and thought: all of them have some plan. They know where they going and how to get there. Their lives are set. I wished I knew where they were living. I was sure there were no cursing elevator ladies and *obeah* women and horrible fathers. Another thought came to me: this library is too organized for somebody like me. To be honest, I felt real sorry for myself then and I left the library after ten minutes or so. As I was walking to the subway, a stupid Mayaro rhyme kept ringing in my head. *Loser, loser, stupid little loser.*

I remained on the subway train for a while and I recalled how, just seven months earlier, I had pretended that all these tired factory workers were really molemen. For a minute or so I wished I could still think this way. Then I landed at Union Station.

I got off there because I didn't want to return early to our apartment and so followed a rush of people out of the train and into the Union building. And the minute I entered the big hall all my loser feelings dropped off. Everybody was walking and walking and moving and moving in a long, never-ending stream. Some had briefcases, and others were dragging suitcases behind them like boxy puppies. Maybe they were leaving the city or going for a vacation or just returning from their jobs, but all this constant motion made everything feel temporary. Even my school worries.

The next evening, sitting on a bench near to a Muffins place I discovered another reason for its appeal: it reminded me of these *Star Wars* bars with all sort of strange aliens sitting right next to each other and not noticing all the snouts and fish faces and extra eyes and antennae right on the opposite table. The walls and ceiling looked like the building where the big X-Men movie fight had taken place and while I was gazing at a flashing schedule screen I pretended that some of the trenchcoat men bent over their laptops and the pretty women reading magazines from behind narrow mole-man glasses were just waiting for some kind of action and would jump out of their coats and throw off their glasses to reveal capes and tights and tall boots.

I wandered around the upstairs floor—where the suitcases were bigger and the people better dressed, as if they were travelling farther than the downstairs crowd—and came through some fancy Spartacus columns to Front Street before I returned to the Muffins place. This building seemed a perfect place for an entrance to a secret underground city (and an hour or so later I walked through a long tunnel that led to an Air Canada Centre).

When I got home it was quite late and I noticed on the fridge a handwritten note with a drawing of a cat saying, "A million little secrets shall tumble from my lips." The cat seemed conceited to be saying this and I felt that the only secret I was interested in was how I could get my father to understand my college worries. I thought he was asleep so I was startled to see the woman coming from his bedroom carrying an ugly little dog. The dog had the same conceited look like the cat. The woman put down the dog and said, "Go, Jezebel, go." The dog wagged its stumpy little tail and walked to the fridge. The woman and my father followed it. The woman sprinkled some of the stuff from a vial beneath the fridge. The dog strolled to the couch with my father and the woman following. Once more she sprinkled the vial over the couch. Then the dog looked up as if it had now noticed me. It came over wagging its tail. Without any warning the woman emptied the vial straight on me. In my surprise I kicked away the dog.

That night I washed my clothes over and over in the basement laundry area, trying to get out the smell of cat shit and ginger. To my surprise when I got back, my father didn't scream at me, and at first I wasn't even sure he was in the apartment. I took a long shower and was about to settle on my foam when I heard, "You was always bad luck. Always." The voice was so soft I felt I had imagined it but then I noticed his cigarette glinting by the porch door.

"I don't believe in luck." I said the words quietly.

"Bitch." He matched my quiet voice.

Cult!

The next morning I saw the woman walking on the main

lane. I don't think she would have noticed me if her dog hadn't starting barking in my direction. She came across and asked, "How is your foot?"

I didn't know how she expected it to be but in any case I told her, "It normal."

"When you do harm to any of God's creatures, that same harm will spring back upon you." She patted the dog and said, "Shh, Jezebel. Everything is going to be all right. Kiss it."

It took a while before I realized she was talking to me. She was holding up one of the dog's paw. "I not going to kiss any dog foot."

"Kiss it." I now saw how much she resembled a slowly boiled frog. Her eyes were bulgy and in the wind her hair seemed like red, wavy seaweeds.

"No. Absolutely not." I backed away.

She kissed the foot herself and told her dog, "Don't worry, dearie. In his next life, he is going to reborn as a dog and every single day, someone will kick him." She said this in a happy voice. "He is just a bad luck boy."

You ugly old troll, you. Froggie too.

A tall black woman with big chunky breasts came up to us. I tried to walk away but the black woman sidestepped and blocked me.

"We have something we would like you to sign," the woman told me. I thought it was some type of nonsense connected to the troll lady so I shook my head. This got the black woman mad and she said to the other woman, "This is the way it is with these people from India and Pakistan. They not interested in anything that don't concern them. This is the way it is with them." The troll lady nodded at this.

I got mad at the two of them, carrying on this conversation as if I wasn't right in front of them. In Trinidad black people were called Creoles but this woman wasn't moving like a Trinidadian Creole one bit. "Look, lady, I not from these places, and I not going to sign any damn paper that I know nothing about. So leave me alone."

The troll lady seemed offended by my tone, but the Creole woman really surprised me by saying, "That is a Trinidadian accent, not so?" She told the troll in a whispering voice, "He worried about his status. The poor boy frighten to put his name on any paper." She fished around in her alligator purse and brought out a crumpled sheet of paper. "What is your name, boy?"

I went through a list of made-up names but eventually told her, "Samuel."

"That is a nice name, boy. An upstanding name. Here, read this when you have the time, Samuel."

"Thanks." I took the paper and hurried away. I opened it at Union and saw a photograph of a Nigerian man and beneath, in bold letters with exclamation after each sentence: No One Is Illegal! Reunite Families! Know Your Rights! Refugees Are People Too! Contact Mr. O Omewale! LLB!

Refugees. I wondered how many people wandering around here were refugees. Was there some way to detect them? Something in their clothes or gestures? What about the Ethiopian man sitting by himself? He was too well dressed and had an expensive briefcase besides. The woman from India with a dot on her forehead? She looked too fat and happy. The pink, stooped man wearing an old coat and hat? He might be too old. I changed benches and focused on another group. The seminar woman said they lived like ghosts and I imagined them, just like the Flash, vibrating at a special frequency that made them mostly invisible. Then another thought hit me. Was it possible that among this crowd there might be someone who *could* tell, and who might be gazing at me this very minute? Soon after I arrived in Canada I had been struck by the short glances as if these people had made their assessments in a second or less but now I scanned all the waiting passengers to determine if anyone was carefully studying me. Perhaps the security guard who was leaning on a counter and munching at a muffin, or the Filipino boy wheeling a cart with newspapers. Even the girl punching letters on her phone.

The next day I chose a bench beneath the stairs. I looked around for a while before my eyes settled on a lanky man whose long legs were crossed like a woman's. He was sitting by himself like a long ghost in his old tweed jacket and a bulging canvas briefcase beside him. It took a while before I recognized him.

Chapter Eleven

THE DEAL

I really believe Sporty had pretended he could not recognize me that day at the Union Station through shame, not his busyness or all his appointments, as he later claimed. But that was Sporty: always pretending, always putting up a big show, always claiming to have some secret in his back pocket. Most Mayaro people got their nicknames from the other villagers but Sporty was the only person who chose his own. I believe it was because everyone called him Homo to suit his last name which was Sapienza. He never answered to the Homo name and after a while he would say, "Hello, you loo-looking for Sporty?" He used to live about ten minutes from my mother's house in Mayaro, in a half-completed teak shack with no windows or doors, right behind Mrs. Bango parlour. When he disappeared from the village, everyone said that he had moved to San Fernando to fleece the rich city folks or had landed in Carrera, the offshore prison.

When I saw him at Union, his face was thinner and he now wore a wild, *ownway* goatee but he still had the habit of holding his head upwards as if he was better than anyone around him. From this angle, his nostrils seemed to fill out his entire face. His legs were folded just like when he used to sit on the steps of his teak house with his face sunk into his *Kid Colt* or *Rawhide Kid* comic book. I was about eleven or so, the age at which my mother had given me the responsibility to buy from Mrs. Bango's parlour, tins of condensed milk or bars of blue carbolic soap or other small items she needed in a hurry.

I believe he lived alone because I never saw anyone else in the house, and he was always by himself, reading his westerns. He must have been about thirty then, and in Mayaro, where all the other men were either in fishing boats or in their gardens, Sporty's idleness made everybody suspicious. I remember my mother, after she had heard from the village grapevine that I had been chatting with him, warning me over and over about "idle, good-for-nothing scamps with big useless heads." But it was just about the time I had started to read the Mandrake and Phantom comics from *The Guardian,* and Sporty always had a big pile of comics on the steps. I think he must have noticed me staring because whenever I was around, he would dig into his pile and sort and rearrange, which made me even more curious. The first words he ever spoke to me were, "Pardnah, these things cost mm-money, you know." It sounded like a threat so I ran off, but the next day, he added, "Two for a doll-a dollar."

"So cheap?" I had asked.

"That is why it will cost you just a sh-shilling for a read."

In my hands were a bar of squishy salted butter and seventy cents change. I hesitated for a while; I always placed the loose change in the cracked teapot next to my mother's Singer and I had never seen her counting the money I brought back from the parlour. "What you have?"

"*Tex-tex-as Rangers. Two Gun Kid. Cherokee Kid. Jonah Hex.*"

"Only westerns? No Mandrake and Phantom?"

"Real men only wear costumes 'round car-carnival time, pardnah. Just one sh-shilling. But nobody forcing you."

It took a week before I walked over and held out my twenty-five cents. "Put it on the st-step." He didn't look at me but delved into his pile and brought up a comic. "Bill-Billy the Kid," he told me. "And be careful with it, please. Wipe your hands, and don't bend back the pa-pages."

I remember the comic being senseless. No one wore costumes like Phantom or had magical powers like Mandrake but Sporty was nodding and making little laughs and saying "*Qui pappa!* That is man," and somehow not stammering at all. When I was finished, he asked what I thought.

"It real boring. Just gun-talk and *badjohn* business."

"You still not getting back your sh-shilling."

I decided to leave him alone but a couple weeks later he called out to me, "Pardnah, I think you might like this one. I get it a few days ago in a sp-special deal."

"How much?"

"The price didn't change."

"I only have fifteen cents."

"I will let you read ha-half."

"What good that will do?"

"You could choose your own ha-half. The beginning or the ending. Is no different from the comics in *The Guardian* where you have to wait mm-months on end to reach the conclusion of the st-story."

That was true; still, I didn't want to waste any money on half of a boring comic. I told him that.

"Okay, I will make you a deal. I will tell you the rest of the st-story myself. The other ha-half."

"Same fifteen cents?"

"Anything mm-more, I will consider a donation."

I knew he was not going to squeeze any more money from me so I walked over reluctantly. As I expected it was boring just like the others. A dusty-looking man sitting by himself in a saloon, challenged he could draw his gun faster than the regular crowd, walked outside with his legs far apart and scattered several gunslingers hidden behind water troughs. When I reached the stapled halfway point, I gave him the money and the comic. He closed it and pretended he was studying the advertisement for X-ray glasses on the back cover. Because he didn't say anything and I felt he would not fulfil his side of the bargain, I asked him, "What happen after the fight?"

"Exactly what you would ex-expect."

"I didn't expect anything. What happened?"

"He became an owlhoot, Pardnah. Moving from one fra-fracas to the other. An inn-innocent and misunderstood hombre on the run. Until a band of Indians ta-take him in." His voice seemed so sad that I didn't pay much attention to his new accent. "But it had this posse of bounty hunters tracking him all the time. There was a big sh-shootout in the end."

"And?"

"He sent all those miserable varmints straight to Boot Hill. Pow! Pow! Badow! They fall like pe-pe-peas. But he had to mm-move on."

"That is all? It sound exactly like all the others."

"You think so?" He seemed to be speaking to himself so I said nothing. "That is the way life is. Innocent and mis-understood men always have to be on the mm-move. They always have to keep one step ahead of the mob-ob who will string them up at the slightest opportunity."

I told him, "I have to get going now."

"You interested in a sp-special deal, pardnah? I could get a pile of comics as big as mine. This wholesaler in Rio Claro clos-ing down. He selling out all his comics for next to nn-nothing."

"I fed up of westerns already."

"That is the thing. If was westerns, I wouldn't be sp-spilling the beans. Is superhero comics."

"Phantom and Mandrake?"

"The latest. And Batman and Justice League and Gr-green Lantern and Captain America. It even have a bl-black superhero too. "

"I don't believe you. How much?"

"Ten dollars for the whole *grop.*"

"Where you expect me to get all that money from?"

"If you really want something, you will find a way. This world don't wait for coward fr-frightened people." He made stealing from my mother sound like a good thing

How could Sporty have forgotten all of this? How could he take his briefcase and hold it tightly against his chest as if I might grab it? And just walk up the step in Union like I was a perfect stranger? It was only when I was entering Regent Park that I considered he might be a refugee.

As soon as I got home, I told my father, "I see somebody from Mayaro in Union today."

"Who?" He was by the kitchen table and I could hear the snap of his cereals as he chewed slowly.

"Sporty from behind Mrs. Bango parlour. He use to stammer a lot. And he had a nickname." After a while, I told him, "Homo."

He continued chewing his corn flakes and I was sure he cracked a small grin. "What he doing here?"

"I really don't know. He didn't talk to me."

"You really don't know?" Usually this tone was the signal for some mocking comment but now he tapped his cigarette against his palm and went to the balcony. It had never occurred to me before but now I wondered if he too missed Mayaro. After he had smoked a couple cigarettes on the balcony, he went into his room.

Later that night while I was washing up the wares, stupid as it was, I imagined my father walking out from his room and talking about some of the other villagers he had known; and me listening carefully until he was finished before I described how Sporty had outsmarted me. I would mention Sporty's surprise at the ten dollars I had scraped up and promising me the best comics from his pile. Telling me, "S-so long, pardnah," as I was leaving, and making all sorts of excuses every time I approached him until the evening I saw the front step of his halfway teak house, empty.

I could have told my father that in the weeks that followed, it looked like Sporty had outsmarted half of the village. He had promised the fishermen new boats from the Venezuelan coast guard and the farmers better prices for their coconuts from some new cooperative. Everyone had paid upfront, and my mother, as if she had known all along about my own arrangement with Sporty, telling me over and over that I should never trust sweet-talkers who promised the moon and stars. After that sort of talk, she always mentioned conscience and pointed to her heart as if it was lodged inside there. The other villagers were not as charitable as they put up crude homemade posters on the telephone poles asking, "Have you seen this Homo?" And "Smartman wanted. Dead or Alive."

A week passed before I saw Sporty at Union again. He was sitting on the selfsame bench next to the cinnamon shop store and dressed in the same old tweed jacket. He was wearing a scarf even in this warm weather. Because he was staring at the electronic schedule on the ceiling monitor—and also because he had been so cold to me during our previous meeting—I decided to leave him alone, but as I was buying a cinnamon bun, I heard someone saying softly, "Pardnah."

When I looked back, I saw Sporty stroking his goatee and staring at the bun in my hand. I walked across and sat next to him. "Your face looks very familiar," he told me.

But he was still staring at my bun and I wondered if I should offer him half. "I met you right here about a—"

"Let me guess. Was it at one of my classes at Ryerson?"

"No, it was—"

"Then could it have been at my seminar at the library?" He shook his head. "No, no. I don't think so. It must have been during my lecture at the annex."

I now saw that it was a towel not a scarf wrapped around his neck. "It was right behind Mrs. Bango parlour in Mayaro. You charged me a shilling to read your westerns." I almost added that he had run off with my ten dollars.

He crossed his legs and shifted closer to me (and to my bun). "Mayaro. Maya-roo." He seemed to be experimenting with the name, and it struck me that he was not stammering one bit. "Do you know there were Indians living there? Not Indians like yourself, mark you, but the real variety. When Columbus landed with his men, these Indians were peeping out from behind every coconut tree. Did you know that?"

"From my primary school *West Indian Reader*."

He seemed disappointed. "That was a long time ago. Much would have changed since. Tell me about Mayaro."

"What you want to know?" I thought of the posters.

"Remind me of the place. The wind breathing through the trees and the sound of coconuts dropping on the mud. *Ta-dup, ta-dup.* The hairy mangrove crabs and the turtles. The evening sky looking like a big *mash-up* rainbow with all these colours leaking down on the sea. The fresh smell of fish and sand in the mornings. *Cascadura* jumping up from the ponds like living clumps of mud. Dew skating down from the big *dasheen* leaves as if they playing with the sunlight. A horsewhip snake slipping down a guava branch as smooth as flowing water. Cassava *pone* cakes and seamoss drinks." To tell the truth, apart from my descriptions to Dilara, I had never thought of Mayaro this way: my strongest recollections were always of my mother getting sick and the couple months at Uncle Boysie's place. Off and on, I would also think of the fishermen in the rumshop and of my short friendship with Loykie, the Amazing Absorbing Boy. But Sporty made me recall these other slices to the village and caused me to miss it even more. I even smelled the fresh fish odour that clung to the sea moss washed ashore in the mornings and the strong woody aroma of the peeled husks from the coconut factory. For a moment, I lost my fear of returning.

"It must have changed a lot," he told me. "That is the way life is. Right now I am changing before your very eyes."

I blurted out, "So you are no longer a refugee?"

He pretended he had not heard me, then he patted his briefcase and I heard a sound like the tinkling of spoons. "All my documents are here. My life's work."

I felt ashamed for trying to trap him. "Everything?"

"My total inventory. If I die tomorrow my entire life can be deciphered from this." He patted it again and now there was a squishy sound.

"It must be very important."

I was glad I didn't mention that his stammering had disappeared because he seemed happy with my remark. He laughed and I noticed his big, yellow front teeth. "Cinnamon cakes always remind me of cassava *pones*, you know. Could be the spices. Can I smell it?"

I held up the bun and he leaned towards it, his nose grazing the crust. I couldn't eat it after this, so I offered it to him. He examined it a bit, bared his teeth like a *manicou* then took a little bite, chewing slowly and smacking. Maybe the bun really reminded him of Mayaro and his Indians because between his toothy nibbles, he told me a story. The story was about these old time Spanish who had recently landed on Guayaguayare, a village next to Mayaro. There was some sort of problem with the local chiefs who were becoming impatient with these foreigners getting in their way and digging up everywhere for gold and silver and making all kind of rosy promises. The grumbling became nastier when these Spanish fellas began to force some of the Indians to build their new homes. It appeared they were here to stay, the Indians realized. One of these building was a big round structure with one door and no windows. When it was finished, the Spanish invited all the chiefs and their wives and children for a big *fête*.

Sporty dusted some crumbs from his goatee and said, "A massacre, you know. Every last one of them."

"The Spanish fellas?"

"The Indians. One door and no windows. Nowhere to escape from. A perfect trap. Some properties are like that." He grew silent after his story and I wondered if he had got it from one of his comics. But in his westerns, it was always the Indians doing the massacring.

After about five minutes of no talking, I told him, "Well, is time for me to go now."

"I suppose so."

His statement confused me because it seemed as if I should now say something else. "To my home in Regent Park."

"Two bedroom?"

"Just one. Small place."

"You live alone?"

"With my father."

He became quiet again and I wondered if he was trying to remember my father but then he asked me, "You could take in b-boarders?"

I was a little surprised at his stammering because he had talked normally during the entire conversation. I told him, "I think my father fed up of even me living there."

"Yes, yes. That is how it goes sometimes." He didn't sound too disappointed. "Why you don't le-leave?"

"To go where?"

"That is always the question, pardnah."

While I was walking to the exit, I glanced back and saw him pushing the remaining bit of bun into his briefcase.

In the night, I told my father, "I think Sporty is a refugee."

I would not have spoken to him but he was sitting before the blank television. As he did not reply immediately I prepared myself for some sarcastic comment. However, he remained quiet. A few minutes later while I was microwaving a bowl of Kraft Dinner I heard him ask something about a letter. I removed the bowl and walked to the kitchen. Did he discover about the money sent by Uncle Boysie? I decided to pretend I had not heard him but now he asked instead about the house in Mayaro. "Boysie mentioned anything about it?"

I shook my head and for the entire five minutes that I sat by the kitchen table he stared at the blank screen. Maybe my mention of refugees had finally made him understand the seriousness of my situation. The next day I was in a better mood than the entire month, and on my way to Union I detoured to the library where I printed out an entire set of application forms for the Alternative Centre. Sporty was at his usual spot with his head bent over some pages set on the top of his briefcase. I decided to buy two buns but when I offered him one, he told me in a busy voice, "Leave it on the bench."

I glanced at the form he was filling out. There were many crosses and scratches as if he couldn't decide on the information. When he paused for a while and tapped his pencil against his leg, I asked him, "What you doing there?"

"I am working on a proposal."

"I have some forms too. They are for classes that will fast track me to college."

He glanced at the rolled-up sheets in my hand. "Mine is important. A very weighty project."

"What it is about?"

"That is a good question. A better question would be 'What it's not about'? You understand? What I am saying, is that it is about everything. A complete history of the last six hundred years. From 1492 to the present date, to be precise."

"That will take a real long time to finish."

"Three months, at least."

"Only that?"

"Pruning is a real art. You have to know what to leave out." He took the bun and held it before him, turning and examining it carefully. "Take a man life, for example. He born, he go to school, he dropout. He move from place to place trying to inspire others. Then he die." He bit into the bun. "End of his history."

"You think anybody will want to read this sort of project?"

"If they are smart, they will lap it up."

I told him, "I mentioned you to my father." He seemed a little worried until I mentioned my father's name.

"Danny. Yes, yes. Left the village a few years before me. Always wondered what happened to him. Smart man." I wanted to tell Sporty he didn't have to *mamaguy* me just because I bought him a bun when he added, "Was developing a special method for making teeth."

"Really?"

"From plastic. Common household items. Cups and such. Melted them in a big ball. Brilliant." He mentioned all of this in little snaps as he crossed out words in his form. I wanted him to talk more of my father but he opened a flap on his briefcase, fiddled around a bit and brought out a jar of whiteout. First, he blanked out a few words then he moved across the form rapidly, until in about a minute or so the entire form was white. "It seems as if I will have to start over. Perhaps I can borrow yours."

"These are for school."

"Of course. It wouldn't work. What course are you taking? May I suggest a course on insects? It was the most interesting programme I taught at Ryerson. Do you know there are ten million species? My favourite was the slinky fly."

"I never heard of them."

"Not surprising. Very hard to track. Other insects wait until the slinky flies build their nest before they chase them away. Always on the move." He pointed his nose in the air and added, "My second favourite is the damsel bug." I was wondering if he might be able to help me with my admission forms when he said, "Sadly I was let go after discussing just fifty-five species. Terrible business. I had more than nine million left." When I left, he was making calculations on his sheet, perhaps checking the exact number of insects remaining in his course.

While I was walking home, I knew I couldn't ask my father once more to sign the form so I decided I would leave it in a spot where he couldn't miss it. I considered the fridge door and the kitchen table before I settled on the television where it would not get lost in the shuffle of free newspapers I sometimes brought to the apartment. Each night when I got home, I checked for a signature, waiting till my father went into the washroom or his bedroom. Though he did not quarrel as before—mostly staring at the blank screen—the form remained unsigned.

I wished I could ask Sporty for some advice or get him talking of my father but he always seemed too busy. One night, about a month after our first meeting, he was in a real bad mood. "They rejected my project," he told me. "They didn't approve the gr-grant." He got up, pushed the bun into his briefcase and walked up the step. Just like that!

I believe this rejection must have hit him hard because he seemed real frazzled for the next week or so. He walked up the stairs with his buns after just a couple minute and I wondered whether this was all he had been waiting for. Then one night I saw him busy once more, scribbling into his form.

"A new project?"

"This world does not wait for those who don't get in line. They are left behind, as a rule." He smiled. "If you pay attention, you will see that every disappointment comes equipped with a loophole. The trick is finding the loophole." He was right about these loopholes: although I needed my father's signature on the college forms, if I was just a couple months older I would have been on my own. I wanted to tell Sporty of the benefits of being a minor but he was busily crossing out lines on his own form. "The loophole could be anywhere," he was saying. "In this particular case, it came in the form of a dream." He looked up, his head held now in its normal position. "Vision would be a better word, actually. Yes, yes, vision." He seemed to be studying some of the bars on the ceiling. "I had this vision of people, plenty people moving. You know what a caravan is?"

"A sorta van or carriage."

"Well, there were thousands of family packed in these caravans. Moving and moving."

"Just like in Union?'

He fetched out a pen from his briefcase and scribbled Union before he continued, "These people were all running away. To somewhere better where they could start over and watch their grandchildren running through the fields collecting damsel bugs and slinky flies." I was about to tell him this project seemed more promising than the previous, when he added, "This journey began thousands of years ago. It started in a jungle and that was the easiest part because these travellers bounced up deserts and plains and mountains and oceans and junks of ice bigger than Canada."

I just had to ask him, "How long this project going to take?'

"This is the problem. You see, this project involve all sort of regions and languages. It not as straightforward as the last one." He glanced down at the form on his briefcase and scratched out some number. "I would say three months, at the very least."

Two weeks later, he took the bun I had bought and told me his outline had been rejected because he could not fulfil some requirement. He was in a real sour mood but by the time he had finished the bun he began to talk once more of his loopholes. Soon he hit on another project. A compilation of all the unknown plants and animals on earth. He mentioned the slinky fly and a couple beetles. "Ignored species, suffering in silence."

Once again, his outline was rejected. This was the pattern for the entire month and although he seemed to recover with each new project, I felt that every rejection had damaged him in some small way. His stammering, though not as bad as before, returned. I tried to help him. "What about refugees?"

He looked at me suspiciously before he began to calculate on a sheet. "There are exactly three hundred and forty-six species of refugees on this planet." He glanced around at the benches opposite and adjusted his figures. "Three hundred and forty-nine."

The next night he said he had to abandon the project as it was too dangerous. He snapped and unsnapped his briefcase's clasps before he asked, "Would you be in-interested in a loan? Just a sm-small sum. I will pay you back as soon as possible."

I thought of his previous scam as I reached into my pocket. "All I have is a ten."

He took the bill and folded it into a tiny nugget. "You may not believe it, but this ten dollars might have sa-saved my life."

He shook his head sorrowfully. I felt a little ashamed for not trusting him. I remembered his question about boarders. "So where you living?"

"Wherever I am when night falls."

"You don't have a regular place?"

"This station isn't that bad. I have all the heat and water and lights that I need." He cheered up. "And in the nights, when it's very quiet, I tap into my visions. The only problem is the men toilets. Filthy. The ladies' is much better. I have learned to pee sitting down. An art in itself."

Maybe it was his worries about not having a regular place to stay or perhaps it was just all the disappointment but the following night Sporty told me, "The plug got pulled." I thought at first that he had been evicted from the station, maybe for going to the ladies' toilets. "The visions have dried up like an old cucumber vine."

This comparison sounded sort of funny but Sporty was not laughing. "What about the loopholes?" I asked him.

"Traps! Nothing more than traps." He patted his brief-case. "This bag have more traps than a crab-catcher van. Tonight when everybody sleeping I going to take it and pelt it ass down the Don-Don Valley."

"What about your documents in there?"

"Traps. Traps!" He almost sounded like my father.

I told him, "I feel the same way too."

"Then you are a fo-fool." He glanced at my hands. "Where is my bun?"

"I ran out of money."

He dusted his briefcase as if there were breadcrumbs there. "Yes, pardnah. That is the way li-life is."

I felt sorry for him. "Maybe you could write something simpler."

"This is the problem with the world today. Everybody want something simple and break down in small pieces. Bu-but I not design that way. That is not my route." He seemed so offended that I was not prepared for his question soon after. "What you have in mind?"

"Maybe something about these Indians that get killed in the round house."

I didn't expect him to take me seriously but he told me immediately, "I see what you getting at. A complete history of what happened to the Indians after the Spanish arrived. I could move from Mayaro to Cuba and Hispaniola." By the end of that conversation, Sporty had extended his project to include Mexico and Venezuela and several other South American countries. And the next time I met him, he told me, "I don't see why I have to limit myself with these jungle Indians. I could move across the plains of America too. Sitting Bull. Crazy Horse. Geronimo." I was sure he got these names from his westerns but he added, "It had a lot of these fellas roaming about in Canada too, you know."

During the next two weeks, he filled me in on the state of his project. "These Indians had a real tough life, you know. They get outsmarted time after time. Chased away from their homes just like the slinky flies. I believe I discover something important, Pardnah. Real important. These people had no idea of trickery. That wasn't part of their package. They lived a straightforward life so when they bounce up anybody dishonest, they goose get cooked. Sitting Duck, not Sitting Bull." As he talked, I felt he was describing his own life. "Now I going to do something honourable. Please, don't protest."

"I not protesting."

He held up a hand as if I was putting up a big argument.

"I going to also put your name on the application. After all, it was you who put the idea in my head. When I get the grant, you will be entitled to half."

"Is you who doing all the work."

"Quite true but is still the right thing to do."

"Is up to you," I told him finally.

"So it's settled then. As the co-applicant, you will have to split half of the hundred dollar application fee. Just fi-fifty dollars. A small sum for a big investment."

"I really don't—"

"Please. Is the le-least I could do. I know you thinking that I giving away this mm-money but I am a man like that. Honest and straightforward. Just like these Indians. In fact, I think I might have some Carib blood in me. Not much, mark you, but enough to make me a straightforward man."

"I don't have that much money on me."

"How mu-much you have?"

"A little more than thirty."

He crossed his legs and leaned forward with his elbows on his briefcase. I heard him mumbling, "One hundred divide by thirty one equal to . . ."

His calculations were talking a while so I told him once more, "You really don't have to include me in any application, you know."

He straightened. "You will get qu-quarter. That sound fair?"

I was sure he was scamming me and I couldn't understand why he was putting up this big show. I was giving him the money because I felt sorry for him, living in Union, waiting for the buns, working on all these proposals, getting turned down time after time. And also because he mentioned Mayaro every now and again. After I handed over the money, he told me, "The universe always ba-ba-balance itself. So far I have identified eight hundred and sixty-six ways." He took out a form from his briefcase and wrote: *Co applicant.* "This is the nice thing about these forms. You don't have to include everybody na-name."

The next week Sporty tried to chisel out some more money from me but I had made up my mind. He mentioned that these arts council people liked proposals about Indian history and that his project was sure to be approved. He told me that he would use his portion of the grant money to rent a small apartment by the Beaches. An old house with gables and two steps leading to a small porch. With a couple flowers in the yard which he would look over as he worked on his project on the front step. He seemed to be describing his house behind Mrs. Bango's parlour. "The most important thing in a man life is property. A piece of the earth. A place he could leave his mark so a hun-hundred years later a passerby will say, 'That is house where Sp-sporty used to live.'"

The next week, the bench he always occupied was empty. I waited for a while. A thin young woman with a ring on her left eyebrow unslung her knapsack and sat next to me. She left after five minutes or so. A Sri Lankan couple with their bags of fries came and began chatting in their language. I felt a little annoyed because they were talking so loudly, as if I wasn't right next to them but after a while, their words seemed small and neatly arranged in straight rows. I thought of a cob of corn.

That same night I realized why my father had been so distracted during the last couple weeks. As I was entering our building, I saw the Creole woman who had given me the form about refugees. She was chatting with a small group and when she spotted me she said, "Samuel, take this sheet and give it to you mother. Tell her we having a meeting this weekend."

I read the sheet in the elevator. It seemed that Regent Park was going to be demolished and its residents placed elsewhere. All of a sudden, I felt real happy. Maybe me and my father would move to a place similar to that described by Sporty, and there we would start over and get to know each other as father and son. He might even resume his inventions. And perhaps years later a passerby would glance at our house and say, "That is where Sam and his father used to live. Father was an inventor and the son was a college student."

When I got into our apartment, my father was not there. I switched on the television. A woman with big juicy breasts was talking about the healing power of special cubes and pyramids. She seemed too pretty for this nonsense but just before I changed channels, I wondered whether the troll-lady mumbo jumbo in our apartment was connected with this Regent Park eviction business. I checked the forms on the set and went to the kitchen. Two minutes later, I returned to look at the forms once more. I felt suddenly that I should not be eating Kraft Dinner that night, maybe something that fancy Canadians ate. Steak or salmon fillet. Several times that night I rechecked the admission form just to make sure that I had not imagined my father's signature at the bottom.

Chapter Twelve

CALL OF THE MOUNTAIN

The next day at Union I looked for Sporty to give him my good news but he was nowhere in sight. I wanted to tell him that my form too had led to success and maybe mention that I forgave his scamming because all he desired was a place of his own; I wanted to say that he should add another number to his figure about the universe balancing out itself. For the next two weeks, I searched up and down for him. One evening I spotted a boy crouched over a comic. He had really spiky hair like the Sham-Wow fella on television and the way he was turning the pages carefully made me feel that he was a comic book collector or something. When I sat next to him, he held the book tightly as if I might pull it away. Still I asked him, "Is the comic interesting?"

"It's a graphic novel," he told me stiffly. "Comics are for kids."

"What's the difference?"

"Graphic novels are not."

He wasn't being helpful but I asked him, "Where did you get it?"

"At an antique shop on Queen Street West." He stated the directions quickly as if he hoped I might leave him alone and go there. And that was exactly what I did. It was close to six when I got there and a stocky man who looked as if he might have been drawn by Jack Kirby was straightening some lamps on a table. The back of the store was packed with old furniture—the kind that people in Mayaro would never give away or sell but keep until they fell apart—and there were rusty tools strung on nails on the wall. At one end of the shop were crates stuffed with books and in one of these I found a pile of comics. Most were familiar, old Marvel and Charlton and even a couple *Turok Son of Stone* but there were also thick glossy comics which I guessed were graphic novels. I pulled out a *Rawhide Kid* and began reading.

"The library is at Bloor."

It was the Jack Kirby man. He had a mean swollen forehead that made him look a little dangerous. "How much is this?"

"Two for a dollar."

"So cheap?"

"Okay, one for a dollar?"

I had no intention of buying the comic so I told him, "It's a first edition. Worth at least twenty-five. These old *Tarzan* and *Submariner* are just as expensive."

He began tapping some sort of old compass against his

palm and by the tenth or so tap, he had offered me a job. Seriously. This is how it went.

First, he introduced himself as Billy Bilkim Barbarossa then he asked me, "What is your name, boy?"

Because he looked like a Mexican bandit, I told him, "Roti Ramirez."

He scratched his beard and I saw a big mole peeping out. He noticed my gaze and hurriedly packed down and smoothened over the hair. "I have never heard of such a name."

"I was born in Trinidad," I told him. "The capital is Port of Spain and the main town is San Fernando. I lived close to Rio Claro."

I tried to think of other Spanish names but he cut me off, "I am not interested in all that. What is your education?"

"I just signed up to finish my high school. The course is at the Centennial College campus." I felt important just to be saying this.

"When do you start?"

"In two months. It's a preparatory—"

"Then you work two months here. Only two." He held up two stubby fingers. "I don't want any big-head college boy here. Now, tell me if you know how to sell."

"Comics?"

"Look, you better get out of my store." He pointed to the door. "Is that all that you can see here?" The gesture changed into a wave at the junk lined up against the walls. "You think it's just junk?" I shook my head. "Nearly every item you see here is attached to a story. And not happy stories either. Death. Divorce. Bankruptcy. Sickness." He removed a rusty hatchet from a coat hanger and I backed away a bit. "Betrayal."

"Everyone is walking around with a broken heart," I told him in the saddest voice I could afford.

"And never forget it," he said, as if it was he rather than Canella who had come up with the idea. "Come back tomorrow."

I couldn't believe my luck. It had taken me weeks before I got the job at the gas station but in less than half an hour, I landed work in a store with comic books and mostly useless items. This was so much better than pumping gas in the cold and gazing at impatient drivers as I cleaned their windscreens and asked about oil changes. And best of all, Barbarossa's antique shop didn't look too different from Uncle Boysie's Everything and Anything place. The universe was really balancing itself. However, the next day Barbarossa seemed surprised to see me in his shop and for a minute I thought he was about to ask me to leave. Worse, I tried to recall the name I had given him but came up blank.

"So, Mr. Roti Ramirez, are you ready to sell today?" Without another word, he walked to a back office and I followed him. His legs didn't match his muscular body and because they were so short, he waddled like the Penguin. Maybe he suffered from big stones that we called *godi* in Trinidad. He hefted a portable heater from his chair and sat. "Rule number one is no haggling. Some of these people come here and believe they can get anything for a dime. Rule number two is you must never mention anything about garage sales or the Salvation Army or pawnshops. Tell them that we bought everything at auction sales. Do you know why?"

"Death and divorce."

"Correct. And rule number three"—he peeped through the door and lowered his voice—"is that you must never chat with Che."

I tried to match his whisper, "Che Guevara?"

He rolled his eyes as if the question had been asked too frequently. The act was unseemly in such a brawny man and I tried not to smile. "His real name is Cherry Xalvat and he is a charlatan of the highest order. Avoid him like the plague."

All day I kept an eye out for someone whose name was either Che or Cherry. I imagined a fat-cheek assassin wearing a beret but there were just three customers: an old woman with a blue purse, blue hair and thick blue veins on her neck; a turtleneck-sweater young man who seemed vexed to see me following him; and a tall Creole lady who just gazed around, jangled her bracelets, and said, "Hmm." At the end of the day Barbarossa asked me what I had sold and when I said nothing he clasped his hands and rested them on his belly. It was the gesture of a man about to utter something but he kept silent. After about three minutes, I left and when I glanced through the glass door, I saw him in the same pose.

Each evening he asked the same question and most times my response was the same but soon I was able to tell him that I had sold a vase or a candleholder or some outdated cookbook. In two weeks or so, I was able to distinguish the idlers and browsers from the genuine shoppers who did not walk around the store gazing at everything but hovered around a particular item. Sometimes they got distracted by some other bit of junk but they always returned to their cherished scrap. I learned to give them space rather than frightening or pressuring them with questions. I soon forgot about Che because there were so many interesting customers here. A few resembled the coffee shop old-timers, but there were a couple of women with sort of frozen expressions who looked as if they were searching for something valuable that their grandparents might have sold by mistake, and some pretty girls who came in packs and giggled as they fingered rings and necklaces. Once I heard a group talking about "a skank" who went around "banging" everybody and "getting laid" each Friday as a rule. These were strange words but I guessed what they were talking about and after they had left, I felt that their expressions seemed more harmless than our Mayaro swearword versions. It made the act itself seem innocent and ordinary. Maybe Barbarossa didn't share this view because he came up and said, "No staring at nipples. The strip joint is on Yonge Street." I was still thinking of the girls when a man wearing shorts came in with a crate of books. He explained in a throat-clearing accent that the books had been bought from Belgium and held them up one by one. The language was strange but there were pictures of castles and flowers and cyclists on the covers. The last book was a Smurfs comic. When I told him that no one would want to buy books written in a foreign language he seemed quite upset and I felt sorry he had taken the time to bring all the books here.

Maybe he had cycled too because his legs were quite muscular. He walked out dejectedly, leaving the box behind, and I saw Barbarossa smiling from the back office. A couple days later, a man with a wicked beard, just like Matapal the fisherman from Mayaro, came into the shop. He removed a banjo from its case, stroked the arm, closed his eyes and stamped his foot a couple times. Barbarossa was not so happy that time and he said I must tell these customers that some music shop was three blocks east.

One evening just before closing time I saw a thin oldish man digging into the case filled with old glasses and shades. I went to replace the jewellery in a nearby box that had been messed up by a group of schoolgirls.

"Can you tell me the cost of this?" His voice sounded fluttery as if there was a butterfly exercising in his throat. And when I turned to him I saw that he had hooked up a round glasses over an aviator shades. With his hat tipped to one side, and his perfectly straight goatee, he looked quite mad.

"The glasses is ten dollars and the shades is fifteen. Genuine aviator."

"Oh, I meant these." He removed the glasses and the shades and I saw a small wire rimmed spectacles barely covering his eyes.

"Ten. Just like the other."

"Oh," he said in his fluttery voice and I immediately put him down as interesting but useless. He blew on the spectacles, wiped it with his thumb, peered through in the direction of Barbarossa's office, wiped it some more and gave it to me.

"It's not suitable, in any case. What I really need is a monocle. I have a glass eye."

"It looks real."

"Thank you. I appreciate that. Do you think I might have it for five?"

"Sorry, sir. It's already discounted." Barbarossa had taught me to say this whenever someone wanted to haggle. He had also told me of *sleepers* which were valuable items sold cheaply by people who didn't realize their rareness. At the time, I thought of terrorists, and sentinels awakening from some deep sleep.

The man took out a kerchief and wiped what may have been the glass eye. "My wife also has a glass eye. My son who I have never seen was born with one too." He straightened his hat and walked away in an upright stride for an old man. As soon as he left, Barbarossa came out of his office. "What did he want?"

"A rimless spectacles. He said he had a glass eye. His wife too."

Barbarossa pointed to his crotch. "His wife glass eye is down here. Peeping out like a Cyclops." I was shocked. I had never heard Barbarossa say anything rude before. "Be careful of him. Remember that."

It was only when I was on the subway that it hit me the glass-eye man might be Che. From then I kept a special lookout for him. It was another two weeks before he returned. He picked up a picture frame and when I went over, he told me, "This is an enchanting picture." I gazed at the empty frame and he continued, "There is a time of the day . . . just before sunset, when you can clearly see the residue of the plucked out picture hovering like an indecisive ghost." He held up the frame. "The light must be just right."

I decided to match him. "Every fish scale has a picture."

The frame shook in his hands. "I must remember that. How much?"

"The frame? It's five dollars."

"It's a pity. I have a picture of my wife the exact size. Would you accept three?"

I was tempted but remembered all of Barbarossa's warnings. "It's genuine mahogany."

He replaced the frame, straightened it and walked away slowly. Immediately Barbarossa came out of his office. "What did he want?"

"The frame for a picture of his wife."

"Why doesn't he hang the picture there?" He pointed to his crotch.

"Was that Mr. Cherry Xalvat?" For the first time I realized the name sounded like a planet from some other dimension.

"No, it's Don Cherry." There are some people for whom sarcasm can't work. It makes them sound just mean. My father was one. Barbarossa was another. Nevertheless, Barbarossa's reluctance to talk of Che made me more curious of this strange man. He came every week, usually on a Thursday and though he never bought anything, he mentioned his wife every time. The horn would remind her of the one she had as a girl that made her voice sound like "freshly squeezed pomegranate juice" and the bell resembled the funnel with which "she summoned the llamas from the mountains."

I stopped reporting these conversations to Barbarossa because I knew where he would point. So I didn't tell him that Che began mentioning some mountain quite regularly or when he told me, "The mountain is calling me, boy."

One Thursday I asked him, "So why don't you return then?"

"But would it still be there?"

"It's hard for a mountain to disappear."

"That's remarkably optimistic." He replaced the brass bird. "I may have believed that once."

When he left I wondered at the relationship with Che and my boss. Why did Barbarossa hate or distrust him so much? Were they long-lost brothers taking different paths like in my mother's Bollywood movies, or did Che steal away Barbarossa's wife? During each of his visit, I tried to pry out some information while he was haggling over some item for his wife but he now seemed more interested in his mountain. I tried to fit him as a jazz man who had to run away after the flood in New Orleans but his fingers seemed too stiff to play a guitar. I also dismissed the thought he might be a retired hitman or a fired lawyer. Besides, he came from some mountain place.

When I was seven or eight, I had gone with my mother and Uncle Boysie to the Port of Spain wharf. My father was somehow connected with that trip because I recall on the way back my uncle talking about how he had "expected exactly that." Maybe my father was supposed to send down some stuff, or come himself on one of the big boats butting the jetty; and when my mother got silent, I wondered whether she, too, was staring at the mountains that seemed so far and near at the same time. There were fluffy baskets of clouds over the highest parts and ravines so steep they seemed to be hacked with a *luchette.* Mr. Chotolal my history teacher had told us that the British people built tunnels there to surprise the French and Spanish ships coming from the other side of the mountain. After one of the classes, Pantamoolie whispered that these tunnels were clogged up with treasure hidden by Bluebeard.

Maybe Che's mountain was frosty like Dr. Bat's, with snow kangaroos and ice catfishes. I was thinking of this when one of Barbarossa's few preferred customers walked out of the office. He was talking to my boss in maybe a French accent about his favourite topic: how Toronto was losing its soul and getting uglier by the day. Usually both of them stood to gaze at one of the paintings of old cottages or lonely lighthouses cramped in a corner. That day after the usual Toronto talk the French fella bit into a nectarine, sniffed a little, wiped his nose with his coat sleeve and said, "Boring place." He said something about jazz festivals in Montreal before he caught me listening. "Where are you from, boy?" he asked.

I didn't like his tone and in any case, I couldn't remember the name of the town I had given Barbarossa so I said, "Regent Park."

"Isn't this city a wearisome place, boy?"

"I met a chimera in the library." I could have mentioned the molemen and Sporty and Mothski and even
Barbarossa himself but my boss began to laugh. It was not a
jolly laughter but the kind people use to cover up some mistake. Like a musical cough. The French fella joined in too
and he pushed down his glasses and wiped his eyes. Soon
after the other fella had left Barbarossa's amusement disappeared and he asked me, "Where do you get foolish ideas
from?" Maybe from my comics, I thought, or growing up in
Mayaro with people talking all the time about *souyoucants*
and *lagahoos*. "This is an antique shop, not comedy club. Yuk
Yuks is down the street."

That night when I returned to our apartment, I heard my
father grumbling, "This place sucking me out." It was the first
time he had spoken to me since I told him I had signed up for
the preparatory course at the Centennial campus in Progress.
All he had said then was "Very nice," and I couldn't figure if it
was a sign of approval or his usual mockery.

I noticed his toes twitching which meant he was thinking. A few minutes later, he asked once more if Uncle Boysie
had written to me about the house in Mayaro. When I said no
he got his cigarettes and walked slowly to the balcony. I don't
know why I felt sorry for him at that point—maybe it was
because he didn't criticize me as usual but just stared at the
mostly blank screen during his smoking intervals. Something
was eating him up and I wished I knew what it was. Maybe he
had looked at all the *Mythbusters* and *MacGyver* reruns and now
had nothing to occupy or distract him.

The next day at work a little lady with an up and down accent told me, "Sometimes these keepsakes we carry around become heavier with each passing day. If we are not careful, we can grow stooped from their weight. We need to unload them." She said it with a smile and as she had a stoop herself I watched carefully when she was leaving but her back did not magically get straighter. There were many people like her who needed a few minutes to talk of their old countries before they parted with their junk.

I wondered if my father had some keepsake that was dragging him down. The following morning as I was leaving for work I asked him, "You have any junk you would like to get rid of?"

He watched me for a good minute, the loose skin beneath his eyes tightening until his features settled into the grim Lee Van Cleef look. I felt he was assessing me while thinking of what to say. "What you talking about?"

"I working in a junk shop. Just temporary."

"See if you could find a clock."

For some reason that put me in a good mood. Apart from the forty dollars on my first week in his apartment, this was the first item he had asked me for. Maybe it would even remind him of the Timex watch he had sent down for me so many years ago. Over the next few days, I rummaged through the new items but there were no clocks. Could be people just threw them away. On Thursday, Che told me, "In every antique shop there is a little secret wrapped into a bigger one. My wife would love this Russian doll."

I had recently suspected that Che was pulling my leg, nevertheless I told him, "I am searching for an old clock."

"Remarkable."

I waited for him to mention something of his wife or his mountain but when he remained quiet, I added, "For my father."

"As I expected. Would you be interested in an exchange?"

It was a good thing that I changed my mind and said to bring whatever he had, because the following Thursday I got my clock and finally found out about Che's mountain. Actually, it was a big pocket watch with the face mounted on two brass dolphins. The chain was so rusty that I was surprised to see the second hand actually moving. When I tried to take it from him he loosened his grasp from the chain one clasp at a time as if we were about to play tug of war. I made a sudden pull and I heard a *rackling* sound like a loose spring. "How much do you want for it?" He gazed around the shop taking his time. I tried to hurry him before Barbarossa emerged from his office. "A glasses or a picture frame?"

"Have you ever wondered why a clock can only go forward and backward? Never sideways."

"If it did then time will stand still."

"Brilliant."

I didn't tell him that any comic reader could figure this out, as he seemed so impressed. "Or maybe we might move in another dimension."

Perhaps I had gone too far because he now seemed bothered. Eventually he told me, "I feel I have been there once."

He grasped the handle of a dagger which was sheathed in a leather sack. "I will take this." He tried to fit the sack behind his belt, gave up and thrust it into his pocket. "Yes, yes. I have been there."

"The mountain is the other dimension?" I pushed the pocket watch into my pocket and took out five dollars.

"Brilliant," he said again and I felt he was just *mamaguying* me because he got a good deal. "It is impossible to properly describe the ridges and breaks and gullies in the mountain, my boy. It was so quiet that sometimes I could hear the clouds moving. Brushing the peaks. Sometimes in the night, I would hear the chatter of tiny animals engaged in a suicide pact." He took a deep breath and I wondered whether he was imitating some habit of his time there. "I cannot adequately describe the people I grew to know so well. I used to pretend they were cloud people but as I became more familiar with them, I discovered a sad truth. A sad truth." I saw him glancing over my shoulder and when I turned, I saw Barbarossa glaring at us. For a minute or so both men appeared like two old boxers sizing up each other, then Che left. Immediately Barbarossa came over.

"What did he want?"

I saw his fingers dangling over his crotch ready to point so I kept quiet about the clock exchange. I told him, "He bought a dagger." I held out the five-dollar bill and Barbarossa hesitated before he took it. There was a strange expression on his face, shock mixed with suspicion. I wondered if he had seen the transaction. For the remainder of that day he was in a bad mood, walking around the shop and peeping outside.

That night I waited impatiently by the kitchen table for my father's arrival. I gazed at the pocket watch before me; the dolphins seeming to be stranded in the tablecloth's wavy brown patterns. My father got home a little after eight-thirty and seemed surprised to see me in the kitchen this early. I had rushed home, bypassing Union. "I got something for you."

"A letter?" He spoke quickly.

"No. A pocket watch."

"Oh." He followed my gaze and scooped up the watch. I saw him looking at the dolphins. He placed the watch against his ear and walked to the television. I wished he might have told me that it was a strange watch or it was exactly what he wanted; nevertheless, every now and again, he shook the watch as if testing. During an advertisement he cleared his throat as if he was about to say something and I felt a bit embarrassed for no reason. Finally, he went into his bedroom. That entire week I pretended that each night he was examining the watch and coming up with ways to improve its design. When next Che came into the shop, he immediately asked about the watch and I put my finger against my lip for I didn't want Barbarossa to know of the transaction. I tried to change the topic. "What sad truth?" He seemed confused. "That you discovered in the mountain. And the cloud people."

I wanted him to reveal they were a secret tribe hidden away like Black Bolt's Inhumans but he said, "Ah yes. It was in Chile." He drew his coat around him as if it was suddenly cold. "They had been chased away from their land by my family who were ranchers." He paused a bit before he launched into the most amazing story. There in the mountain, he fell in love with one of these displaced women and soon he joined a ragtag group of guerrillas fighting against the rich ranchers, his family included. One night a daring plan was hatched: a selected group would journey to the capital, mix with the crowd and kill the president during one of his "bogus lectures delivered from the palace's balcony." According to Che, the assassination failed because the police had been tipped off, and only two of the group escaped. Deep in the jungle there was a showdown between the two survivors. "It slowly dawned on me that the man next to me, a brute of a peasant, coarse in every possible way, was actually an informant who had sold us out. Each night I slept with a dagger next to me. One morning it was gone and so was the traitor."

"What happened then?" I asked impatiently as he seemed lost in his thoughts.

He bowed like an actor in one of those carriage-and-sword movies. "Here I am before you."

"And the woman?"

"I never saw her again."

"Is that who you wanted the Russian doll for?"

"You might say that, yes. You might say that." Again, he sounded like an old-time actor.

"And the traitor?"

He took a deep breath. "It's of no consequence. We must forget the old battles. If we don't then we—"

"Grow stooped from their weight?"

"Remarkable. Remarkable." And with that, he left. This was a long conversation and during the day, I noticed Barbarossa watching me, his tiny eyes dull beneath his swollen forehead.

During the following weeks, it seemed that Che's relating his story had somehow cleared his mind and put him in a good mood, for now instead of constantly talking of his wife he frequently hummed a Spanish song, "*Guantanamera guajira Guantanamera.*" His fluttery voice made the song seem sadder than the versions I had heard often on the Trinidad radio stations. Once while Barbarossa was staring out suspiciously from his office Che closed his eyes and sang, louder than ever: *Yo soy un hombre sincere/De donde crece la palma/ Y antes de morirme quiero/Echar mis versos del alma.* I asked him its meaning and he told me, "I am an honest man/From where the palm tree grows/And before dying I want/To share the verses of my soul."

He had a good singing voice and I couldn't understand why Barbarossa was so annoyed afterwards. "This is not Massey Hall. Please explain that to—"

"Che?"

He walked away, grumbling.

I couldn't picture palm trees growing on a mountain but I felt it was a beautiful song with a catchy rhythm. Sometimes I found myself humming a line at work and Barbarossa would come up to me immediately as if he had super-hearing.

During my last week at the shop, I asked Che if he was going to return to his mountain any time. I told him that I too was leaving this place soon. He shook my hand and bowed like these Mexican actors on television. Then in the same dramatic way, he pointed to his chest and said, "My mountain, it is here. In the morning, I smell the grassdews and in the night, I hear the clouds brushing the trees. But when I die my body must be carried to the highest peak to be laid next to my wife's grave." He said something in Spanish and when I asked its meaning he said, "My grave must be caressed by the purest fog. No snow shall fall on its dirt."

"How will your body get there? So high up?"

"By mule." He pointed to Barbarossa's office.

Chapter Thirteen

VAMPIRES IN THE MIST

The night after my first class at the Centennial campus, I really missed my mother. My father, caught up in whatever was worrying him, didn't seem too interested that the programme would fast track me to a high school diploma. (Though I shouldn't complain, as his silence was a real improvement from his mockery.) My mother, though, would have been even prouder than the few times I surprised her with a high grade at Mayaro Composite. The preparatory course was mostly boring, as it repeated a lot of my subjects from Mayaro Composite and I couldn't wait to be a bona fide college boy. There were a few oldish people in the class, which was surprising, and sometimes when our English and history teacher—a chubby, smiling lady who wrote "Mrs. Dragan" on the board but told us to call her Jolie—was mentioning some Canadian history fact, I would see these old people listening real attentively. Me, I sometimes pictured

Mrs. Dragan trying her best to keep her flames in check and when she smoothened her dress to sit I pretended she was fluffing down the scales on her bottom. The boys who were my age seemed quite bored of her lectures but the older students, many with foreign accents, were always jotting down notes and asking questions. In Trinidad, everyone would say that they were slackers or were in the class to avoid housework or something.

At the end of my first week, I wished even more that my mother was alive and here in Canada, so I could return to her in a tidy apartment and say, "Remember when you used to say that I was wasting my time with these stupid made-up books?" Maybe she would bend her head a little to the side and say in a tired voice that could signal either resignation or approval, I could never tell, "Yes, son. I couldn't see that." And I would explain that, although the pay was no better than any of the others, my most interesting job ever was at the Queen Bee movie shop, which rented only these old B movies with pirates and cowboys and monsters posing and crouching against dusty sepia backgrounds. I would tell her, "See, I got this job because of my knowledge of comic books. And it's perfect too because I just work on Wednesdays and weekends."

Two years before I came to Canada, before I even knew she was ill or would soon die, she gathered all my old comics, *Green Lantern* and *The Legion of Super-Heroes* and *The Inhumans* and *X-Men*—all the comics I liked, illustrated by Mike Mignola and Gene Colan and Klaus Janson—and burnt them right outside the back step. I was so mad that I told her that I was leaving, never to return. I rushed out from the house to the beach, still in my school uniform. I would have been fourteen, and looking back at it now, I can't believe I was so childish, and that my mother always fell so easily into this game of me running away. Did she not expect that I would return home once I got bored from walking along the beach and throwing seaballs into the water?

I never understood why she hated my comics so much, or my monthly trips to Liberty cinema in Rio Claro to look at these old pirate and gladiator movies, because she herself would often have a Bollywood movie in the VCR while she was sewing by the living room window. Her only explanation was that this make-believe world I was falling into spelled real trouble. A dreamland, she said. As if her Bollywood dramas were any better.

Queen Bee video store never stocked Indian movies, although I don't think anyone would have noticed them in between the old *Yang Yu* karate films and the Hammer vampire movies and the cheesy space flicks with their bathtub rockets and dustbin robots. The owner of the store, Mr. Konrad Schmidlap, was one of the stillest persons I had ever seen. His severe lips and nose looked as if they had been soldered to his bony face, and he moved like a gloomy pigeon whenever he was inspecting the shelves. I felt that his knees were trembling with each step, though I would never tell him that because he seemed hard of hearing. He reminded me a little of Peter Cushing from these old vampire movies.

When I had inquired about a job in his place, he seemed so blank that I immediately regretted entering his store. It was a good thing I remained though because during his interview, he asked just three questions. The first two, about my previous experience and my age, were easy enough, but his last question was completely unexpected. He asked me why aliens always travelled about in pods. Although his voice was stony, I felt this was some sort of joke, so just as seriously I told him that aliens used mother-ships or saucers to travel from planet to planet. They used the pods to hibernate inside until they were ready to harvest. I wanted to laugh at what I had said but Mr. Schmidlap crooked a finger and I followed him to his little corner desk.

"Do you think you can harvest these?" he asked, pointing to a stack of old videos in boxes. Later, I debated whether he had made a joke, because while I was arranging the videos on the shelves he shot out a quick, grating sound, which sounded like a stubborn gear grinding. After my first week, he showed me how to file the movies in index cards, and set me behind the counter. To tell the truth, that made me feel important and a couple times, when the shop was nearly empty, I quietly practised a few expressions in Barbarossa's fussy manner for the customers who had returned their movies late or who were lingering to view the posters. "You think this is a place for viewing pictures? The art gallery is in Front Street. Next!"

Many of the people who strayed into the shop were young men with thoughtful sleepy eyes and little beards and canvas knapsacks. They usually asked for movies by Bunuel and Cassavetes and Polanski—which we never stocked—before they moved to the horror section. They may have been college students and sometimes I felt like mentioning in an offhand manner that in a single term I would be taking their courses. By the end of my second weekend, I was able to recognize the regular customers. There was a middle-aged man with a small chin squashed against his neck who liked these old movies that all began with "Carry On" and even older cartoons. He talked about Woody Woodpecker and Tweety Bird as if they were real and were his longtime friends. He was always complaining about a nasty girl and at first I felt it might be a co-worker or something, but I later realized it was the little girl who was always pulling away the football from Charlie Brown. "Such a little bitch. I believe she grew up to become a prime minister." He had a low-pitched British accent and I wished he would say through his nose something like "Pip, pip, old chap. Tally ho." Another customer, who was ancient enough to have *limed* with Roy and Norbert at the coffee shop on Parliament Street, only borrowed these seventies blue movies, which Mr. Schmidlap kept in a special drawer below the counter. He described some of these movies but used words like mons veneris and pudenda that somehow made them seem less porny. One of his favourite was *The Devil in Miss Jones.*

One evening as I was about to close up, Dr. Bat walked in. At first I couldn't recognize him as he was wearing an oversized hat that covered half his face. I was about to call out to him when a woman in a sari escorting two boys said something to him in Hindi. He spotted me then and seemed a bit embarrassed I had seen him with Madam Bat and the Baby Bats. He hung back when Madam Bat asked if there were Bollywood movies here. When I said there weren't any, she asked, waggling her head, why the shop's name was Queen Bee. I said the B stood a kind of old-fashioned movie, not for Bollywood. She didn't seem to believe me so she walked down the middle aisle with her Baby Bats.

"How is Paul?" I asked Dr. Bat.

"He returned to birthplace for pedigree property redresses."

"Newfoundland?"

"Alberta. Chinooks and such." Just then Madam Bat returned and Dr. Bat walked away hurriedly.

I guessed Dr. Bat was talking about some property Paul had returned to claim; and in the night when my father asked me once more about any letter from Uncle Boysie, I wondered if he had his eyes on the house in Mayaro. But why would he, since he was living in Canada? Two days later during Mrs. Dragan's description of the "two Canadian solitudes" (which was very boring in spite of its nice title) I noticed the boy in the seat before me drawing in his copybook instead of taking notes. I had seen him before, always sitting by himself. He had droopy eyes, his hair was cut into uneven tufts, and one nostril was flatter than the other. After the class, I asked him if he was drawing a comic book. He seemed startled I had discovered him and I remembered my own irritation at the chimera peering at my letter. I decided to leave him alone but as I was stuffing my books into my bag he said it was a picture of their old house in Cuba. As he didn't have an accent I asked him if he was from there and he said he arrived in Canada, with his grandmother and two sisters, when he was four.

"What about your parents?" I asked. He opened his book to his drawing and I noticed two stick people staring out from separate windows. I guessed his parents were still in Cuba. "What's that in the yard?"

"Goats," he said as if it should be obvious the squares with tails and boxy heads were animals. "And that is a turkey." He pointed to a fan.

Maybe the Cuban boy's drawing was still in my mind during the weekend because the minute this old Filipino fella with raisin bumps all over his face came into the video shop, I had this idea that he said little prayers while he was cutting off the necks of turkeys. To bless their souls or something. He had a very flat face as if he used to regularly roll off the bed to fall on his face when he was a baby. He returned on Wednesday and on the following weekend and I soon began to think of him as Mr. Real because he used this phrase so often. The name on his card was Toktok Magboo and it was easy to guess his taste in movies from his clothes as he was always dressed in a long grey overcoat and a felt hat, and even in the late evenings he wore a tinted horn-rimmed glasses. His thick eyebrows seemed like grey mushrooms sprouting from behind his glasses. But for his dark brown colour and his accent, he could easily have sprung from one of the B movies he always requested every Tuesday and Friday.

He returned his movies promptly although there was really no need to because nobody else wanted films like *Plan B from Outer Space* and *Broccoli Banzai* and *Nazi Ballerinas* and *Vampires in the Mist.* Besides, they were all videos. Once he was standing behind a girl who was returning *Electra,* with his copy of *The Japanese Pit.* After the girl had left, he said, "These special eppects is too much nonsense. Who will believe such a thing?" He raised both hands above his head like a comic book superhero preparing to fly off. "Good twattle." He sounded a bit like the old porn movie man. I glanced at his video case. A woman was running away from a group of Japanese armed with enormous swords but right toward a pond crowded with skeletons. Up in the completely red sky was a low flying airplane with a rope dangling from somewhere behind a propeller. When he noticed my gaze, he had said, "Pom this I get all my inspiration." I did not understand what he meant but from then on, I began to stare at his brand of movies on the shelves. Occasionally, when Mr. Schmidlap was not there, I would pop one into the VCR.

They were the stupidest films I had ever seen. Nearly all had women with big overflowing breasts and curly red hair and wide-open eyes. These women were forever getting in trouble with monsters that crept out from ponds and stalked out from tombs and dropped from spaceships. Thankfully, they were saved in the nick of time by men who didn't talk much but mostly chewed at their cigarettes. I just couldn't understand the hold of these plastic monsters and toy submarines and dirty unshaved men on Mr. Magboo but during each of his visit, just to make conversation, I mentioned some stupid piece of a movie.

He liked that. He revealed to me his favourite actors and their special lines that he repeated in his singsong voice. It was a bit difficult to follow him as he changed the letters f and v into p and b but I gathered that he liked the English Hammer movies with Peter Cushing who always looked half-dead telling Vincent Price "Begone, spawn of Satan or face my wrath." I think Vincent Price was his favourite actor, although he also liked Christopher Lee and Boris Karloff. Even though I didn't really enjoy Mr. Magboo's movies, at least I was able to fulfil my side of the conversation whenever he mentioned some scene or memorable line like, "Sorry, Nancy, I'm a loner. That's the way it gotta be. Parewell." Some of the movie phrases, similar to comic book dialogue, stuck in my head and I wished I had some friend to practise them on. *Quick! To the air chamber. God help us all if this doesn't work. Resistance is futile. You will be assimilated.*

I used a couple of them in an essay where we had to describe a memorable event. Mrs. Dragan was not impressed and she asked how long ago I had learned English. I said that it was all we spoke in Trinidad and she stared at me as if I was lying. She liked the Cuban boy's essay and when she returned it, he was beaming. After the class, I asked what he had written and he talked about his family's early days in Canada when his grandmother would take the whole bunch of them for rides on the subway train. "She didn't have much money so we rode the trains for hours on end. To me it was an excursion."

His name was Javier and as we walked to the Centennial College Loop, I noticed he had a limp. When we got there, a couple girls were waiting for their bus. One was tall and real pretty. Her bottom crack and the tattoo above it was showing and when I mentioned this to Javier, he stared at the ground as if he was embarrassed. I believed he did not have many friends. Still, he got an A in his essay and I felt his grandmother would be pleased.

I don't think Mr. Magboo too had many friends because he began staying longer during each visit to the video store. I soon grew used to his long overcoat and his accent and the little discussion of the movies we had seen. I didn't say much during these conversations but as I grew more familiar with his movies, I felt that we were seeing them in different ways. After he had left, while I was rewinding his videos I would pause the film every now and again, searching for the magical pets or the hidden codes or the mysterious dark-skinned woman Mr. Magboo had mentioned but I could spot none of them. I wondered whether these movies were stranger than they seemed, especially since Mr. Magboo's additions seemed reasonable and even a bit interesting. Also, whenever I asked him about these hidden scenes, he never hesitated in describing their connection with the plot. He finished off his explanations with the usual, "It's real, buddy," as if that would convince me.

All of this was very puzzling. It was like searching for a stranger in a crowd, or maybe looking for the Waldo man on a crowded beach. After work, I would frequently puzzle over Mr. Magboo's extra scenes. Stupid thoughts came into my head, like perhaps he had some special video player that could pick up all the deleted scenes. I even asked him if he had seen earlier copies of these films but he shook his head and said that life was too short and there were too many good movies.

One evening on my way to class, I dozed off in the train and dreamed I saw Mr. Magboo running away from a sabre-toothed tiger. By the time I got off at the Warden subway station and took the 102A bus, a *grop* of screaming red-hair ladies were running alongside Mr. Magboo. Throughout the entire class I pictured them being chased all over the place by giant spiders and space blobs, and when Mrs. Dragan asked a question about a big-pappy name Diefenbaker I could not answer. It was Javier instead who provided the correct response. I was a little embarrassed so on our way to the bus terminal I mentioned the distractions of Mr. Magboo's movies. Javier acted as if all of this was quite normal and he mentioned some Spanish writer fella who described goats chatting with their owners and the ghosts of husbands lying in bed with their former wives. It sounded just like my *Crypt* comics but I did not bring this up.

That weekend I waited impatiently for Mr. Magboo. When he got there, I told him I had seen a randy ghost in one of his movies. There was a goat too and while he gazed at me in puzzle, I threw in a couple other animals. It's payback time, buddy, I thought. See if you can match this. *Bictory!*

He then described the baby Cyclops and the flame-spitting bunny monster and the giant bat with a winch instead of a tail. I accepted defeat. Finally, he asked about a movie he had previously requested. "Find please *Bampires in the Mist.*" He pushed up his lips as if they were fangs there.

After he left I mentioned this movie to Mr. Schmidlap. He went through his index cards, slowly, one at a time, and after ten minutes or so I regretted asking him anything. The next day I decided to take a trip to the Pacific Mall in Markham, where Mr. Schmidlap bought many of his movies. On the Steeles bus I wondered if I was going out of my way to get a stupid film for a crazy old Filipino because he reminded me of these old Mayaro fishermen like Matapal, who were forever making up stories of necklaces found inside fishes, or simply to get to the bottom of these missing-scene mystery.

The mall was more crowded than any I had seen before and there were Chinese people walking all over the place. All the stores had Chinese signs and I wondered what kinds of secret potions and magic herbs were hidden in boxes inside these places but as I got closer, I saw cellphones, cameras and gadgets with red blinking lights. The mall with its boxy shops was different from those elsewhere in the city and I lost my way a few times but the other customers, speaking in their high-pitched, scraping voices, moved skilfully from store to store. They all looked very rich, I don't know why. Finally, I found the video store at the end of the mall. I asked the worker there, a short man with his hair plastered over his bald patch, for *Vampires in the Mist.*

"Eh? Damn Piss?" It took a while before I realized he was joking because his old-baby face remained serious. When I repeated the name of the movie slowly, I knew he was going to continue his horrible joke as he dipped into a huge box and flipped through stacks of movie cases. "Aha," he said with his head still in the box. "Umpire Want Kiss." He laughed with small nibbling sounds the way a small animal might but I was more interested in the DVD case in his hand. "Five dollars. Just for you."

"Only five dollars?"

"Okay. Ten then. Brand new. Direct import." I gave him five dollars. As I was leaving, he shouted, "We got this kind of movie too." He placed his hands behind his head and pushed his waist backward and forward. It was funny because he still had the serious look on his old-baby face.

I could barely wait for Mr. Magboo's next visit, and the minute I spotted him shuffling through the door I held up the DVD case. He took it, gazed at the cheaply photocopied jacket, opened the case and gave it back. "Not work on home telebision, buddy."

He looked deeply disappointed. "Why?" I asked him.

"Bideo, bideo only."

"You don't have a DVD player?"

"Upstairs only. Not my concern."

"Don't you want it then?" He shook his head and I felt I had wasted my time going to Pacific Mall. During his Wednesday visit, I didn't bother to chat too much and after he left I felt I should have explained that it was not because of the DVD business but only my preoccupation with a recent essay that would count for 25 percent of my final mark. The class had to write a three-page paper with the title, "The person who most influenced my life"; and during the entire week, I had been stuck. I thought first of all about my mother but I felt embarrassed to reveal how she was afraid I would run away like my father, how she burned my comics, and all the parables she threw my way. I thought next of Uncle Boysie but felt the teacher would laugh at his crude Mayaro suppositions. Finally, my mind turned to my father.

In Mayaro, I sometimes pretended that his absence was no big thing, and that it gave me more freedom to *lime* and knockabout with no drunken quarrelsome father hindering my every move, but now, thinking of the essay, I realized that every significant event of my life had been marked by his absence: passing my common entrance and listening to the other successful boys boast of the presents given to them by their parents; my first day at Mayaro Composite, walking by myself and gazing at the other students dropped off from their fathers' cars; discovering my friend Loykie, the Amazing Absorbing Boy, living deep in the swamp and trying to make sense of his disease all by myself; receiving birthday presents my mother pretended had been sent by my father (even though I had previously seen these same items in Uncle Boysie's shop); moving to my uncle's house after my mother died and depending on him to straighten my life. It seemed that my father had influenced me more by his absence than if I had seen his face every day of my life.

In the end, I wrote of my mother.

As I expected Javier got the highest mark and he was asked to read his essay aloud. He had written of his grandmother who took care of him and his sisters ever since they came to Canada. She used to work all over the place but when she returned tired in the evenings she always put on a happy face for all of them. Sometimes she told them stories from Cuba, one of a creature called a "Curupira" that protected the forests. According to Javier's essay, his grandmother was uneducated and could barely speak English even though she had lived in Canada for fourteen years. She had a laugh like "coins tinkling on the floor."

When he was finished, everybody clapped, the teacher the loudest. After class, I said that his grandmother seemed an interesting person and he asked if I wanted to meet her. I didn't know what to say; no one had invited me to their house before. We walked quietly for a while and I told him that his Curupira creature was similar to the Trinidadian *Douennes*. He asked about my grade and I said I had passed though I did not mention the teacher's comment about "not focusing enough on positive details." Maybe she just wanted happy stories.

I reread the essay at home and I saw that the teacher was right: it seemed as if I had concentrated too much on my father's disappearance and on my mother's sickness. When my father came home, he asked immediately, "That is a letter?"

"Is an essay from class."

"So is not a letter from Boysie?" He looked at me suspiciously.

I don't know what came over me but I said, "Read it for yourself."

He glanced at the title and the grade, seemed about to return it but instead walked to the balcony with the essay. After five minutes or so, I wondered what section he was now reading. Was it the paragraph where I mentioned that most of the Mayaro people felt my mother was real pretty? Where I described her glancing out of the front window while viewing her Bollywood movies? How I missed not having a father around whenever the other boys boasted about their hunting and fishing trips? The five minutes stretched into ten and when he returned, the essay was neatly folded. He placed it on the table before me, carefully set a cup above it—as if a sudden gust might ruffle the pages—and without a single word walked out of the apartment.

That night was one of my loneliest in Canada. I couldn't understand this, as I had been alone in the apartment so many times previously. I had a job, a friend, and would soon be in regular college. Then it hit me: Javier's description of his grandmother and his sisters and all the stories running through their house made this apartment seem dry and bare by comparison. Later, on the foam, I felt that people might be happier if they had nothing to compare to their own situations.

The mood followed me the next day in Queen Bee. I stared at the old movies and remembered Mr. Magboo saying that "upstairs was none of his business." I fished out his index card and wrote down his address: 4 Chartland Boulevard. That night I left with his address in my pocket and an old DVD player Mr. Schmidlap rented for fifteen dollars a week. As an employee, I got it for three weeks. The next morning I set off for Chartland Boulevard, but by the time I got to the Scarborough Town Centre I wondered if Mr. Magboo might be mad at my appearance with no invitation at his apartment. An hour later, when I got off the Brimley bus, I began to hope he was out, maybe taking a stroll or in the pharmacy or some other old people place. Chartland Boulevard was lined on both sides with big, grey houses. Maybe I had the wrong address, I thought hopefully. Perhaps the bus driver had stopped miles away because of my constant reminders to him about the address. I always imagined Mr. Magboo as living in an old dingy high-rise or some retirement home where he looked at his movies alone in a little room. His house was at the end of the crescent. There were fruit trees at the sides and a Lexus parked on the long driveway. I was sure I had made a mistake but when I rang the doorbell, the woman who came out looked a lot like Mr. Magboo, even with her fancy jacket and mauve hair. "Yes?" She had a polite voice but her eyes looked over me quickly and I felt she was already thinking of some excuse.

"I am looking for Mr. Magboo," I told her quickly.

"He's out at work." She stepped away from the door.

"He works?"

I thought she was going to shut the door but instead she said, "Yes, I am about to join him. I am already late." She had none of Mr. Magboo's accent.

"Could you give this to him then?" I held out the DVD player.

"Oh, Dad. Did he rent this?"

"It's a loan from the shop. He is a regular customer."

"Wait here." She shut the door. I felt foolish. Maybe she was calling the police. I almost walked away but when she opened the door, I saw Mr. Magboo with her. He was in pyjamas and seemed confused by my presence. He glanced from me to the woman who told him, "I am going to the office. If Mike calls tell him I will be home at five." Then she got in the car and drove off.

"I brought this for you." Mr. Magboo still seemed confused so I added, "It's a DVD player for *Vampires in the Mist.*"

"For me?"

"A temporary gift."

He shuffled into the house and because the door was left open, I followed him down to the basement apartment. He walked slowly, holding the railing and breathing through his mouth, as if he was tired. I wondered why I had never noticed any of this at the video store. Because of this new mood of his, I didn't know if he was simply going down for his afternoon nap and would be surprised that I was following him. He opened the door to the apartment and eased himself into a couch. The place had an odd smell, like mouldy socks and nasty old-people bottoms. "The light switch is by the wall," he said. I wanted to leave.

I switched on the light and all at once the place looked exactly as I might have imagined. Seated next to Mr. Magboo on the old plaid couch was an enormous orange cat that looked as if it could materialize here and there like Nightcrawler from *The X-Men.* The coffee table was really an old chest and on its top was an assortment of metallic action figures I had never seen before. The rest of the furniture, the rocking chair and the black table and the four-poster bed stuck in the corner, was out-of-date and dusty looking. But most interesting of all, were the pictures stuck on the wall. There were sea monsters and slit-eyed aliens and huge bats and all the usual red-hair women with their mouths wide open. I removed my hand from my nose and told Mr. Magboo, "You have even more posters than our video store." He stroked the cat but didn't reply and once more I felt he was not happy with this uninvited visit. "Well, I have to go now. Enjoy the movie."

"Wait. You hook it up."

While I was attaching the cables, he stroked his orange cat and said softly, "Aah, Igor. Today you get a special gift." He seemed especially happy when the movie appeared on the screen and he sat forward on the couch saying to Igor, "It's real, buddy. It's real." The only time he slumped back was when he heard the upstairs door closing and footsteps creaking on the floor. He glanced at his cat and said something in Filipino to the animal. After ten minutes or so, he told me, "They don't hear me any more."

"Who?"

"Entire pamily. But mostly grandson."

"Because you are busy with your interesting movies?"

He didn't like this light remark one bit. He got up from the couch and walked over to the table and fiddled with an old lamp that flickered before it settled into a buzzing half-glow. "For fifty-six years I live happy in Manila. One by one, all my children disappear to Canada and Australia and Singapore.

Years pass. Wipe die. Then I get a letter from Angela, my daughter here. Come up, she say. This place is design for retire people. Lakes and parks and libraries and no mugging. So I come." He pulled a chair and sat next to me. The dim light traced and deepened his wrinkles. He was squinting as if the lamp was bothering his eyes. "Pipteen years ago. Pipteen."

"It don't sound so bad."

He tapped the base of the lamp to hush its buzzing. "Angela and husband Mario were busy all the time but I had two grandson to care. I take them to school and in evenings, we play games and listen to songs and laugh-laugh until parents came in nights. I say to myself, 'Toktok, in truth the letters don't lie.'" As he spoke, I noticed Mr. Magboo's accent was becoming stronger and stronger. He got up.

"What happened?"

"They grow up, buddy." He raised his hand from his waist to his shoulder then above his head. "No use for this old man again. Nobody want to call me by my Toktok nickname again. They even give me new Canadian name por when I pick up children from school. Costco."

I was disappointed. "Toktok is not your real name?"

"In Manila ebbybody have nickname. I don't lie. It's real." He laughed, which was the saddest thing about the conversation. "Now I become a low-rate creepy-crawly swampy monster."

When I left Mr. Magboo I worried I had awakened his deep resentment about his family. He had been happy just viewing his movies. The film we had viewed had a scene of a mummy strangling an entire family and I had this horrible image of Mr. Magboo climbing up the stairs with his bandages trailing, and strangling his family who had ignored him once his usefulness was over. In most of the B movies it was often an innocent act that led to the awakening of the creature.

After the next class at Centennial, I mentioned this fear to Javier and he just laughed. He told me old people played with a different set of rules and once you understood these rules, everything was usually okay. I felt he was talking of his grandmother. Maybe she was not as pleasant as his essay depicted. Before the bus arrived, he invited me once again to his home.

But Javier was right. That weekend Mr Magboo walked in with a list of movies written in a *crapo*-foot handwriting. "Now I look at all these mobies in DBD." His tiredness was completely gone. "And this you send to mobie people." He brought out a clutch of rolled-up papers from his coat pocket.

"What are those?"

"All the stories I make. For mobie people. You post for me."

"But I don't know the producers—"

"You get it from case." He gave me a twenty-dollar bill. "For stamp."

"Look, I just work in a video store. That is all." I returned the money.

"You not send?"

"I am just a video clerk," I pleaded.

He became angry. I saw his eyebrows disappearing behind his glasses. He said the world was filled with stupid, ungrateful young people. He wished a sabre-tooth or a volcano god could be let loose on all of us. His hands were trembling as he left with his movies and his money. But he returned on Wednesday with the rolled up scripts, the money, and the complaints about young people. Midway through his accusations I decided to take the money and return it when he was in a better mood. I would think of some excuse later. He seemed happy and wondered whether they might get Boris Karloff or Humphrey Bogart to play the lead roles.

"These people are in a coffin somewhere," I told him.

"Exactly so."

I decided to not argue.

He brought more scripts during his subsequent visit and I felt guilty for placing the entire bunch in Mr. Schmidlap's drawer. My guilt increased as he chatted happily about the proposed movies and their long dead actors and enquired why he had not yet received any replies. I decided to use his money to help pay off Mr Schmidlap for the DVD player but each time he visited my guilt increased. One weekend while I was looking at sweaters in the Donation Centre, I saw a red cape hanging on the wall. This was the week after Hallowe'en and I got the cape for just three dollars. When I gave it to Mr. Magboo during his next visit, he tried it on immediately and flashed a smile like the Count on Sesame Street. A woman in the store pulled her son closer. Mr. Magboo left with the cape hanging from his neck. The next week he arrived with the cape flowing after him. I didn't know what to say. At least it suited him.

When one week then two passed with no visit from Mr. Magboo, I pictured him wandering around some park with his cape blowing behind him and terrified children running away and bawling. Maybe his family had placed him in some home for old, crazy people. I tried to reassure myself that it was only an old man wearing a cape. Who on the bus or the subway will notice? The answer was everybody. Especially the police. I prepared myself for a visit to his home.

I never visited because Mr. Magboo appeared one Saturday with his cape and a new hat. Something else was new and as he got closer, I saw it was the obviously fake Fu Manchu moustache, so lopsided he seemed to be scowling and grinning at the same time. He also had a cane that he used to stylishly adjust his hat. I noted his broad smile and decided he had gone completely mad. "I haven't seen you for two weeks," I managed to say.

"Because I become busy. Berry busy, buddy." I wondered whether his daughter had a new baby. "When you give me cape, I went straight to CBC to complain about movies they steal."

"With the cape?"

"I think it might have magic powers. Because just outside the building a man say to me, 'Hurry up. We going shoot soon.' So I pollow other men with tight pants and bows-arrows."

"You were in a movie?"

"Many, buddy. They call me . . . what is the word?" He thought for a while. "Something like leffobers."

"Extras? Is that it?" I might have sounded a bit excited.

He leaned closer to me and whispered, "It's real, buddy. You better believe it." I think this was his extra voice. He was about to leave the shop when he hesitated and said, "Parewell, priend." Outside, he swirled his cape and vanished into the crowd. I never saw him again.

Or rather, I never saw him in real again, for I was sure that in a couple television shows I spotted him running away from explosions and bears, and once, sleeping inside a purple pod.

During the first week of December, with barely a month left for the completion of my preparatory course, I received a letter from Uncle Boysie. He said he intended to spend Christmas in Canada and itemized some intended sights that would not have been out of place in Mr. Magboo's movies. He wanted to see cats frozen on trees and against windows, and playful Eskimos, and André the Giant battling midgets. Most worrisome, he instructed me to describe for him immediately after his arrival, "a regular Canadian" so he would be able to fit in.

Chapter Fourteen

THE FEDERATION OF FOWLS

When I showed my father Uncle Boysie's letter he began to curse straightaway. "Why the bitch coming here for? Anybody invite him?" He glanced at me suspiciously before he continued. "He lie if he feel this is *mash-up* Mayaro with *commess* and *bacchanal* on all sides. Regular Canadian, my ass." It was only when I ventured that he might be coming to straighten out the house business that my father cooled down a little. "Eh? You think so? But he could have done that right in Mayaro," he said in a weak and indecisive voice. I could see that he was conflicted (to use Mrs. Dragan's word for second-generation immigrants.)

I turned to her for an answer to Uncle Boysie's question. We were discussing multiculturalism—a favourite topic of hers—when I asked, "Miss, how would you describe a typical Canadian?" I saw her struggling and immediately regretted the question. She was sly though as she tried to turn the table.

"You are originally from Trinidad, not so? How would you describe a typical Trinidadian?"

I recalled Uncle Boysie's gripes. "Someone who likes *bacchanal* and carnival."

"I see. Is there a typical Latin American?" She walked to the back of the class.

Javier answered. Stories and a history of struggle.

She turned to other places and students, most likely from these spots, provided answers. Poetry and Guinness. Caste divisions and "sparkling poverty." Tea, crumpets and a dry sense of humour. Inventiveness and patriotism. I believe some of these normally quiet students felt it was a game as they went on and on. The teacher didn't play though and when she abruptly moved on to another topic I decided that there was no such creature as a regular Canadian. I would have to tell Uncle Boysie that.

Nevertheless, I thought of my uncle's question in Mr. Schmidlap's video store. I had to discount the owner first of all because he was too gloomy and he seemed on the verge of expiry. One by one I also dismissed the regular customers. Too porny. Too tame. Too crazy. Too foreign.

Which left one tiny sliver of hope. Danton. His full name was Danton Madrigal and he regularly mentioned Canadian places like Owen Sound—which he called "the elephant's bottom" because of how it appeared on the map—and Longlac and Haliburton and Bolton. I felt that all these spots were far away so I was surprised when he revealed that he frequently visited his old friends there.

His first appearance in Queen Bee coincided with the flurry of meetings in Regent Park, organized by people worried about where they would be moved, so—just in case—I always listened carefully to his descriptions of places that seemed both strange and interesting. His farmhouses and abandoned copper mines and Indian reservations and bundles of rivers. It was only later that I began to also notice his appearance, the tiny eyes peeping from behind round wire glasses and the few grains of hair on his head pulled into a tight ponytail. His round face reminded me of parakeets from Trinidad but I would never mention this to him, because first of all, he never gave me a chance to put in a word and secondly, I could never tell what was going through his mind. In the beginning, it was difficult to catch up with him because he was always jumping from topic to topic. Sometimes he would be talking about a movie explosion and then switch to some accident in Owen Sound. He had many accidents with motorbikes and boats and these little snow-cars. These accidents never went well for him because he talked about the insurance companies and police as if they were movie crooks.

The weekend after I asked Mrs. Dragan about typical Canadians he came into the shop riding one of these scooter chairs used by old people. I thought he had another accident but the minute he entered, he parked his chair next to the row of science fiction movies and jumped right off. "What do you think?" he asked me. "Like my new car?"

"What happened?"

"What happened, my friend, is that I got tired of walking."
He laughed in his scratchy way and I spotted Mr. Schmidlap
awakening from his nap in his corner table.

"I thought you had another accident."

"Samuel, you crack me up." He usually said that whenever I asked a question he found, for whatever reason, funny.
He leaned across the counter toward me. "Don't tell anyone
but it's payback time."

I tried to recall his long list of enemies. Doctors, lawyers,
insurance people, police, and more mysteriously, a shadowy
group he believed was controlling everything from electric-
ity to water. He hinted the group was based inside one of the
big buildings on Bay Street. He called them "the federation of
fowls" and he once mentioned he had rigged up his computer
to tap into their network. When I mentioned that conversation to Javier, he said that Danton belonged to a special kind
of mad men who were dangerous because they didn't know
they were crazy.

"Want to go for a spin? C'mon, it's faster than most
bikes." This was another thing about Danton: I never knew
when he was joking or not. He walked across to the science
fiction aisle and returned a couple minutes later with a movie
named *Vendetta*. "Seen it about five times," he told me.

"It that good?"

"It that good?" He imitated my accent and laughed. "Yes,
Samuel. It could be my life story." As usual he shifted to the
fowl federation before he got going on another of his favourite
topics: how nice things were in the sixties with everybody

singing and dancing as if the *fête* wouldn't end. He went on about these people like Jerry Garcia and the Grateful Dead and Jimi Hendrix, as if he knew them personally before he said suddenly, "I think the scooter has made me too mellow. This is very dangerous."

He left before I could ask him about a typical Canadian.

He came every weekend so when he returned *Vendetta* and borrowed *The Parallax View* I decided to pretend more interest in his federation business. That was a mistake.

He told me, "You've been thinking, Samuel. That's a good sign. I think you've just booked a place in the commune."

"Which commune?"

"The one I am forming, silly." He pointed to his scooter. "And believe it or not, that is the key."

"Really?" I think this was my most common word in our conversation.

"Yes, really. Do you want to know how it's the key?" His little eyes seemed soft and watery behind his glasses. "You have to promise not to tell a soul about this. It's payback time."

"But for what?"

"You haven't been listening to me, Samuel. For the false reports, losing my job and my entire pension, my divorce, garnishing my wages, the accidents, the insurance guys. Should I also mention the cabal?"

"What's a cabal?" It sounded like a tiny exit at the end of a long tunnel.

"Do you see that asshole with a briefcase outside? Well, he's part of it. Everyone in that building across the street too. And the one next to it." I noticed his finger pointing to building after building. I wanted to ask if everybody in Toronto with a briefcase was in his cabal but he seemed too angry then. I remembered he had said once that dreams couldn't find a place to grow in the city because there was too much concrete. "I hold all of them responsible for my present condition." He got on his scooter and gazed up at me. "The federation of fucking fowls."

He went on for another twenty minutes; and during that week whenever I spotted anybody with a briefcase and a suit, I thought of his cabal. The journalists who descended on Regent Park. The two politicians who collected a list of petitions. Even the little group formed to fight the relocation. I felt that their leader was a huge bald-headed man with pinstriped clothes and shining shoes. Someone like Kingpin from *Daredevil.*

When next I saw Danton he was on foot but his glasses had been replaced by dark shades and he was limping on a walking stick. I was about to open the store for the day and did not recognize him until he pushed his stick through the half-open door. "Trying to ignore me, Samuel?"

"I didn't make you out with your shades and stick."

"I didn't make you out." He laughed and pulled back his ponytail tight. "That's good though. It means it's working."

"Doing some undercover work?" I asked him lightly.

"You give me too much credit." He pushed a finger behind one of the black lenses and rubbed. I could hear his eyelids clacking. "It's my eyes. They are developing holes."

I felt I should challenge him. "Take off your glasses and let me see."

His little smile got stale all of a sudden. "You can't see them, silly. They are not visible to anyone but myself."

"So you see these holes from the inside then?"

"Exactly. There's about five in all."

"It sound painful."

"Well, Samuel, I am used to that. But it's more inconvenient than painful. For instance, I might be looking at that row of movies and completely miss the one I'm searching for."

"That happens to me sometimes."

"This morning a cyclist almost ran me over. He was in my blind spot."

Now I don't want to sound heartless or anything but Danton had told me so many bad-luck stories, this new one just rubbed off me. "You think the cyclist might be from the cabal?"

He stared at me from behind his shades before he said, "That's good. Very good. You are beginning to understand the matrix. Can I trust you with something? Don't tell anyone, but I think they are on to me."

"The fowl federation?"

"You know of them?"

"You told me about a dozen times."

"Yes, I may have. I think the holes are spreading upwards. I seem to have these memory lapses." He took a deep breath. "Time is running out, Samuel. I have to move fast. I need all the help I can get."

"What do you want me to do?"

"Keep your eyes open. Someone wants something from me."

Me too! But it was too late, he had already left.

I think it was then that I noticed this man wearing a brown plaid hat. He was drinking a Tim Horton's coffee and the minute Danton pulled off, he did the same, slowing down every time Danton stalled, speeding up whenever Danton quickened his pace.

I too had to move fast: it was just two weeks before Christmas and Uncle Boysie's arrival. Things were picking up in Regent Park also, as notices of community meetings were daily stuck on the lamp poles. And every night as a rule my father asked me if Uncle Boysie was still coming or had changed his mind. The week before the end of the semester I got an airmail from the mailbox downstairs and when I gave it to my father he seemed relieved to read that Uncle Boysie intended to come on New Year's Day instead of Christmas because "the flights cheaper as nobody does want to fly on that day."

The flight postponement was a reprieve but Uncle Boysie's question about typical Canadians lingered in my mind. Auntie Umbrella had asked the same question and when I babbled on about albinos she didn't seem satisfied. I couldn't be blamed then as I was sort of green, but now, nine months later, I felt I should be more informed. I couldn't once again bring up the topic in the class so I looked for clues on the streets and in the newspapers. In the *Sun,* a whole batch of journalists was complaining that "Christmas was under threat" but all they mentioned was a couple of people refusing to sing carols and say, "Merry Christmas." I decided these reporters were like the old-timers from Coffee Time, Roy and the others who were always grumbling about how things were changing and making up their own stories to prove this.

Soon after my first visit to downtown Toronto I had watched everyone walking all apart and wondered if they belonged to different clubs that met on weekends, where they would throw off their quietness and mingle to make clubby jokes. I had to laugh at the notion, just a couple months earlier, that I would always be an outcast here until I managed to join one of these groups. I had invented all types of nonsense clubs and pretended that I had managed to scam my way to an invitation.

I now decided to return to the library and suffer myself through one of the downstairs seminars. After two useless seminars on architecture and writing (during which a short man with snarling whiskers declared that "The novel is dead, stabbed through the heart by brittle coquettish munchkins") I lucked upon a meeting discussing diversity. The speaker, whose name was Mr. Pelicano—he was thin and lanky and the complete opposite of a pelican—began by building a house. He talked about grouts and trowels and tiles and single-colour buckets. When he was finished he said proudly, "There you have it. A perfect mosaic." He never mentioned who this builder was, gazing at his materializing house.

The next day Danton came to the video store with his right arm and his left foot heavily bandaged. "I hope you are keeping watch," he said, placing on the counter his three films: *Blow Out. Winter Kills. Three Days of the Condor.*

"What happened, man. You look like you returned from a war."

"Samuel, you crack me up." Then he got more serious. "You see that gentleman before the coffee shop? The insurance guy?" He glanced at the Tim Horton's man who was tracking him. "I don't pay him any attention. Do you know why? Because he is not the enemy. He is not even a foot soldier. The generals are on the top floors of all the buildings you pass every day. That gentleman, Samuel, is just a pawn."

"A pawn for who?"

"For the generals."

"Which generals, exactly?"

"The ones on the top floors, silly."

"The federation of fowls?"

"Did I mention them to you? Anyways, I may have to take a little break. Lay low for a while."

"Are you going to Owen Sound?"

He placed a finger against his lips. "Not so loud. There are spies everywhere. I think Schmidlap used to be in the SS. Spent some time in Argentina before he came here. Can I tell you a secret?" He did not wait for a reply. "I am working on a movie too. It's set in the future. Everyone is dying from some mysterious ailment. All the scientists are stumped. Everyone but for this—" he leaned over and whispered "—this counterinsurgent. He discovered it was because technology had allowed everyone to complete their tasks faster. You know the rest."

"Not really."

"C'mon, Samuel. Attention spans diminished. Minds grew conditioned to more abbreviated tasks. It was only a short time before the body caught up. You understand? The counter-insurgent was mocked for this view and so, single-handedly, he set about destroying computers. He sabotaged trains and elevators and sports cars and soon he set his sights on the federation of fowls. It was a grand battle." He chuckled. And I thought of never-ending comic book explosions with thousands of vowels.

I didn't get the opportunity to ask Danton about a typical Canadian because he never returned to Queen Bee. But on the day my classes ended, a week before Christmas, I was sitting on a bench not too far from the CBC building. On a nearby bench there were two men from Afghanistan. I was listening to their manner of clipping and hardening their words as if placing a little shield around each sentence. One of the men, who was tall and resembled my mother's Bollywood actors, was listening quietly to his friend while staring at two dead birds not too far from the couple. Perhaps like me he was wondering if some animal, maybe a sewer rat, had dragged them here. Just then there was a little thud and a bird landed on the same spot. The tall Afghan looked up at a glass tower and his friend went to the bird. He scooped it up and held it in his open palm like an offering. He walked away with the bird in his hand, his friend trailing him.

I sat there for another fifteen or twenty minutes, as it was not too cold that day. Flurries were drifting down in merry little spirals. Everyone was walking quickly, perhaps to put up their Christmas decorations or visit family or whatever Canadians did in preparation for Christmas. I thought of all the people I had met in my ten months here. The coffee-shop old-timers. The chimera. Barbarossa. Danton. The seminar speakers. The Regent Park crowd. My father. All the worriers.

I got up. By the time I got to Regent Park I felt I had an answer for my uncle. A typical Canadian—or at least those I had met—was someone who fussed all the time. About everything. Toronto was getting too modern and ugly. Toronto was stuck in the past. Too many immigrants. Too few. Foreign people were living all by themselves. Foreign people were walking bold-bold in places that shouldn't concern them. Too many American shows. Too few. Too much hockey violence. Too little. Too hot. Too cold.

When I entered our apartment I saw my father hunched up before the television, worried and frightened like anything. I wondered what was going through his mind. From his posture I felt he might be repeating, *Trapped! Trapped!* Not too long ago, I felt close to hating him—now I just felt sorry for him.

Chapter Fifteen

CARMEN ISADORA CIENFUEGOS
AND THE MAGIC LANTERN

Maybe I was becoming a regular Canadian, because once school was closed and I *limed* around Regent Park, I too began to worry. It could be because I was in such close and constant quarters with my father; and worse, observing each day different groups fretting about the end of the neighbourhood they had lived in most of their lives. This was surprising, as I had never thought of Regent Park as a community, maybe because living with my father encouraged me to feel it was a place to escape from. Once I heard the Creole woman, who had given me the sheet about refugees, saying, "Just imagine that I have to start over again at my age. With strangers on all sides. That is nastiness. Real nastiness. But God don't sleep." She had shouted, "You hear that, Samuel? The man upstairs don't ever sleep." She sounded a bit like Auntie Umbrella.

I was also worried about the preparatory course. What if I failed? Maybe I had antagonized the teacher with my silly questions and not concentrating enough on agreeable aspects of the city. I had tried to be positive on the ISU essay I submitted on the last day of class. We had to write three pages on our favourite season and I chose fall because of all the shimmery comic-book colours: a dazzling red dash here, a splash of yellow there, a sparkle of orange peeping out like Mayaro fireflies. In Mayaro, mostly everything was green. Here the fall colours seemed wizardly and unreal. I included all of this in my essay, and three days before Christmas, when I went to Centennial to collect my grades I was worried like anything.

I got an A minus for the essay, the highest mark I had received in my entire life. I met Javier in the office and he told me he got the same grade (though he had written of spring as a time of renewal). We walked together to the loop and he asked if I had decided on my regular college course. I told him I had not, but it was exciting to have reached the stage where I could be asked such a question. He said he planned to sign up for a diploma in Police Foundations. I thought of his limp but said nothing. Just before his bus arrived, he once again invited me to his grandmother's place.

I recalled Javier's question on the bus but could not settle on a suitable course. By the time I reached Regent Park some of my excitement had dribbled away. It was a real grey day and everybody seemed weighed down by the gloom, walking with their heads down and looking real sour and bothered. In Trinidad, people sometimes felt lazy during overcast days, keeping inside their houses and peeping through the windows at the rain pelting down the sprouting, but here, they seemed to lose all life, moving like abruptly hardened sponges.

The mood followed me the next day. I tried to imagine what was going on in Mayaro during this Christmas season. Most likely, the fishermen were strumming their cuatros at some *parang fête*, stopping only for a drink of rum. Uncle Boysie's shop would be busy with children eyeing all his dusty wound-up toys on the highest shelves. Carollers would be going from house to house; and from all the windows and jalousies and louvres would drift the mingled aroma of sorrel and punch à crème and seasoned meat. In the week before Christmas, our own kitchen smelled of all kinds of cakes and curried duck and apples bought from the Mayaro market.

In Mayaro, I always associated apples with Christmas. The fruits were packed in soft cardboard that preserved their fragrance. Once I used to dream of these Christmas postcards with snowy cottages, and reindeer, and children in red caps and galoshes building snowmen while dogs wearing funny coats looked on.

The next morning when I headed out, I guess I was trying to recapture that feeling. I saw children packaged so tightly they lumbered like chubby little robots, and just before Parliament Street I was startled by two boys skating down an embankment. I returned about an hour later to an empty apartment. I placed the bottle of wine I had bought for my father on top of the fridge and turned on the television. Two grey-hair women were saying something about goose fat and doughnuts and pies. They were in a studio kitchen and on the walls were hollies looking like wreaths. But the women themselves appeared happy as if they had been waiting their entire lives to talk about goose fat and doughnuts. Maybe these things could only be enjoyed from afar as a fantasy, or if you were born here.

On Christmas Eve, my father returned late in the night and went straight to his room as if he was avoiding me. After a while, I unrolled the foam but my mind kept returning to Mayaro, and to my mother. I thought of all my friends from school there speculating on their presents and stealing pieces of their mothers' pastries from the kitchen; and closer, the Regent Park families that came from every part of the globe huddling around and maybe not saying much but just comforted by each other's presence. In Pickering Javier's grandmother might be telling him and his sisters some Cuban story while they listened to music similar to our *parang* streaming from the radio. I wished my mother was alive, even if she was away from me. I could still write her and boast of my classes and my grades and all these interesting people that popped up everywhere. When I was eight we had sat together before the television on Christmas Eve and looked at the entire *Nutcracker* movie.

Ten minutes or so later I got up abruptly, ashamed that my father might hear my croaky sounds (the same as when I had tried to stop crying at my mother's funeral). I opened the balcony door a crack and noticed the Christmas lights on a couple windows and porches. When I eventually fell asleep,

I dreamed of snowy cottages along the Mayaro beach and nut-cracker dancers jumping to the rhythm of cuatros and grey-hair women explaining how to prepare sorrel and punch à crème.

The next morning—maybe because of the dreams—I was temporarily confused to awaken on a piece of foam. My father was in the kitchen wearing a coat. I told him, "You don't have to go out today, you know."

He hesitated by the doorway. "I will be back in a while."

"I bought a bottle of wine for you."

"Yeah." He had a furtive look on his face and just for a second I pretended he was rushing to get me a last-minute present.

During the period when my mother still believed my father would return to our house in Mayaro I used to see her, particularly after her conversations with some village woman, gazing out of the window, with her hands flat on the ledge. A couple times I pictured her spotting him from a distance and rushing out to help drag the heavy suitcases to our house, and once they were opened, saying, "Oh gosh, Danny, this is such a nice dress. It so silky. What material is it?" Laying everything on the couch and saying, "Like you buy out half of Canada or what?"

This was my first real Christmas with my father—as I had no recollection of him in Mayaro putting up Christmas tree lights or anything. Once I had asked for a microscope for Christmas. It was just after I had discovered *The Wonder Book of Wonders* and I imagined me and my father—who was in a lab coat and had unruly hair like a scientist—doing all kinds of crazy experiments. Instead I got a cheap telescope from Uncle Boysie's shop and on my way from school I had pointed it to the ocean and pretended the barges were pirate ships. Closer to home I focused on semps and bullfinches on the telephone poles. They seemed so close I felt I could stroke them. A week before I moved to Canada I had left it for the Amazing Absorbing Boy so he could gaze out at strangers intruding into his swamp.

I tried to push away all these memories by strolling through the building. The doors were shut and there was no one on the stairs or in the elevator. On the last floor, I spotted the woman who had called me an asshole. She was standing with her cat before her open door, smoking. I quickened my pace but noticed that all the inside walls in her apartment were painted in black. Maybe it was some kind of protest, or perhaps she followed a strange religion. I don't think she recognized me but when I reached the end of the hall she said, "Merry Christmas." I didn't answer quickly so she added, "It's Christmas, asshole."

"Then you should get that cat a damn new owner." I was surprised at how loud my voice sounded on the stairway. Just like her ringing curses. Maybe she was standing before her door just to provoke people. For some reason that made me smile: the picture of this fat lady with her cat just waiting to curse everyone who passed by. Or she could be my own special nemesis like the Catwoman or the Joker.

My father returned a little after midday, the same sly and uncomfortable look he had left with still on his face.

I wondered if he had been visiting some woman, maybe the ugly red-hair troll. Once a family who had rented a beach house on Plaisance were sitting on a couple of folding chairs facing the ocean. I overheard a man with a big belly flopping over his trunk saying that Trinidadians always returned with the ugliest foreigners. "Is like they does go to some ugly people street and propose to the *fuss* woman they spot. The very fuss." A woman who might have been his wife pressed her fingers against her lips and shot out a laugh, each note higher than the last, as if she was playing a mouth organ. Her big bottom jiggled as she ho-hoed.

My father went to the balcony, smoked a couple cigarettes before he returned to switch on the television.

"Happy Christmas," I told him.

"Yeah." He switched from channel to channel. Most had people praying. I had once seen a television documentary about a man who had three separate families that were unaware of each other's existence. I dismissed that thought swiftly: my father couldn't even keep up with one family. "You want to call your uncle?" At first I wasn't sure whether he was mumbling to the television but he glanced quickly at me by the table and added, "Just for a minute or two."

As the phone was right next to the television I couldn't help notice him watching me point-blank as I dialled over and over. Each time I got a busy signal—I guessed too many people were calling their families in Trinidad—I saw his face tightening. Maybe he just wanted me to call so Uncle Boysie could tell me something of our old house. Eventually I gave up and a couple minutes later, he went into his room. I heard his mattress creaking as if he was shifting from side to side.

Around three in the afternoon, I got out a pen intending to write a letter to Uncle Boysie but realized he would be here by the time the letter arrived in Mayaro. I took out my Centennial booklets, read of the real college courses, put them away and walked around the living room a few times. I wondered how the place would look with photographs. This got me thinking once more of our old house and of my mother so I quickly turned on the television. People were still praying as if they had nothing better to do. I felt really, really bored. Some years earlier, I had watched two men carrying a neighbour, Popo's son, into his house. It was a Christmas day and the men were holding his arms and legs and swinging him like a sugar bag. They noticed me gazing and shouted merrily, "Today Popo boy come a man. You don't tunna man till you ass get drunk and tote home." I don't know why I missed that sort of spectacle too.

The next morning I decided to take up Javier's invitation. He lived in Pickering so I had to take the eastbound Go Train at Union. On the train I got out his directions I had written on the back of an old transfer ticket. He said the house was on Liverpool Road, close to the station, but I must have walked about half an hour before I actually got to his address. I wondered how he managed this distance with his limp. The house was on the brink of a gentle hill. This was the first strange thing about the house, as Toronto seemed mostly flat and I just assumed it was like that all over. The curve reminded me of Bucket Corner just after Rio Claro. The second strange aspect to the house was the number of plants the family had managed to squeeze into the small yard. Most were winter-dead, so I couldn't tell if they bore fruits or flowers.

The third unusual feature of the house was the girl in the living room. She was sitting on a spongy-looking sofa and her legs were curled up below her bottom. While I was talking to Javier—who seemed surprised at my visit in spite of his numerous invitations—I sneaked a couple glances at her and met her eyes looking at me point-blank. Each time I was forced to look away. When Javier went to get his grandmother, I fished around for something to say but it was the girl who asked the first question. Now I had a legitimate reason to gaze at her. She had tattoos of butterfly wings on her wrists and some kind of trailing plant on her ankles. As she was sitting, it was difficult to get a good gauge on her shape but she reminded me of these tough breed of girls from Mayaro Composite who wouldn't give me a second glance, preferring instead to hang out with taxi drivers twice their age. She asked her question again, with a wicked smile this time. I guess she was probably accustomed to boys casting little glances at her breasts.

"Yes, I am Javier's friend," I told her. "He's very smart."

"Javier?" She put her hands to her mouth and her eyes widened. When Javier returned with a short woman who looked like a pale, grey-hair version of Auntie Umbrella, she repeated my statement to both. The old lady, who had a cane, said something in Spanish and the girl responded also in that language. From the tone of their voices, it seemed like an argument. This was the pattern for the next fifteen minutes as the four of us sat in the living room. I wished I could understand Spanish so I could tell if Javier and the girl were translating for the old woman what I had just said in English. Finally, the lady leaned on her cane, uttered a tiny groan and got up. She spoke swiftly gesturing with her free hand. Go away fast, old lady, I thought, which was unfair because of all the sacrifices she made, according to her grandson's essay. Now the girl got up to guide the lady to a dark hall and I saw tattoos of what seemed like lotus flowers creeping down the back of her pants, to her nice round bottom. There was also a tiny hummingbird on one shoulder. Maybe because of the way this girl was swaying her bottom, I remembered some of the terms used by the schoolgirls in Barbarossa's antique shop, and I felt that banging her would be like making love to a pond. With her lotus flowers and trailing vines and birds. I crossed my legs hurriedly and placed the sheet with directions on my lap. Think of something else quickly, I told myself. "Do you miss your parents at Christmas?" I asked Javier.

"Not so much again. But Carmen does. She's a year younger than me."

The girl returned and Javier repeated my question to her. "You?" she asked.

"I miss the village mostly. My mother passed away."

"So do you live with your dad, then?"

"We . . . we share the same apartment," I told her.

"Meaning?" She sat on the arm of the sofa, next to her brother and stared down at me.

"I hardly see him."

"Why not?"

"I will bring him for my next visit and you can ask him yourself." I didn't like all these questions but Carmen laughed at my answer. She may have felt it was a joke or something. Her brother looked embarrassed.

"Sam likes superheroes," he told her.

I expected this tough girl to laugh at this but she asked me, "Really? Who is your favourite?"

"The Amazing Absorbing Boy."

"I have never heard of him." She leaned forward and I noticed the gold nose ring that matched her colour exactly.

"He lives in a swamp."

"Swamp Thing?"

"A swamp in Mayaro. My village."

"Ay, caramba!" she told her brother, laughing. "Your friend is funny." All of a sudden she seemed prettier and more interesting. It could be because she seemed to be paying me attention or because of the curve of her lips as she smiled or maybe just her poking out nipples as she leaned forward. She looked a bit like Rogue from X-Men. Now she flopped down on the sofa and sat cross-legged like a Trinidad pundit.

"What do you miss the most of Cuba?"

Carmen answered. "My parents."

"How come they remained in Cuba?"

After a while Javier said, "They were killed. That's why we left."

"Didn't you know?" Carmen asked. She leaned her head onto her brother's shoulder. It seemed a private scene and I wondered if all siblings behaved like this. I felt sorry for asking the question and during dinner, I felt that her mood had changed. I tried to hurry up but when I was leaving, Carmen walked out of the house with me. She said something to her brother—who was standing on the doorstep—and translated for me: Tell Grandma I will be back in two hours. She was going to the Pickering Town Centre, she told me, and as we walked in the direction of the Go station, it struck me that this was the first time I was strolling with a girl. Really strolling. In Mayaro where neighbours were always gazing from their windows it was impossible to publicly put the moves on a girl. I couldn't count my detour with Canella, as I was too tipsy at the time, and Dilara was always accompanied by her friend. In any case, Canella was maybe eight years or so older than me, and Dilara was too remote.

This girl was different from both women. Canella was tall and assured and Dilara was delicate and bird-like. Carmen was medium everything and even though she appeared rough-and-tumble, I felt it hid an interesting softness. I was glad she decided to sit with me in the coffee shop until the arrival of the westbound train; and sitting there, I wished Pantamoolie and the other Mayaro boys could see me. Once Pantamoolie had told me that Spanish girls were hot-blooded and up for anything.

In half an hour or less, I felt the reputation may have been undeserved. Her full name, she said, was Carmen Isadora

Cienfuegos. She told me that when she graduated from Pine Ridge Secondary in a couple months she wanted to volunteer at some old people place before she started college. It was because of her grandmother, who was suffering from early-stage Alzheimer's. Now the old woman talked constantly of Cuba and of Carmen's parents as if they were still living. "Do you know what she used to tell us when we were kids? We had a small gas lantern, the only thing we brought from Cuba, and in the nights she would place it in our bedroom and say it possessed a special kind of light. One that would summon our parents' spirits no matter where they were roaming."

"In brightest day, in blackest night . . ."

"Yes?" she asked.

"Another type of lantern. From a comic book."

"Tell me about it."

I missed the next train and the one after. I didn't care. When I got to Regent Park it was already dark. I pretended the streetlights were magic lanterns and all these people walking about sneaked little glances to see whoever they had left behind. I believe I saw my mother dressed up as in the week before her death. But her cheeks were not bony and she was not wearing an ill-fitted wig but looked as pretty as I had ever seen her. I even heard a tiny bit of Nutcracker music.

Chapter Sixteen

UNCLE BOYSIE AND THE PINK PUSSYAH

T he first thing Uncle Boysie told me as we were leaving the airport was, "This *mingpiling* scrawny bit of fur floating around, people does make so much fuss about?"

"Is not real snow," I told him. "Is flurries."

"Furries? How come I never hear about them?" He glanced at me as if I was involved in creating a bogus Canada for Mayaro people. But soon he turned his attention to the other passengers on the Airport Express. "How come it have so much grey-hair people around here? They never hear about dye or what?" And a few minutes later. "Why everybody so quiet? Like they in a witness protection programme or what?" He was speaking loudly, in the Trinidadian manner, and when he asked if there was some pundit convention at the airport, I had to quietly explain they were all Sikhs who wore turbans and dressed like Trinidadian pundits.

On the 401 highway he inquired if there were loads of

rubbish and broken-down shacks hidden behind all the fancy buildings like in Trinidad and I told him I didn't think so. He had not changed one bit, although it was strange seeing him in an expensive fur coat, white hat and two-toned shoes. He looked like a mobster, through and through, and while we were walking to our apartment building I noticed people staring at him. This affection—if it was that— was not returned by my uncle as he watched the big iron garbage units by the parking lots and the overturned shopping carts and the drawings on the walls and the young people smoking in little groups around the boardwalk and the clothes on some of the balconies. "I thought you say it didn't have no hide-away *mash-up* place? What is this then? And where all these people from? Trinidad?"

"All over. And they going to pull down the entire place soon."

"What you mean pull down?"

"Relocate everybody elsewhere."

"Oho. That is why all of a sudden you father get a tick in he bottom. Running away at the first sign of trouble. The *neemakaram* home?"

He was at home and the biggest surprise to me was how quiet and nervous he appeared. He seemed almost afraid of my uncle. My father was taller and maybe a couple years younger but Uncle Boysie had the kind of thick neck and solid-looking fat that in Trinidad gave him the mark of a *badjohn*. "You mean to say that this is the best place you could find to live, Danny?" he asked my father. "And where all the machine and fancy unit you invent? Where the talking bicycle and the furniture that does follow you around the place and the teeth make from plastic?" He pretended to be peering around. "You father was a big inventor in Trinidad, you know," he told me. "But the only thing he invent was a scheme to get out of the island."

He heaved one of his suitcases on the kitchen table, unzipped it and began digging inside. "Aha. They didn't find this." He pulled out a bottle of Puncheon from one of the pockets, uncorked it and took a big swig. "For the cold." He plucked out some T-shirts and threw one at my father and another at me. "These bitches and them seize three-quarter of me luggage in the airport. All me curry *chataigne* and *mauby* and herbs I does use for the constipation. Is a good thing they didn't poke inside me bottom. That is what they do with these Guyanese in JFK, you know. Prospecting for park-up gold." He pulled out two envelopes from a mess of yellowish underwear. "Customs people don't like to dig around too much in smelly jockey shorts and thing."

My father was walking from one end of the living room to the other but when Uncle Boysie placed the envelopes on the kitchen table, he immediately stopped his pacing. But my uncle leaned back on his chair and unloosened the top button on his trouser, which meant he was in one of his talkative moods. He began by mentioning all the crime in Trinidad, the rise of Colombian and Mexican drug gangs, kidnapping children for money, and the government big boys building huge walls to hide-away the slums. "The country have too much money, if you ask me. It give people a whole new setta vice."

He reached for the two envelopes but only to replace them in his coat pocket. I wondered if he was torturing my father but it seemed he still had a lot to spill about Trinidad. Everybody was going mad one by one: the prime minister wanted to build a palace for himself on one of the smaller islands off the east coast; the leader of the opposition claimed to receive visions that directed him to travel about in a horse-drawn buggy rather than his car; the police commissioner complained that a few smartass journalists who were forever complaining about bribes—rather than using the proper word, gifts—were giving the practice a bad name.

My father went to the balcony for a smoke and Uncle Boysie gazed at him. "How two of allyou making out, boy?" His voice was softer now.

"We okay, uncle."

"I don't expect you to complain. You not like that." He got quiet for a couple minutes before he asked, "How college going?"

"I had to finish a preparatory course first. Sort of finish high school."

"You pass?"

I nodded.

"When you will begin then?"

"In the beginning of February."

"A month or so away. So you will have to buy uniform and thing soon."

"They don't wear uniform here."

"Eh? No uniform? You sure is a real college? What about the fees?"

"I trying to save up from my work."

He got out the envelopes once more from his pocket. Now I too was curious about their contents. "So where you does sleep, Sammy?" I felt embarrassed to mention the foam but my uncle followed my gaze to the rolled-up bundle against the living room wall. "Later on we will take a little vacation in a hotel. It have any nearby?"

"They might be expensive, uncle."

"You don't worry you head about that, Sammy. You working?"

"Yeah. In a video store. Three days. Wednesday and weekends."

"It look like I have a lot to do in these ten days." He called out to my father who came immediately. "I have something for you, Mister Persad." Uncle Boysie fetched a glasses from a case in his shirt pocket, adjusted it over his bulky nose, and read the names on the envelopes carefully before he gave the thicker one to my father. I saw him scrutinizing my father with the same suspicious expression as when one of his Mayaro customers asked for an extension on their credit. Without removing his gaze from my father, who was chewing his lower lip nervously—which made him look younger, almost like an *ownway* schoolboy—Uncle Boysie said, "Sammy, tonight you will sleep in the bedroom. Me and you father have a lot to discuss."

That night was the first in ten months I slept on a real bed. But I was not as comfortable as I should have been. Visions of my father and uncle quarrelling and fighting and one throwing the other off the balcony flashed through my mind. I listened carefully for some commotion from the living room and when I heard little sopping sounds—like a baby sucking air from an empty bottle—I was mystified. I placed my head against the wall but still could not figure what was going on. Finally I decided to pretend I was getting something from the fridge.

My father and uncle were in the living room, my uncle sitting on the foam and my father on the couch. My father was crying. Sobbing like a baby, with his hands rubbing his eyes. It took a while for the shock to wear off but when it did, I felt disgust, pure and simple. I know it sounds bad on my part but the sight of a big man crying in this quiet weak way, with his shoulders bobbing, just didn't seem right. I didn't care what it was that had set him off. And that night in my father's room I tried to imagine what had happened. Did Uncle Boysie threaten him? Was it connected in some way with the envelope? I thought of something else: this was just the first night of Uncle Boysie's ten-day stay.

I slept badly that night, alert to any kind of commotion, and I awoke later than usual so I had to rush to the bathroom to hurriedly bathe. When I left, my uncle was snoring loudly on the foam and my father was coiled up on the couch. I was relieved because I wasn't in the mood to face either of them. I got to work almost an hour late and Mr. Schmidlap rapped his wristwatch gloomily and glanced at me. That entire day I tried to figure out what had led my father to cry so openly and worried about what might be going on in the Regent Park apartment. After work, on the streetcar, different scenes flashed through my mind, but the one that I wasn't prepared for when I returned to the apartment was the sight of Uncle Boysie sitting on our couch and dressed in a London Fog trench coat, black serge pants and white gloves. He also had on a broad, striped tie. On his head was a Panama straw hat that tourists to Trinidad usually wore. The only thing missing was a butterfly net. In fact he looked exactly like a tourist but dressed for the wrong climate.

"Where you going?" I asked him, glancing around to make sure there was no unconscious body lying around.

"Montreal."

"This time of the evening? And wearing that? You know how far Montreal is from here?"

"You have a aunt living they, boy. You mother cousin. She married some bottomhole, I can't remember his name." He fished into his coat pocket, maybe for the address. I realized he was thinking of the country's size in Trinidadian terms, where "extra long trips" were any that exceeded an hour.

"Montreal is nearly six hours away by train."

"So I dress up for nothing then? What it have closer?"

"What you looking for?"

"It have any nearby rumshop?"

I felt this was his aim all along but I had to tell him, "I don't think so. In any case they might be closed up by now."

"What about these joints?"

"What sort of joints?"

"Joints, nah man. Pussyahs."

"Strip joints?"

"Righto pappyo." He grinned.

"I think I usually pass one on Yonge Street."

"Pass? Only pass?"

"I believe you have to be eighteen to go in."

"You not eighteen yet? Look how tall you get in one year."

"I will turn eighteen in February."

"Listen, boy, you is a man once you does pee froth. Now tell me if you prefer the outfit I land in or this one?" He changed hurriedly; and on our way to the Dundas streetcar he told me, "Consider tonight a early birthday gift." I glanced at his fur coat and hat and prepared myself for the worst. But he was in completely different mood from the previous night and I wasn't sure if he was playing when he called Union Station *Onion Station,* or when he glanced at a poster of the Maple Leafs and said, *hawk-key,* stretching the first syllable as if he was clearing his throat. When we got off at the Yonge station he pulled his coat tightly around him and asked, "Like you in a hurry to get to the place or what?"

"Everybody does walk fast here. Cause it so cold."

"It damn cold in truth. I feeling it right through me pyjamas."

"You wearing pyjamas under your pants?"

"I prepared for anything."

I didn't know what he was talking about and I was afraid to ask. I slowed my pace to match my uncle's but the minute he spotted the sign, Pink Pussycats, the letters flashing in red and yellow, it was I who had to keep up with him. His face lit up as he passed under the billboard with a flashing naked woman. I followed him inside. He chose a front table. A woman with nothing on top came over and asked for our order. Uncle Boysie looked at her breasts as if he was fixing to feast. I almost bolted when he leaned over like if he was planning to smell the woman's breasts, but he tipped his hat in an old-fashioned way and someone at a nearby table applauded, either at the woman or Uncle Boysie's courtesy. I felt embarrassed to be sitting right next to him as he bawled out, "Pussyah, girl!" and "Wine and shake it good," and "Clamp that pole tight." By the end of the night, I was sure he had spent more than a hundred dollars but he didn't seem too concerned. A man who was dressed almost the same as my uncle kept glancing at him suspiciously. On our way back Uncle Boysie talked endlessly about the different variety of breasts he had seen and about where these women had shaved and what he would do if he had a girlfriend like one of the strippers. Then he got back to the breasts. "I prefer mine like grapefruit. The watermelon variety does look nice but in a couple years they does turn to long papaw. The coconut type not too bad either but they too kissmeass stiff. I like them to jiggle." He mentioned several other fruits, and insisted on calling the place "the Pink Pussyah." I had never seen this side to him and I wondered if his monthly restocking trips to Port of Spain had been all business. Or his weekend journeys to San Fernando to see Abdullah the Butcher wrestle.

Then he moved to bottoms. He said very seriously, "You know the bottom is the best part of a woman. It give you a good idea of what kinda shape she in. It have nothing better in the world than a nice rosy little bottom. It does get me stiff just talking about it. Imagine that, at my age." He began to talk about one of his girlfriends and in his tipsy way, asked if I had ever screwed a Canadian. We were on the streetcar at the time and he was talking loudly. Two old women glanced at us nastily and Uncle Boysie whispered (thankfully), "Look at them two old bat. They get old and they close up shop now. But they still hot like hell, just give them a chance." He winked at the old women and they looked away quickly.

Maybe his mood latched on to me because when he asked again if I had a girlfriend I told him I did and—trying to make her exotic—mentioned all her tattoos. All of a sudden his old "uncle voice" returned. "Eh? Tattoos? She will eat you raw." I remained quiet after that. He stuck with the uncle voice as we were making our way to our building, almost as if we had not spent the last two hours gazing at naked women bending backward, forward, and sideways. In the elevator he said, "You father just disappear this morning. Maybe we should have carried him with us tonight. Woulda be good therapy."

"What therapy?" I asked as I opened the door.

"Something for he nervousness." He gazed around. "Like he gone again. You accustom to this aloneness, boy?"

"Is not all that bad."

"But you alone here in the nights. Nobody to call if any trouble strike. Surrounded by strangers. You know any of these people next door?"

"Everybody here does keep to themselves."

"Yes, I notice that." He placed his hat on the television and sat on the couch. "But you and all practically grow up by youself. No father, no brother, no sister, and hardly any friends too. Was a good preparation for this Cyanadian life. You open the envelope I give to you?"

"I thought it was for my birthday."

"It have a thousand in it. The government tightening up on foreign exchange now so whatever I give you will have to be in instalments."

"You don't have to give me anything, Uncle Boysie."

"And what I will do with all me money? Give it to who?" He loosened his trouser button. "You know something, Sammy? You is the first person in the family who so ambitious. I can't figger out where you get it from. I can't figger it out. Eh?" I wasn't sure if he was asking me a question but I remembered that less than two years earlier Miss Charles, our English teacher at Mayaro Composite, had hinted that most orphans were doomed to become pickpockets and petty thieves. Pantamoolie, my friend, had cast them as willing victims, as he claimed to know of a bunch that had sold kidneys and hearts and stones to rich Germans. But I had thought of other orphans, Batman and Spider-Man, and most of the X-Men and the Legion who had refused to give in; each eventually locating their special power and patiently understanding how to properly use it. Sometimes I placed Loykie in this category, even though he had a mother.

Uncle Boysie was saying, "You mother woulda be happy, boy. Happy like pappy that you working and studying with some plan in mind. You know . . ." He paused.

"Know what?" I had to ask him.

"You know, Sylvie . . . you mother always wanted you to come up here but deep down in she heart, she was worried like hell that you would end up like you father. When she first get sick she give me a letter for you father. She make me promise over and over that I would tell him to send for you and God will punish me if I lie, so I have to tell you that I hold back on that letter for months. Had it right below me cash register all the time. I believe Sylvie write it when she realize that . . ." His voice went a little downhill. "In that sick state, still pretending that he was regularly sending down money. Is only one thing that make me contact you father. One."

Because he got quiet I prodded him, "What, Uncle Boysie?"

"When you father pick up he ass and leave, the plan was that he would send for the two of allyou. One year run into two, and two into three, and still you mother keep telling everybody that it was just a matter of time. I think she stop believing after a while and it was just shame that full she mouth with that talk. Sometimes when I take a little too much grog . . . late-late in the night I does feel that she didn't dead from any damn cancer. She just get tired of waiting." He crossed his legs and pulled up his socks. "After a while Sylvie wasn't sure what she was waiting for. She just fall in the habit."

For a full five minutes I went over the question that had been bothering me for as long as I could remember. I felt embarrassed to ask but decided I might never get the opportunity again. "In the beginning, did my parent ever . . ." But I couldn't continue.

Maybe Uncle Boysie knew what was going through my mind because he answered right off the bat, as if he had come to Canada especially to reveal this to me. "You father was always walking around with his head in the cloud as if he was better than everybody else. He used to wear these raincoats in the hot sun. Once he borrow or buy a old Vauxhall and even after it was haul away by the wrecker he continue wearing fancy driving gloves. He always wanted to be different. One time he decide to open up a dentist business and for a month in Mayaro it had teeth flying out from people mouth or splitting in two or clamping shut on a piece of meat. Nearly kill half the village." He smiled a bit but immediately got serious once more. "That was when he meet you mother. But I didn't like it. I didn't like it one bit. I do some investigations."

I had to prod him as he seemed lost in his recollection. "What you found out?"

"Well, boy, I discover that you father was born in Sangre Grande and he had no idea who his own father was. But you know how *mauvais langue* Trinidad is, so it had a ton of rumours. According to these rumour, his father was anybody from the Portogee shopkeeper to a drunkard fella who was always falling down on the road. Anyways, I find out that you father get kick around from captain to cook when he was growing up. From pillar to post."

"And what about Auntie Umbrella?"

"She get adopt by some Cyanadian missionary. Adopt or servant, I really can't say. But I think she had a different father. Some black stumpy fella, most likely."

"How come nobody ever tell me any of this before?"

"Eh? You know how worried I use to be that you mother might one day reveal this to you. But she and all probably didn't believe anything bad about him. At least not in the beginning." And right there in the living room Uncle Boysie told me how my father would come to his shop where my mother was working at the time, and chat her up with all his big ideas. "One day I get out me *gilpin* and threaten to *planass* him on the spot if he didn't stop his foolishness. The next morning you mother disappear. You sure you want to hear all this, boy?"

"Yes, yes."

"All right then. You is a big man now. You peeing froth. You going to strip place and thing. So as I was saying, I look up and down the island for two weeks before I discover she was in Sangre Grande with you father. I send down a police pardner to rough him up a little bit and bring back you mother home. I thought that was the end of it but you mother begin to sulk like anything. As if I was public enemy number one. She was about eighteen or nineteen then. I had no choice, Sammy."

Uncle Boysie told me how he bought the property on Church Street, renovated the old house on the premise and set up my parents there. He patiently described the process—replacing wood with concrete, building a soakaway at the back, augmenting the foundation, changing the roof, repainting—which was not interesting at all so I interrupted to ask what had caused my father to leave.

"What happen was that he start feeling tie-down. He start complaining about ball and chain." I remembered an earlier statement of my uncle in which he had likened a dreamer with no dreams to a madman. But I also wondered if it was because my father had been kicked around from captain to cook himself. "Everything I expected to happen, happen. The one thing I didn't predict was that after he leave, you mother would blame herself for everything. That was why she never complain. And why she use to act as if one day he would come back to her. She had no choice. Sometimes it make us happier to believe something we know is a damn lie because we does come out better in that picture. Like you and you Timex watch. I know you always believe you father send it down for you but I buy it from a fella in Port of Spain. Everybody use to call him Iron Mike because his entire hand was covered in metal watchbands. Anyways, that is old-time news. You must be throw away that watch years now." He shook his head and in a suddenly jovial voice added, "You see what one night in the Pink Pussyah does do? Make me tongue get loose and *ownway*. Is a dangerous place. Maybe we should visit some other pussyah place instead." He got up wearily, removed his coat and draped it against the sofa, and unrolled the foam.

"I think you should use the bedroom tonight," I told him. He seemed about to protest so I said, "I have to get up early tomorrow and I don't want to disturb you."

Even though he asked, "You sure, boy?" I could see he was relieved.

As he was walking to the bedroom I asked him, "The envelope you gave my father . . . was it the deed for the house in Mayaro?"

"Yeah. My part of the bargain." He pulled in the door.

In the night I wondered if my father had been crying the previous day when he learned my mother had been waiting and waiting and waiting. I wanted to believe that. Just like I wanted to believe the Timex watch had been his gift.

Chapter Seventeen

GOAT AND SIT

The next morning I heard Uncle Boysie quarrelling in the bathroom. "How long I blasted have to wait for the warm water to appear?"

"Just leave it on for a while."

Five minutes or so later I got worried. I knocked then opened the door. Uncle Boysie was in the bathtub, the water lapping his neck and bales of steam swirling around his head. He looked like a fat ogre resting in a grotto. An hour later he was outfitted in his fur coat, his hair slicked back like a gangster, and smelling of coconut oil. He started whistling a calypso in the elevator and I was struck once more by the shift in his mood. In the lobby I noticed the Creole woman gazing from her mailbox to him and she seemed a little confused when he told her, "Is a fine day outside, madam lady senorita. Weather for leather." It was cold and grey and clammy looking with the sort of dampness that seeped past coats and trousers.

"So where you want to go today, Uncle Boysie?"

"Maybe we could check out a wrestling match with André the Giant.

"I think he died."

"Scheme, boy, scheme. He will come back in a couple months as André the Midget." I decided to not argue. At the corner of Dundas he noticed a little white dog with a sweater and asked, "So what them puppy does wear in summer? Bikini and sliders?" In the streetcar I inquired about his proposed itinerary once more and he asked, "How far this bus does go?"

"To the subway going south to Union. From there you could take a train."

"To Montreal?"

I decided to not mention Via Rail. "To Oshawa in the east."

"But ain't Ottawa close to Montreal?"

"That is a different place."

In Union Station he kept bouncing into busy travellers and I was afraid he might begin to quarrel but he was in a good mood. Reading the Go Transit sign, he said, "Goat-and-sit," as if he expected the station to be lined with animals waiting for the next train. We bought two coffees and the woman, plump-ish with a pleasant face, told him, "Have a nice day, hon."

At the counter he startled the young black clerk by saying, "Two tickets, hon." Once we had settled on the upper berth I explained that "hon" was not typically a man-to-man thing. But he was busy gazing at the bulldozers and excavators. "Like they pulling down the city or what?" he asked. And a couple minutes later, "Look at all them 'bandon train park up in that old garage. I wonder if they will sell them?" He speculated on how he might use them in Trinidad: a couple carriages on the Churchill-Roosevelt Highway stocked with *doubles* and delicacies, and a few close to the Mayaro market loaded up with soursop and sapodilla and coconuts. I had this vision of green and white carriages lining all the roads in Trinidad with vendors peeping from the windows. Auntie Umbrella had showed me a side to Canada that I had pushed aside because of my worries at the time, but Uncle Boysie was focusing only on the odd aspects. "That lake frozen no ass, boy. It look like a piece of the sky just drop off and land they." And later. "But ay ay, how all them house so similar? You could easily go to the wrong house by mistake. Different pussyah." He glanced at a huge sign. "Wait a minute, Gooberdhan from Rio Claro have business here too?"

"Is Gooberham."

"And what I say?" When we approached Pickering I was tempted to visit Javier and Carmen but remembered Uncle Boysie saying that my tattoo girl would eat me raw. Soon we approached Ajax and I felt a bit of regret about leaving Carmen's city. "How you so quiet, boy? Pussyah get you tongue or what?" I forced a little smile for his sake. The train stopped in Oshawa where we bought two westbound tickets. In Burlington we took another train and in an hour and a half we were once more in Oshawa. I worried about the number of times we were going to repeat our trip but soon Uncle Boysie began to snore quite loudly. I wondered how many of the nearby travellers were also contemplating if this modern train had suddenly reverted to an old chugging engine.

I believe his sleepy mood remained with him because when we got home and he spotted my father before the television he yawned and asked, "I thought you was back in Mayaro already, boy." My father smiled sheepishly. I wished they would chat about my father's time in Mayaro and bring up small lumps of information I had no idea about but Uncle Boysie said, "This travelling does make you real sleepy. I could use the bedroom, Sammy?"

A few minutes later my father asked me, "So allyou meet anybody in particular?"

"No. We was just travelling. Uncle Boysie was thinking about importing the abandoned carriages to use as vendor stalls in Trinidad."

A couple months earlier he might have mentioned something about "oompa loompa" or "assness" but all he said was, "He have the money. He could afford it." I tried to gauge from his voice if there was any bitterness or sarcasm but it seemed just a plain statement. I wondered if I was losing the ability to read him.

"Uncle Boysie was telling me about your teeth business in Trinidad."

"Yeah? What he say?"

"That you couldn't get the right adhesive so you had to use *laglee*. The sap from *chataigne* tree."

"People don't eat properly in Mayaro. Eat mostly with their front teeth. Like rodents." It was a criticism but still the funniest thing he had ever said. In the television MacGyver was slowly mixing some ingredients to blow a hole in a concrete wall. A worried woman was watching a ticking bomb. "Time running out," my father said, his eyes fixed on the screen. A few minutes later he unrolled the blanket at his side and wrapped himself, tucking the ends around his shoulders. I switched off the lights, spread the foam and fell asleep to the woman's increasingly hysterical voice.

During the following days I took Uncle Boysie to the Exhibition Place, and the St. Lawrence Market, and the Skydome, and Harbourfront where he sat on a bench facing the lake and ate four hot dogs, one after the other. Each day, though, he got quieter and I didn't know if it was the temperature, or sadness that his vacation was coming to an end. He inquired over and over about my college and my finances and whether I could manage here all by myself. He even asked if I might be more comfortable in Mayaro. I didn't want to mention my loneliness of a week earlier so I told him that there were far more opportunities in Canada. He seemed relieved. Later at an art gallery I felt that my occasional sadness really stemmed from a series of disconnected pictures—the Julie mango tree in full bloom, fishermen pulling their seine in the mornings, my mother by the sewing machine watching my approach from school, the Amazing Absorbing Boy hidden in the swamp—that were like panels from different comic books.

In any case I didn't want to think of Mayaro at this time. Uncle Boysie had done so much for me and I wanted him to enjoy the couple days remaining. Two days before his departure I asked him if there was some place he would like to visit before he left. I even offered a hint. Pussyah. Even though he glanced at me suspiciously, we landed that night at the Pink Pussycat place once more. The dancers came on and did their routines but Uncle Boysie didn't shout encouragement as before. We left in less than an hour. In the streetcar he told me, "All this excitement not right for a man my age." From his voice I guessed something specific was on his mind so I waited for some kind of explanation. "This week pass fast, boy. I only have one day again. I leaving on Sunday, you know." He looked at me and I nodded. "But I will be lying if I tell you that I not worried."

"You shouldn't worry about—"

He held up a hand. "Let me finish. You might think this is just a old man talking *chupidness* but I always consider you like a son." He took a deep breath and drew his coat more tightly around him. "This place cold no ass, boy. I don't know how you does manage here. With the coldness and you job and you big time studies. And with you father. You know how he surviving here?" I didn't know what he was referring to so I shook my head. "He does get a little cheque every month from some kinda workman compensation for a breakdown a couple years aback."

"What sort of breakdown?"

"Nerves."

"Nerves?"

"I don't know how to describe it. I used to hear about a couple people in Trinidad with the same problem. Is like a situation halfway between normal and mad and season up with plenty acting. Remember one of them place we pass on the train? With-me or something."

"Whitby?"

"Yeah. He was in a hospital there for people with nerves. People who"—he hesitated—"couldn't cope."

He got quiet.

"Trap. Trap. Oompa loompa."

"What you say, Sammy?"

"Nothing uncle."

We got off from the streetcar and walked towards the apartment. "I tell you father that he have to fix up this sponsorship business before he leave."

"Leave Regent Park?" I was still thinking of my father at some psychiatric place in Whitby.

"Canada."

"He leaving?"

"Take it easy, take it easy." He placed a hand on my shoulder. "You remember that envelope I give him the first night? Well, you know it was the deed to the property in Mayaro. I can't tell you how it *hut* me heart to give him that but it was you mother wish. She say that he never return when she was living but he might come back when she dead. The property in both of allyou name." I felt this conversation between my father and uncle had taken place on the day I saw my father crying. I had seen Uncle Boysie deal with a couple of his workers and I knew how rough he could be. I wondered at the threats he had made to my father.

When we got to the apartment I hoped that my father would be home but Uncle Boysie said, "The lagahoo gone again. God might punish me for this but I hope he have a hard time in Mayaro. Every time he spot you mother sewing machine or she decorations or the flowers she plant all over the place. You does think about she?"

Nearly every day. But I told him, "Not directly."

I really didn't want to talk about my mother, not even with Uncle Boysie, who was closer to her than anyone else. In the days after her funeral when I was in Uncle Boysie's place I had this feeling that she was still in the small house tending her bougainvillea and crotons and hibiscus; I pretended that I was on an extended holiday, no different from the occasional weekends I sometimes spent at my uncle's place. She had died during my term exams, and on the day of my final subject, chemistry, I passed by the house.

The bougainvillea had grown taller—and briefly I had this picture that they were straining to look for her—and wispy silvery vines had invaded the clump of crotons, but apart from this, the house seemed the same. I had stood at the front entrance for maybe ten minutes, trying to convince myself that my mother was gone and at the same time nourishing the tiny dust of hope that it was all a dream.

I had heard many times that the spirit of dead people never wanted to leave in a hurry and I wondered what I would do if I saw the machine pedalling by itself. One of the windows was partially open and when I went to shut it, a pigeon flapped out from the outside ledge. That window was where

I sometimes saw her on my way from school. I looked at the coconut trees and listened to the faint sound of the sea, carried by the breeze in little gasps. It sounded like a distant moaning. I remained there, on her chair, until I saw the shadows loosened and thrown across the trees like a big black bag. I wondered what may have been going through her mind as she sat there, evening after evening. That night, while I was walking to my uncle's place, I felt that there were these tiny pieces of me that had turned to ice and others that were hot and burning up. Like the Composite Superman, except that my powers were of Iceman and the Human Torch.

Other fantasies, other super hero powers, like that of the unfeeling android, Vision, and the Silver Surfer, who had no home and was forced to roam the universe, danced in my head during the nine months I stayed by Uncle Boysie's place; until the day of my flight to Canada, when I imagined that I was flying over solid blocks of ice to my Fortress of Solitude. My own little sanctuary, away from all the problems in the world.

As I sat by the kitchen table with Uncle Boysie, I thought of my friend, Loykie, the Amazing Absorbing Boy, with whom I would swap all these superhero fantasies. He was the only other boy who knew all the comic book heroes. He lived twenty minutes away and had no other friend. "So what happened to Loykie?"

"Who?"

"Loykie," I told Uncle Boysie. "The boy who came with his mother to Mayaro a good few years ago. They used to live in the swamp. They came out a couple times with Loykie covered with a sugar bag."

"The boy with the skin disease?"

"Yes, him."

"He drown a couple month ago."

"He drown? Loykie? You sure?"

"Yeah. They never find his body."

The evening before his departure, I took my uncle to Sears and Honest Ed's and the dollar stores, where he picked up all sort of cheap useless items like bird feeders and laser pointers and plastic dog bones. At the end of our shopping trip, Uncle Boysie looked like a big *mash-up* flower with his colourful shopping bags spread out on all sides. When we stopped at a Tim Hortons his bags took up an entire table. I ordered two coffees and Uncle Boysie told me that my father had signed and submitted my sponsorship forms. "Finally he do something for you. But I had to push him." He said the problem with my father was that he never got out from his make-believe world and so he could never change. Although I knew where my uncle was coming from, all his talk of change just got me thinking once again of the Amazing Absorbing Boy, who would pretend that he could transform himself into the same material of whatever he touched, and for a moment I pretended he was sitting at the corner table, all by himself and touching the cup and the table and the wall and turning into paper and wood and concrete.

Chapter Eighteen

THE AGE OF IMPROVISATION

I missed Uncle Boysie more than I had anticipated. He had never taken me to a hotel as he promised and I had never explained to him what a typical Canadian might be. Nevertheless, I felt he had achieved what he came for, which was getting my father to sponsor me. He said that my father's agreement was really part of a bargain into which he had been pushed but I pretended he had intended to sponsor me all along. Maybe because of my fabrication I began to see little broken up pieces of friendliness pushed by him my way. Mainly small murmurings about the demolition going on in Regent Park. But it could be that Uncle Boysie had changed him from being a cold and faraway stranger into someone who wore fancy gloves in Trinidad and who suffered from nerves and who spent time at a psychiatric place. I couldn't forgive him but I knew him better. Most evenings when I returned from Queen Bee I would see him smoking in the balcony and surveying the demolition.

Every week some new section of Regent Park was torn down. There were bulldozers and backhoes and excavators and small Bobcats ripping down walls and tearing up sidewalks and piling mounds of rubble all over the place. When I was a boy, long before I discovered the DC and Marvel worlds and the thick *Classics Illustrated;* even before my interest in sharks and dinosaurs, I used to be fascinated with all these machines that seemed like iron monsters with huge arms and jaws. Together with the other Mayaro boys, I had fashioned clumsy trucks and vans with empty sardine cans as trays and bobbins for wheels. Sometimes I imagined that I was driving one of the forklifts at the coconut-husking factory near to the Amazing Absorbing Boy's swamp.

I don't think the other Regent Park residents were as thrilled with the machines because every other day I saw some new notice on our door mentioning another meeting to protest the "forced relocation to market value condominiums," and the "unwarranted attack on poor people," and even one about police brutality. Important officials came and had their pictures taken with some of the petitioners and promised this and that but the machines continued their tramping and levelling. Immigrant focus groups and advisory committees were formed and the members also had their pictures in the *Star* and the *Sun,* appearing mad and worried and determined. Once the Creole woman knocked on our door and asked for my father. I told her truthfully that I had not seen him for the last two days, and because she remained by the door just shaking her head I added that he planned to return soon to Trinidad.

It seemed as if she was just waiting to hear this because she gave me a long speech about how Canada was a perfect place until you bounced up your first hurdle. "Is then and only then you realize that you don't have a neighbour you could call from across the road to help fix your car. Or a third cousin to check out that loose wiring or fix the leak below the sink. Is you and you alone and with every passing minute the place start getting colder and the ice slipperier and the smiles more frozen and the pace of everybody faster. You hear me, Samuel? Like if they running away from you. This place perfect if you have money and if you luck hold out but if that is not the case then *crapo* smoke you pipe. Ah Lord Lord Lord." She had a Caribbean accent but it was difficult to determine if it was Trinidadian.

"So you going back?"

"Going back, Samuel? Go back to what? My life here."

In the following days I thought of what she had said. She was right about the coldness though. January went away slowly and in February the cold seemed newborn and frisky, as if had not been hanging around for the last three months. In Trinidad, I believed winter lasted only one month and that it went away with the Christmas carols, but every week the days got shorter, the nights falling at the same time that the fishermen in Mayaro were preparing for their last haul and the *dasheen* planters were still toiling in their fields. It was so still on some evenings, with no breeze ruffling the trees or shovelling up dust from the road, I felt that an invisible ray had frozen everything in place.

It seemed as if I had spent far more than a year in Canada, maybe because so much had happened ever since I landed in my father's apartment. Things were tough in the beginning, really tough, but I really had to count myself as lucky. Uncle Boysie's money had been granted at the correct time, as was his agreement with my father that led to me being sponsored. According to the Creole lady, "*crapo* would have smoked my pipe" if I wasn't being sponsored, as it would have been impossible to pay the tuition fees.

Same with the choice of a programme. For months I had bothered my head with courses in baking and electronics and even dentistry but the correct course was right before my eyes. At least when I was in Queen Bee. And so I signed up for a diploma in Communication and Culture, where half of the courses had something or the other to do with films. I knew I had made the correct choice when on the first day of class, a short Chinese man with the neatest moustache in the biggest head I had ever seen wrote his name on the board. Dr. Michael Yee Fang.

Dr. Fang's course was on internet films and during the first week he showed us more than two dozen five-minute films, some of which he claimed had been shot on cellphones. He said that soon films and books and television shows would have to be shorter because nobody wanted to be tied down to the same thing for too long. Maybe my father was from the future. In any case, this was much better than watching movies from the pit in Liberty cinema in Rio Claro as people there were always shout-ing at the actors and flicking cigarettes at the screen whenever a villain appeared. Every month there was a small fire in the cinema. Once when Dr. Fang was carrying on about all these new internet films and streaming videos and compression techniques I remembered Danton's proposed movie about everyone dying at a young age because their minds had grown accustomed to only handling short tasks. Dr. Fang said this was the age of improvisation and that anyone who could not adapt would be annihilated. It was an interesting comic-book word and for a minute or so I imagined Dr. Doom or Lex Luthor saying it. Dr. Fang, though, spoke in a quiet normal way (except for the word "usually" which he could never pronounce).

Another course was on propaganda. This was taught by a old bald-pated man who was always fanning himself with his lecture notes. His skin was thin and oily and it reminded me of the pale paper with which Mayaro grocery owners wrapped butter and cheese. He wore the same pants and grey coat to every class and his stop-and-start voice alone was enough to send me into a deep sleep. Worse, he gave us extra long reading lists that he expected to be covered for the subsequent class. In Trinidad whenever anyone used the term propaganda it was to express disbelief. People would say, "Nah, man. That is just propaganda," if they were told that so-and-so wife was fooling around. I tried to make this class interesting by digging up other Trinidadian examples, and sometimes I had to force myself to not smile when I recalled the lies told by Pantamoolie and my other friends at Mayaro Composite.

The most interesting course by far was that on folklore, and not only because it was taught by a pretty lady who wore only shades of green, and who scattered her fingers across her cheek as she leaned forward on her desk and gazed at us; I liked this course because it was the only one where I had a special knowledge of nonsense superstitions like shape shifting *lagahoos* and ball-of-fire *souyoucants*. The teacher's name was Miss Latanya Lemptiski and she commanded us to only use her first name. She looked too pretty to be a real professor.

On the third week of her class she wrote *avatar* on the board. I thought she was going to lecture about Hindu gods but instead she licked her finger, flipped through her loose notes and began talking about video games. I felt sort of bad, as this was the first time I didn't have a clue what she was talking about. As some of the other students began to boast about their Playstation games and their own avatars I realized how green I was in this field. I never owned a Playstation or Xbox or the other toys the students spoke about. I began to focus instead on Latanya's light green blouse with no top button and on her habit of licking her finger whenever she intended to turn a page. Then she mentioned doppelgangers.

The Xbox crowd seemed mystified but she got my attention instantly. I had come across these doppelganger impostors in comic book series like *Crisis on Infinite Earths* and in the Frank Miller *Batman* books and Chris Claremont *X Men* annuals. Nearly every superhero had his or her own doppelganger. Superman had Bizarro, Wolverine had Sabretooth, Spider-Man had Venom and the Justice League had an entire alternate universe. I was disappointed when that class came to an end.

While I was walking to the subway I pretended that all these people with their necks pulled into their coats had duplicates running around in a warm beach, and when I got home and spotted my father staring as usual from the balcony I imagined he was creating his own doppelganger that smiled and grew excited as it paused from its inventions to look out of a window at swaying cornbirds' nests and spindly heliconias. That night I wanted to talk to him of my class so I remained by the kitchen table and when he slid shut the balcony door, rubbed his hands and sat before the television I told him we had studied avatars in class. He seemed puzzled so I repeated the teacher's statement about shapeshifters that could replace a real person so perfectly that no one, not even family, was able to detect it was an imposter. He seemed to be thinking about this but then he leaned forward and turned on the television. MacGyver was making some kind of walkie-talkie with a cordless phone. "That wouldn't work," my father said. "You going about it the wrong way. If was me I would have used a nine volt adaptor from the radio. The entire thing will blow up when you plug it in to phone the police."

The next day at work I phoned Javier but got his grandmother who said something in Spanish. I was about to hang up when I heard another voice on the extension. I said I had called for Javier and during a pause I mentioned our classes together at the Centennial campus.

"Sam? I thought you had abandoned us and gone back to your swampy boy."

I felt a little tickle in my stomach from hearing Carmen's musical voice. "Abandon you, my dear? How could I?"

"What?"

"Oh God, sorry. I was looking at a movie poster on the wall." I felt if I continued I would begin to stammer like Sporty.

"Really? Are you in a cinema?"

"I work in a video store."

"Cool. Can you get me a movie with Javier—" She began to giggle. "Javier Bardem, the actor, silly." We chatted for close to half an hour. She told me that her brother was now in Durham College doing his law enforcement course and she was volunteering at Heathcliff Retirement Home where many of the old people had Alzheimer's just like her grandmother. "It's so sad. They can't recognize anyone." She now believed that the only thing separating adults from children was memories. This was impressive and soon she cheered up and said I should not be "a stranger." I said I was busy with my college courses but I would definitely call again. I would have liked to chat longer but she had to go to her retirement home.

"Abandon you, my dear." It was Mr. Schmidlap. I had no idea he had been listening and I couldn't tell from his face whether he was joking or chastising.

"A friend," I told him. "Her grandmother has Alzheimer's."

He blinked slowly twice and returned to his corner table. Just before we were closing I went over to him and said I would have to leave the job, as I needed to devote more time to my assignments. He put his hands into his jacket pocket as if we were going to have a long conversation. I mentioned the difficult propaganda course and threw out some names recently mentioned by the professor. Zedong. Rumsfeld. Goebbels. He blinked slowly, one-two-pause, one-two-stop, as if we were communicating in code. To tell the truth I felt sorry for him then and I wondered if old people had a hard time dealing with any upset to their schedule. On Saturday, my last day at work, I brought him a Thor action figure. I got it for only five dollars at Barbarossa's shop. When I had entered the shop my old boss was telling a young girl with glasses that seemed to be clenching her face that some speed dating centre was four blocks west. I almost walked out of the place as the girl look quite frightened by Barbarossa's loud voice and big head but he spotted me and said, "Mr. Roti Ramirez, if you come back expecting your old job, the position is taken." When I told him I was just browsing he turned his attention once more to the nervous girl.

I bought the Thor figure only because there was nothing else in the shop that suited Mr. Schmidlap and when I gave it to him I had no idea if he would be offended by the rust on the cast iron knees and the peeling paint on the face and the missing hammer but he held it and stroked it and turned it this way and that before he placed it on his corner table.

Latanya finally got to the gods in her next folklore class. She said that these old-time religions were packed with shapeshifters. She mentioned Circe and Pan and Anansi from Africa. The interesting thing about these shapeshifters, according to her, was that they were always up to some sort of mischief, never caring about the consequences. They were quite smart, too, as they had to rely mostly on trickery while battling gods who threw thunderbolts and erupted volcanoes. During her following class she focused on fairy tales I had read in primary school. Who would have imagined that these imps and sprites and wraiths and genies were so important, "altering the balance of power" according to Latanya? She made them seem like the good guys and as she read from her notes I imagined she had a few hidden in her cupboard and a couple pushed under her bed. I was startled when at that exact moment she said that we all had our own shapeshifters.

She gazed at the puzzled students and clarified that every single person had at some time or the other met a shapeshifter. She threw out some names: Shelley and Donne and Goethe, who had bounced up shapeshifters pointing to this or that path. This didn't help and quite a few hands went up, most likely for clarification. And as she explained I felt that her eyes flickered on me as if she had read my mind and knew my biggest secret by far.

Chapter Nineteen

THE AMAZING ABSORBING BOY

The first time I heard of him was from the rumours at Mayaro Composite. A couple of my friends mentioned this boy who had moved with his mother to a house about twenty minutes from ours. The only way to get there was by an access road long abandoned by regular vehicles, and used mostly by hunters returning from the forest and fishermen who sought out the scaly *cascadura*, which liked to live in those swampy areas. It seemed an odd place to live, as all the nasty yellow waste from the coconut-husking factory drained into that corner of the swamp. One of the boys reported that he was the same age as us, about thirteen or so, and we expected him to soon show up at school, and when he did not, the rumours began.

We heard that his mother was a *souyoucant,* who could shed her skin and change into a ball of fire; that his father was an escaped murderer who was hidden away in the house too;

that they had skipped away from Chacachacare, the offshore leper colony; that they were pygmies. When all these interesting stories were exhausted, the class began to speculate on the family's background. Day by day, the family changed from Portuguese to high-caste Indians to Chinese to mixed race *cocopanyols* and finally to albinos. Once Goose, who was an even bigger liar than Pantamoolie, said the father was an old scaly alligator that visited the mother each night. Then one morning, the class prefect, whose father was a game warden, said that the family name was Loykie. This didn't help one bit because it was the sort of name that could apply to nearly all the races in Trinidad. Low Kee, Loakie, Lokhi, Loukoue. I preferred Loykie because its pronunciation reminded me of a character from *Tales of Asgard,* found at the end of *Thor* comics. The only student who claimed to have actually seen him was Pantamoolie. He told us that the boy was swinging from vine to vine like Tarzan and each time he hit a tree by mistake he made a screeching sound like a baby dinosaur.

After a while the rumours dried up as new bits of *mauvais langue* displaced the news of this strange family. In school, me and my friends turned our attention to the girls in class who were sprouting breasts and wearing makeup and hiking up their skirts and swinging their bottoms as they walked. After classes, we would improve on the stories we had heard of some of these girls, but every now and again while I was reading a comic, my thoughts drifted to this invisible family. One Saturday morning I stole one of my mother's curtain from the bottom of her dresser and headed for the road where the family lived. I crossed a ravine by stepping on a couple of river stones, as the smelly yellow stuff from the coconut factory was flowing sluggishly in the water. I walked along the riverbank dodging the prickly *grugru* palms and stinging nettles until I got to a shallow basin where the exposed roots of a silk cotton tree looked like huge gnarled fingers. I held the ends of the curtains tightly and dragged it across the shallow end of the basin but caught just a couple tiny guppies that I threw back into the water. I went further upstream and trawled the curtain, catching a river shrimp and a spiteful baby crab that raised its *gundee* at me. Once more I followed the ravine, looking for a deepish patch where there might be sardines, and if I was lucky, a couple *cascadura*. About twenty minutes or so later, I noticed a muddy ribbon of water that meant someone was fishing further up. I climbed onto the bank and followed the ribbon to its source, but whoever had been fishing upstream had left in a hurry. I returned the next day but it was the same story.

This went on for about three weekends (my mother by then was becoming suspicious about the missing curtains from her drawer so I had to substitute a doily) and I felt this mysterious fisherman was playing with me. One evening I shouted out, "Hello. Who there?"

I repeated the question and was about to leave when I heard from a clump of balisier, "Me."

"Who is me?" There was no reply so I shouted once more, "What you doing here?"

"I searching for *crapo*-fish."

"Tadpole? Why you catching tadpole?"

I got the answer the next weekend. "I does mind them."

"Why? They not good to eat."

This went on for close to a month; me asking the question and this fella answering from inside the balisier. Finally I asked him, "Why you hiding inside the bush?"

"I like it here."

"I don't believe you. Who could ever like a nasty place like this?"

"Okay then. I catching caterpillars."

"That just as stupid like catching tadpoles." I added a little taunt. "I feel you does eat them. Make a nice soup."

The leaves of the balisier shook a bit and I heard a small chuckle. "Caterpillar soup! Who ever hear of that?" I saw the long leaves parting and he came out, almost stumbling over the knotted roots. Even though he was some distance away and the meagre light was shredded into tiny ribbons by the bamboo overhead, I felt that I had come face to face with the freakish Thing from *The Fantastic Four*. I grabbed my doily and ran as fast as I could.

Three days later I told my mother I was going to a cricket practice in the recreation ground. As soon as I passed the factory I retraced my route till I came to the silk cotton tree. I must have shouted hello for half an hour before I got a reply. "You don't have to bawl so. You will frighten away all the river moroccoys."

"Moroccoys could hear?"

"Better than me and you."

"How you know that?"

"I have a couple as pets. And they could run real fast when nobody watching them. Climbing up tree even."

"Bring them for me to see."

"They don't like strangers."

"Just like you? Why you always hiding in the shadow?"

"From the sun. It make my skin itch and burn."

"Why your skin like that? And what is your real name?"

"Stop asking all these foolish questions." He retreated back to the balisier clump and said nothing after that.

During the next visit I decided I would ask no further questions but just looking at him the words spilled out. After a long silence he said he had some disease that sounded like Harlequin. I asked if had anything to do with the romance novels the girls in my class read. I believed he laughed at that, although it could have been the hollow sound made by the bamboo as they scraped against each other. He asked about the girls in my class and I dropped some names. Did I have a girlfriend?

A couple, I lied.

He asked me to describe the main one and I combined a couple of the girls in one big sexy description. Rita and Saroop daughter and Tammy who everyone called Tammyflu as she was always sniffling. Did I ever kiss her, he wanted to know, and when I said yes he asked how she tasted. Like chewing gum, I replied quickly, and just to break this long list of lies I asked once more why he was living in this swampy place. He told me he was searching for a Hogzilla. Then he changed his mind and said it was an Alligatorzilla. We began talking about comics. I told him that my favourite was the Phantom, who took his father's role with none of the jungle people suspecting the substitution. His favourite was Green Lantern. While I was making my way out of the swamp I wondered if his choice had been made because the entire place was so green. Everything but the yellow slush from the coconut factory. I remembered that yellow was the only colour immune to his hero's powers.

Soon we began talking mostly of superheroes. One week he changed his mind and said his favourite was now the Martian Manhunter. I tried to match that by bringing up the Watcher, who was always around whenever there was serious trouble but who could not interfere even if an entire planet was threatened. He then hit upon the Silver Surfer.

He was good at this game. During every encounter, I waited for him to mention the scaly Thing but he always selected superheroes who were not really popular but who had incredible powers. Finally he chose the Amazing Man and stuck with that. I had no idea who this character was, and it took a while before I was able to buy a comic that featured him. His real name was Will Everett and he was a black man who could transform into the substance of whatever he touched. In the comic I'd bought, he was tricked into touching glass and he was shattered but my new friend told me that the character had died a couple times before but was always revived by the comic book writers.

A couple weeks later I brought a comic featuring Crusher Creel, the Absorbing Man. This was a Marvel character and his powers were similar to the DC Amazing Man. At the end of the story, he was tricked into touching water. My friend didn't like this character as much, maybe because he was a villain, but he was fascinated by the water death. "This is the perfect trick. Changing to water. He could be in any ocean in the world." I had to point out that the character had died, but he didn't buy it. "All he have to do is reconstitute." It was a big word and I guessed he had picked it up from one of his *Amazing Man* comics. "These absorbing people can't die. They just change from one thing to the other."

That was true. We soon discovered other superheroes with similar powers. They all had obvious names like Parasite and Copycat and Chameleon, and they treated their power as a blessing and a curse. My friend explained why. "Sometimes you might touch something ugly. Or dangerous. Or something that you don't know too much about and then begin to show-off with this new power. It easy to get tricked then." I waited for him to say he had touched an alligator. "But still, is the best power in the world, if you know how to use it. You could beat Superman just by becoming like him."

"But is not a real power," I told him. "Is just imitating."

"No, is more than that," he said after a while. "Every time you change you keep a little dust of that substance inside you." I had never read of that and I felt he had just made it up. I noticed too that he was talking as if he had these absorbing powers himself. I began thinking of him as the Amazing Absorbing Boy.

I kept our meetings a secret for more than a year, but during a boastful speech by the game warden's son about some big manatee his father had caught, I blurted out my weekly encounter with the Amazing Absorbing Boy. I told my classmates that his orange-red skin was covered with scales that were so thick, when he knocked on them, they made a hollow sound. Nothing could harm him, I said. He was as tough as an alligator. His best power, though, was his ability to control all the scaly animals in the forest, all the *tattou* and moroccoy and *cascadura*. Everyone laughed and I realized this was the kind of story we routinely made up to pass the time. I knew then I would have to get him out of the swamp.

During the following weeks I tried to tempt him with descriptions of the beach early in the morning, and Mrs. Bango's parlour stuffed with cakes and sweeties, and all the stores at the Mayaro junction, many with comics hanging on clothesline over the hunting knives and fishing hooks, and the fancy houses being built by these American oil people; during all this time, I felt like one of these circus people who captured hairy women and wolf boys to display in cages. In the end I was glad that he resisted my traps, time and again, with his mother's strict warnings.

My friends never swallowed my exaggerated descriptions but word soon reached my mother through the village-gram. As I expected, she hit me with her usual talk about making up fancy stories just like my father, but one morning after she had discovered the clump of muddy curtains below my bed, she asked about the boy. She listened patiently and though she didn't say whether she believed or not, at the end of my little speech, she asked where this family got their food from, if they never came out from the swamp. The next evening I noticed a parcel with two currants roll on the kitchen table. I believed my mother had left it there for me to take for the boy and on my way to the swamp I passed by Mrs. Bango's parlour and bought some tamarind balls and paradise plums and a couple packs of powdery *chilli bibi*.

In my haste that day I forgot my doily, but the minute I got to the silk cotton tree I asked the Amazing Absorbing Boy where he got his food from. He said that they fished and set traps and grew their own food. I told him I had brought a gift and he told me to leave it by the bank. The next day the bag was empty but for the ants running all over.

"How it tasted?" I asked him.

"Real nice. Better than *balata* and *caimite*."

I felt guilty for not bringing any snacks that day and tried to change the subject. I asked if he could wear shirts. He explained that the cloth chafed against his scales. I asked if he had been born this way and he said that he had, just like his father. People used to pelt his father with stones. I believe he preferred our super-hero talk to this line of questioning and when, for two weeks, he did not respond to my call from the ravine, I felt he had decided to avoid me. But then, braps, just like that, he turned up again, standing before the balisier patch. He told me that he had been in the San Fernando hospital for some treatment. He talked a bit of his disease and said that his father, who had left him boxes of comics, had disappeared when he was seven and he never knew if it was from shame or if he had been killed. I remember pretending that maybe his father had not learned to use his absorbing powers properly.

From then on, he disappeared during the last weekend of every month. I wondered why no one had seen him and his mother on their way to the hospital and, sometimes, I imagined the drunk and sleepy passengers in the 11:30 Guaya late-bus, bawling down the place when the Amazing Absorbing Boy and his mother got on board.

When they did show up, the reaction of the Mayaro people was completely different. I was *liming* by Mrs. Bango parlour at the time when I heard a terrible commotion. People were shouting from their houses and dogs were barking and children were bawling. At first I thought it was another rumshop fight that had spilled onto the road, but I could hear no cussing, no egging on the fighters; this was a different sort of commotion.

I rushed with the other *limers* to the roadside and saw a plumpish woman, her face covered with a broad white hat holding the hand of a stooped creature. The creature was completely covered with a robe or maybe a tunic made from stitched sugar bags, and a hat that hid his face. The only parts of his body uncovered were his hands and his ankles and it was impossible to miss the alligator scales. Women ran back to their galleries, from where they called out to their children, who in turn ran back shrieking as the pair drew closer. Bill, the sergeant, was hiding behind a standpipe and even Mano the village *badjohn* was ducking and peeping from behind his bicycle. Then there was complete silence, even from the dogs. I believe everyone was struck by the weight of this event that they would relate years later to their children and grandchildren. It was better than an appearance by the prime minister; maybe a visit by the pope or the queen could compare. As my friend passed the parlour, his hat turned slowly in my direction but everyone was too excited to notice.

There was the same excitement during their other trips through the village, and it soon became like a little carnival, or these biannual visits by the Ministry of Agriculture people to show their films. It was a nice, free pappyshow for the villagers, who noted that they had not yet bitten or attacked anyone. Some of the villagers began referring to him as Moroccoy Man and the *Cascadura* and once I heard a neighbour threatening her son by saying, "If you continue coming out last in test I will make the *tattou* bite you *duncy* little head off." However, I stuck with the name I had chosen during our superhero chats, a combination of the Absorbing Man and the Amazing Man. I never asked him about these trips and he never mentioned them, but from my school friends I heard that he had been seen wandering around the beach and other places I had mentioned to him, dressed in his sugar-bag robe. I felt he was lucky that he had landed up in a place like Mayaro, where people were superstitious and simple and excited by everything different. Where he wouldn't be pelted, like his father. Once he said that the jellyfish on the beach looked like a dead baby and when I asked him how he knew that, he said that a few years earlier he had seen a tiny body floating in the yellow sludge from the coconut factory.

The last time I met him was at my mother's wake. It was late in the night and I was in the little canvas tent before our house. Uncle Boysie and a few others had just left to make preparations for the funeral the next day and there were just a couple old men sleeping on the wooden folding chairs. I, too, was sleeping when I heard a voice to my back. I thought I was dreaming because at this close range, his voice sounded like someone sucking in air and suffocating. I know this will be hard to believe but, sitting right behind me, the Amazing Absorbing Boy told me a story about a woman who had been buried in a field of bullgrass and whenever the wind blew through the tall grass, people would hear the sound of her voice. Singing all her favourite songs. I guessed this was another angle to his Absorbing People stories, or maybe a version of something his mother told him after his father's death, but for some reason, it removed a small slice of my sadness. Not that I believed him or anything, but I liked the idea suggested by his story; that there were always these little pieces left behind, dancing around and joining and connecting and forming new objects. I thought of this while I walked along the beach in the nights, gazing at the waves and trying to get my mother's death out of my mind. It crossed my mind, too, when I returned to our house on the day of my chemistry exam.

As I said, I never saw him again, not even when I went to give him the news of my departure to Canada. I shouted and shouted by the ravine but he never showed up. I even said that my father was an inventor and he might be able to build a machine that would turn his scales into shining glass. Or maybe a new set of skin made from the rubber tree sap. He would use this skin whenever he visited the village, I bawled out to the balisier clump. I even hit on an invisible dye from the *roucou* tree. Still, no answer. Finally on the weekend before my flight, I left an old telescope and a single sheet of paper tucked in a balisier's arm, where I felt he'd be sure to spot it. On the sheet was a four-panel comic book drawing of a boy touching an Eskimo and a big block of ice and a polar bear and a tree with red zigzag leaves. The boy's eyes were big and wide with excitement like the people from *Archie* comics and I hoped he understood that it was supposed to be funny.

The minute I put up my hands and I saw everyone in class gazing at me, I knew I could not tell them this true story of my friend, the Amazing Absorbing Boy. Why? Because then I would also have to mention my first silly thought when Uncle Boysie told me he had drowned, that he would soon reconstitute; because I guessed they would not believe, or worse, would be more interested in this disease of his; because when you really got down to it, he was no more a shapeshifter than I was.

And while the class was waiting and growing impatient I discovered something about the Amazing Absorbing Boy's favourite superheroes: I always felt their most notable traits were their colours, black and blue and silver, and they were all outsiders who were scorned and feared, but at that exact moment, I realized that all of them had been killed off over and over and over.

In the end I told the class about the *lagahoos* who, at nightfall, changed their human forms into that of dogs and donkeys, and terrorized all the poor villagers. Every village had their own *lagahoo*, and in Mayaro, ours was Amos. Everyone seemed satisfied with my answer and Latanya asked me to spell the word as she wrote it on the board.

Chapter Twenty

FIREFLIES

After this little drift back to Mayaro, my thoughts returned, more and more, to my old village. And while the bulldozers were tearing up Regent Park and this big machine with a ball and chain (just like that used by the Absorbing Man when he fought Thor) was knocking down walls; while the older people watched on worriedly from their balconies; while more committees were formed and petitions circulated; during all this time, I was in a place far, far away. In the beginning, this place was warm and humid and there were all these insect sounds in the nights, as if they were carrying on this long conversation behind our house, somewhere in the field of cassava bordered by wild heliconias with their pale yellow flowers (which from a distance looked like frozen baby cornbirds). There were little dirty rumshops close to the beach where the fishermen came to spin their stories, and a Chinese shop where bees and flies buzzed over the bags of sugar and casks of molasses.

But soon something strange happened to this picture I had created of Mayaro. One morning as I was leaving our apartment, when the rumble of the machines had already begun, a shoe museum popped up, right alongside Mrs. Bango parlour. The next day, waterfront trails appeared along the beach, and in less than a week, there were huge glassy buildings along the Mayaro junction and the fish stalls had been replaced with a huge market that sold Greek and Italian and Jewish and Indian food. Soon there were rows of red-leaf trees hidden beneath the coconut palms. Sometimes on the streetcar I imagined some Toronto landmark like Union Station plumb in the middle of the village.

I wondered if my father was also contemplating some version of this combined scenery in preparation for his move to Mayaro and a couple evenings when he returned with hats and caps, the Goodwill tags still attached, I felt he was practising to be a Trinidadian *saga boy*. He wore the hats as he was watching *MacGyver* and each style transformed him from pimp to swindler to drug dealer to Pink Panther spy. Once when he was wearing a bucket hat pulled low over his forehead like Gilligan I noticed him examining what looked like a burn mark on his left hand. It was just above his wrist and I was about to ask how it had happened when I realized it was a tattoo. He was rubbing the tattoo and smirking at MacGyver as if this was some private joke between them. I shifted my position on the table to get a better view. The tattoo seemed to be of a big eye and when I went to the balcony the eye seemed to be following my move. When I returned I swallowed and told him, "That is a nice tattoo."

"Eh? Oh this? Is a flying saucer."

I guessed this was another aspect of his preparation for Mayaro, as most people his age wore tattoos of ships and anchors and rockets, but I pretended it was his final salute to my world.

In the middle of March I visited Javier and once more Carmen accompanied me to the Pickering Go Station. There I told her the story of my friend the Amazing Absorbing Boy and though she had been joking just a few minutes earlier about "the swampy boy" she got quiet and said it was the saddest thing she had heard for a long while. I told her jokingly that she should give me her magic lantern so that I could see him in its dim glow; instead she leaned over and gave me a hug that lasted for five minutes or more. I felt really happy and peaceful then even though I did not squeeze her breast or anything.

It was a very cold night and on the return trip I saw that all the trees were covered with ice. It seemed as if puffs of smoke had frozen and exploded into millions of tiny sparks that were clinging to all the trees and buildings. They looked like fireflies granted one last night of life before they died and they were partying like mad. Maybe it was the gloomy but magical scenery, but I thought of all the people I had met here who I would never see again. In Trinidad I was sure to bounce them up in the beach or some road but it seemed that in Canada I got to know everyone more from their absence, long after they had disappeared. In any case, I had plenty practice with this. As the train approached Toronto I saw the pack of bulldozers once more and I remembered Uncle Boysie, in describing the same scene, had remarked that the city looked as if it was being eaten up from the edges. I had thought then of a comic book word, *contagion,* and imagined some slowly spreading alien spore, but now I tried to see the place from his eyes. I wondered what it would look like in ten or twenty years and if like the coffee-shop old-timers I too would complain about everything that had been torn down and lost forever. In Mayaro nothing really changed; people lived and died in the same house and arguments between neighbours lasted for years but here it seemed that every week something new was added. No wonder the chimera fella from the library could never finish his Toronto poem.

I guess all these thoughts were swinging through my head because my professors at Centennial were forever talking about adaptation and improvisation. My courses there finished at the end of May and even though I was relieved to have passed all three I was surprised at the early completion date. In Trinidad classes always ended in July. For two weeks I walked around the city and noticed what I had previously missed—every street had its own style. Before everything had seemed big and shiny and connected but I saw buildings that could have popped straight out of some dingy section of San Fernando and others that seemed so ancient and grand with their turrets and fancy windows and solid walls, it was easy to imagine ghosts roaming around in secret passages.

During one of these strolls I walked into Barbarossa's shop, but as he was harassing a new employee, a boy who resembled Javier, I left quickly. Twenty minutes later I wandered into Queen Bee and Mr. Schmidlap glanced from behind his Thor statue and crooked his finger at me. When I walked over he asked where I had disappeared during the last two months and I wondered whether he had Alzheimer's like Carmen's grandmother. I returned the next evening and took my place behind the counter.

Soon winter went away and everything smelled fresh and grassy. In Mayaro, the old people always said this odour signalled that a snake was nearby but here instead of snakes there were squirrels and birds and hundreds of geese. The geese looked real plump and tasty and I wondered if anyone had ever pushed one of them into a bag and rushed to his apartment for a nice meal.

A couple of the Regent Park residents began moving out to other areas. Those who remained were real worried about their own impending move with all the new travel costs, and splitting up from neighbours and friends, and losing the parks and roads they knew so well. One night I heard a very tall man saying to a woman who reached his shoulder, "Press-shure. Is true press-shure we facing." Another night I saw a group of people gathered around a big notice stuck on our apartment doorway. The Creole woman was quarrelling with a small Sri Lankan man with a perfectly straight moustache. I think it was a nasty argument because they began to call each other really insultive names. Soon two groups formed around the two quarrelling people, Creole people on one side and Sri Lankans on the other. I was a little surprised because I was sure I had spotted some of those now on opposite sides chatting in the laundry room. I left in a hurry and returned late in the night to see what they had been arguing about. The notice said that our apartment was scheduled to be demolished in six months.

The next day my father disappeared. That same evening after work I walked to Union and bought a return ticket to its furthest northward destination. The bus stopped at Barrie and when I got back to Union it was close to midnight. A few young women, some with backpacks, dropped out here and there and I thought that in Trinidad they would never travel alone this late. Earlier that week Uncle Boysie had written to ask about my father. At the end of the letter he mentioned some little girl whose body was found in a cornfield because her mother had been unable to pay the ransom. A week later I wrote my reply. I said that my father would probably be in Mayaro by the time this letter arrived—which surprised me, as I had not concluded this before. I thanked him for the money sent and said that my interview with the immigration people would be in four months. The next day, once more on the Go Bus, I was sure that my father was gone for good.

Soon I began to choose new routes, travelling further too. Sometimes, I would pass a rundown little town with old shabby building and tired people roaming around the single convenience store, and I would pretend that my father had moved to one of these places, and that he was sitting at that very instant, as the train sped by, on the balcony of a grubby townhouse, smoking and trying to fill in the blank spots in his life and wondering where all the years had gone. But on the return trip, I would see him in Mayaro, in the house that was probably overgrown with all my mother's plants. I wondered what he would think if he heard her murmuring and singing every time the night breeze hit the field of cassava. Most likely he would feel that it was a warbling bullfinch or a *picoplat*.

Maybe it was fitting that my interview for landed immigrant status was conducted by a man who looked a lot like a Canadian animal. The dark circles beneath his eyes made him look exactly like a raccoon but as the interview progressed, they also gave him a cynical and suspicious appearance. In any case I had nothing to hide and I told him of my mother's death and I repeated my age and spelled Mayaro and my father's name as he glanced at the documents before him. He mentioned an engineer from India who had married his own sister he then brought over, and others who sponsored complete strangers, claiming they were their children. I was thinking of this when he asked about my education and I said that I had recently started my second semester at Centennial. How long had I been in Canada he asked? The minute I answered and noticed his suspicious glance I felt that I too could hardly believe I had been here for almost two years.

Soon after my arrival in Canada, I had been filled with wonder and confusion at this new place. At the end of my first week, my father had told me that I had to learn the rules real fast to survive. Now after all this time, I still didn't have a clue what he was talking about. I had come to Canada, expecting I would get to know this person who had left his *Wonder Book of Wonders* and his crazy half-finished inventions behind, but after twenty months, I still didn't know any more of him. I didn't know the type of job he had before his breakdown, what led to his crack-up, if he had a girlfriend, why he was so angry in the beginning, if he felt any little piece of regret about leaving my mother, and things like that. Maybe, if he had remained here, he would have landed up in a coffee shop like the one on Parliament Street, where he would complain about everything and blame everybody but himself. He was like the Spectre or the Shadow or one of these comic-book characters who had no friends or family and slipped in and out of dimensions to change into either hero or villain according to the crisis they faced.

Summer slipped away and the place grew colder but I continued travelling. Sometimes I took several buses to extend the distance; and I discovered that past all the crowded cities with crisscrossing streets, past the shabby smaller towns where my father might be cornered, even past the long stretches of trees and rocks and cultivated fields, there were these old farmhouses with sloping red roofs and wobbly wooden fences and cattle grazing in the surrounding fields. I felt there were ravines in the back of the fields with salmon and cod—and even *cascadura*!—jumping about. And while I was gazing at these peaceful places I would remember my first weeks at Regent Park when I was so comforted by the familiar there, I was afraid to step outside to the strange Bizarro world.

I tried to imagine what lay beyond, all the places Danton had mentioned. North Bay and Timmins and Longlac. Maybe I was too accustomed to small villages and towns because the only way I could wrap my head around places that stretched for hundreds, maybe thousands, of miles was by viewing them as comic-book scenes. With big flapping banners of mist swirling across icy lakes and tiny nibbling animals making freaky *coot-coot* sounds as they scrambled from hole to hole. And snowfall so thick it erased everything else so I could make anything I wanted of the scene. Sometimes there were strange people hiding behind trees, not showing their faces but tracking every move I made. At other times, I pictured crazy old men by their windows aiming their guns at snapping turtles in a pond, or religious scamps with bundles of wives holding pitchforks and babies, or trappers and lumberjacks feasting on moose. Whatever lay out there I wanted to see it all, panel by panel. And when I was finished, I wanted to push on. I couldn't wait for Regent Park to disappear. I even mentioned this in a letter to Uncle Boysie and in his reply—where he stated that my father had not yet showed up in Mayaro—he warned me I should get my foot back on the ground and finish my studies.

He said that I should be careful I didn't fall into a make-believe world like my father and mother, and even though I knew where he was coming from, sometimes, when I am travelling and my mind is slipping all over the place, I would feel that he didn't understand that my world wasn't make-believe but was a patch of every amazing thing I had touched and absorbed, a dust here and a dust there.

GLOSSARY OF TRINIDADIAN VOCABULARY

Word definitions are quite fluid in a Trinidadian context as they depend upon other variables, such as the tone in which a word is expressed. Below are some definitions of Trinidadian words used in this novel.

B

bacchanal. Confusion and scandal.

badjohn. A criminal or violent person.

balata. Hardwood tree found in the forest, used to make furniture and floors.

barra. A kind of flatbread made from chickpeas, used to make *doubles,* a type of sandwich.

C

caimite. Round, dark purple fruit, also called *star apple.*

carite. A popular and tasty fish. Used in fish broth.

cascadura. An edible fresh water fish with bony placoid scales.

channa. Chick peas.

chilli bibi. A dusty snack made with parch (roasted) corn, sugar and cinnamon.

chupidness. Like stupidness but less of a rebuke.

chataigne. A large prickly fruit with edible seeds. Similar to the chestnut.

cocopanyols. Descendants of settlers from Venezuela who intermarried with other ethnic groups in Trinidad. Also *cocoa-panyols.*

commess. Confusion. Frequently refers to scandalous behaviour. Also *commesse.*

crapo. From the French crapaud, meaning 'toad.' Also *crappo.*

crapo-foot handwriting. Poor penmanship.

D

dasheen. Tuberous root of the taro plant.

doubles. Popular street food in Trinidad, made with chickpeas and *barra.*

douennes. The ghosts of children not christened before their deaths. Also *douens.*

downcourage. Frustrate.

duncy. Stupid. Illiterate.

F

fête. Like *bacchanal,* commonly found in English-language dictionaries.

flambeau. A torch with a bottle base.

G

gilpin. A large cutlass. Also *guilpin.*

grop. Bunch, group, or gathering. Also *grap.*

grugru. A palm tree with small edible nuts.

gundee. Crab's claws. Also *gundy.*

H

horning. Committing adultery, being unfaithful.

J

jumbies. Ghosts, often evoked to frighten children.

K

kitecutting. Trying to cut the string of an opponent's kite with a piece of broken bottle.

L

lackarbeech. To duck school or work. Also *l'ecole biche.*

lagahoo. A shapeshifting creature. Often an old man who lives alone and who transforms in the night into an animal.

laglee. Sticky sap from the breadfruit tree. Dried and used to trap birds.

lime/liming. A casual gathering to pass the time.

locho. A lazy drifter. Also *loacho.*

luchette. A digging tool. Once used by road workers.

M

macco. A busy body. Also used to describe a showy object. Also *maco*

maljeau(x). Evil eye. Also *mal yeux.*

mamaguy. Flatter.

manicou. An opossum

mash up. Wreck, ruin; or a combination of different elements.

mauby. A bitter drink made from bark and several spices that is reputed to have medicinal qualities.

mauvais-langue / languing. Spreading gossip or rumours.

mingpiling. Small and skinny. Also *ming piling.*

mooma. Mother.

N

neemakaram. Ungrateful or a betrayal.

nowhereian. A wanderer.

O

obeah. A type of folk magic.

ownway/ownwayness. Stubborn and headstrong.

P

parang. Spanish influenced music, mostly with guitars and maracas, popular during Christmas.

picong. A kind of friendly heckling.

picoplat. Seed-eating bird with a distinctive warble.

planass. A blow with the flat side of a cutlass. Also *planasse.*

pommecythere. An edible fruit, acidic when green but extremely sweet when it ripens. Also called *golden apple.*

pone. Sticky golden cake made from cassava and coconut.

pothound. A stray dog. Often a term of insult.

R

rackling. Jangling metallic sound, as of broken machinery.

roti. A type of flatbread.

roucou. A red dye from the similarly named tree. Also *roukou.*

S

scooch. A game that involves trying to hit an opponent's body with a softball.

saga boy. A ladies' man. Also *sharpman.*

shadow beni. A leafy herb similar in taste to cilantro, but with a stronger flavour. Also *shado beni.*

skeffy. Scheming.

souyoucant. A vampire-like creature. Typically an old woman.

squingy. Wrinkled.

sweetmouth. Flattery.

T

tattou. Armadillo.

W

windball cricket. Softball cricket with few rules.

Z

zwill. A toy made from flattened metal bottle caps.

ACKNOWLEDGMENTS

Thanks to The Canada Council and The Ontario Arts Council. Also to Diane Martin, Michelle MacAleese, Jennifer Lum, Michael Cho, Doris Cowan, Scott Sellers and Hilary McMahon.

RABINDRANATH MAHARAJ is the author of three previous novels: *A Perfect Pledge,* which was a finalist for the Regional Commonwealth Writers' Prize for Best Book and the Rogers Writers' Trust Fiction Prize; *The Lagahoo's Apprentice,* which was a *Globe and Mail* and *Toronto Star* notable book of the year; and *Homer in Flight,* which was nominated for the Chapters/Books in Canada First Novel Award; and two collections of short stories, *The Book of Ifs and Buts* and *The Interloper,* which was nominated for a Regional Commonwealth Prize for Best First Book. Rabindranath Maharaj was born in Trinidad and now lives in Ajax, Ontario.